PRAISE FOR **THE WORST THING**

"Who says a nice girl can't write a convincing psychopath? In *The Worst Thing*, Nora Gaskin introduces Ape, a character so real, so broken, so deliciously creepy ("Are you scared?" he asks one of his victims. "I need you to be scared.") you won't be able to look away from him. You might even catch yourself secretly, guiltily admiring him. You surely won't forget him."

– Kim Church, author of *Byrd*

"*The Worst Thing* is a tight, spare novel of suspense, reminiscent of Ruth Rendell. With a bad guy Gaskin fashions from the inside out, whose demise you will root for even as you come to understand his needs, this story has the depth and substance of one that will be read for years to come."

– Jenny Milchman, *USA Today* bestselling and Mary Higgins Clark award-winning author

"Nora Gaskin's new book, *The Worst Thing*, is the gripping story of a traumatic crime and how it affects the lives of everyone associated with it, from the police to a building handyman. It has all the plot twists and turns you want from an absorbing crime novel, but the book's real strength is in its characters. Most of the main characters are women who are tested and respond in ways that are human and believable. The men feel like real people too. The ending is equally real. Highly recommended."

– Sarah Shaber, award-winning author of the Louise Pearlie WWII mysteries

"Shadowy foreboding and well-earned emotions lured me into Kellah and Angie's world, while the fascinating back-stories, absence of gore, and realistic police work insured that I enjoyed every word. A tightly woven, highly readable thriller about motivated, original characters."

– **Karen Pullen**, author of *Cold Feet* and *Cold Heart*

"Chills down your spine! Prickles on the back of your neck! *The Worst Thing* is a thriller's thriller. You will never again meet a tattooed man without looking back over your shoulder. Nora Gaskin creates characters so alive and breathing you truly feel they step right off the pages. *The Worst Thing* is fantastic writing full of foolproof plotting and downright scary . . . an absolute page turner."

–**Ruth Moose**, teacher, published poet and short-story writer, award-winning author of mysteries *Doing It at the Dixie Dew* and *Wedding Bell Blues.*

"A twisty plot with complex characters. I couldn't turn the pages fast enough!"

– **J.D. Allen**, author of *19 Souls*, the first in the Sin City Investigations series

THE WORST THING

-a novel-

NORA GASKIN

The Worst Thing
Copyright © Nora Gaskin Esthimer, 2018

ISNB: print, 978-0-9991958-5-7
       ebook, 978-9991958-6-4

Library of Congress Control Number: 2018902443

All rights reserved. The contents of this book are the intellectual property of Nora Gaskin Esthimer. Except for brief excerpts for reviews of the work, no portion of the text can be reproduced in any form without written permission of the publisher. Please contact Lystra Books & Literary Services at the address given below.

Author's photo by Barbara Tyroler, www.barbaratyroler.com

Book design by Kelly Prelipp Lojk

LYSTRA BOOKS
& Literary Services

Published by Lystra Books & Literary Services, LLC
391 Lystra Estates Drive, Chapel Hill, NC 27517
lystrabooks@gmail.com

To Steve,
the best thing

ALSO BY NORA GASKIN

Until Proven: A Mystery in 2 Parts

*Time of Death: The True Tale of a Quest for Justice
in 1960s Chapel Hill*

EDITED BY NORA GASKIN

Carolina Crimes: 21 Tales of Need, Greed and Dirty Deeds
Published by Down & Out Books

PART 1

Convergence

1

MARCH 2012

Albert went in the back door. Bitch Mom was in the living room with the TV on, Dr. Phil laying down the law to somebody. His dad had hated that guy. He yelled at the TV like the man could hear him, mocked the suits and ties and fumed about how unfair the world was that this fat idiot got rich and famous. Maybe the IRS should check old Phil out. And all the time, Mom kept watching, kept cranking up the volume. Albert wondered why she still bothered, since she didn't have Dad there to aggravate anymore.

It hurt Albert's head to think about all that. He went through the room without speaking and went upstairs. The sound of Dr. Phil's voice followed him. "Do you want to know what I think?" That was always the question, and hell no, he did not. He got to his room and closed the door before the doctor delivered his opinion.

As loud as Phil's voice was, Dad's was just as loud in Albert's head. "He's got the devil's own luck."

That's what Dad said about people who had what he wanted.

Mom had done laundry and dumped his clean clothes outside his door. He had finally gotten through to her that he didn't want her in his room. Ever. But did that mean she couldn't fold his stuff? Couldn't put it down on a clean sheet to keep it off the floor she never vacuumed? He pushed the door open, stepped over the pile, and put his backpack down on the table by the window. Before he went back for the clothes, he tugged at the bedspread and smoothed it. Then he picked things up one at a time and spread each pair of pants, each T-shirt, each sock, out on the bed so he could examine it. It would serve Bitch Mom right if he put everything back in the laundry basket and made her wash it all again.

It made him mad, because he wanted to take a shower—the first thing he did after work—and she made him waste all this time. He folded each piece and put it away. Then he had to inspect the bedspread again. Finally, he stripped off his work clothes. He got dirty working for the moving company, and he was sure the boss, Joe Biggers, gave him the filthiest jobs. Biggers was married to Mom's cousin. He didn't like Albert, wanted to drive him away, but was too scared of the women to fire him.

Albert bundled the clothes he took off, and as he passed the stairs on his way to the bathroom, dropped them over the rail. Let her pick them up.

He stood in front of the bathroom mirror. His scalp was sweaty from wearing a watch cap all day. That was Biggers's fault, too. He said he didn't want customers seeing the tattoo on the back of Albert's head. He peeled the cap off and felt his skin. Stubbly. He put a new blade in his razor and shaved while he was in the shower. When his chin and cheeks were smooth enough, he ran the razor in an arc over his ear. When he shaved his face, it sounded like fine sandpaper on finished wood. His scalp made a louder, coarser noise, but the hairless skin felt good. Smooth. Clean. He rubbed shaving cream all over his head and ran the blade over it in slow careful strokes, forehead to neck. When he was done, when he was satisfied that he'd gotten every hair, he stepped out of the tub, washed the soap and dirt down the drain, then showered again.

When he wiped the steam off the mirror, he liked what he saw. His skull glowed pink. He took the hand mirror and looked at the back of his head. He loved his tattoo. The big gorilla with fangs and rage. The guys at work called him Ape, because of Darwin. Had they ever seen a hairless ape? Stupid guys. This tattoo was one big fuck-you to them.

He dressed and picked up the knife he liked to have in his pocket when he was home. A small one, just one blade so it folded slim, didn't take up space, but he felt its weight. It was the first knife he ever got, when he was still a kid. There was the night Bitch Mom and Dad got in a huge fight. It moved all over the house, Albert having to go from room to room to stay ahead of it. He was hiding in the storage room off the kitchen when they got there, when Dad raised a fist and Mom opened a drawer and pulled out a knife. She'd never done that before. Dad backed up. "Whoa, whoa, put that thing down." The fight ended. Dad left the house.

Albert watched Mom pour a drink and heard her feet on the stairs. She went to bed. She didn't even look for Albert or call to find out where he was. He stayed hidden for a while. When he came out, he studied the knife she'd left on the table. The fights made him shake all over, but now he knew this thing had the power to make them stop. Dad was scared of this thing.

The next day, Albert stole a little pocketknife from the

He ate the sandwich and drank some water. He felt good. He took his laptop out of its locked case and set it on the desk. He opened it and cleaned the screen, then the keyboard, before he turned it on. He wanted to know what old knives were worth. And yeah, tomorrow was payday. Dad never had money, but Albert, he was nothing like old Dad.

Later, if he couldn't sleep, he'd go for a drive. He'd make a swing by the building where his dad's old restaurant had once been, before the IRS shut it down. If he didn't keep an eye on it, some old homeless wino bedded down in the doorway. Sometimes Albert thought it was his old man's ghost inside that cardboard shack, under the sleeping bag that was so rotten Albert wouldn't touch it. But ghosts didn't bother him. A ghost was a nothing.

Albert wasn't afraid of his old man any more. Not afraid of Bitch Mom, either. But when he drove around, he liked to think what it would be like to have somebody in the van with him. Somebody who said his name and when they saw the wino-ghost, told him, that's not you. That'll never be you.

He finished looking at knives on the Internet, closed down the laptop, and locked it away. Maybe tonight when he opened the door to the van, she'd be there and she'd say, "Where have you been? I've been waiting."

2

Kellah listened to Angie and the other models chat in the back of the limo, until the driver started the engine and closed the window between the front and back. She could still hear the voices but as a wordless murmur. Angie had talked her into coming along for the photo shoot at the last minute so there wasn't room for her, except up front with the driver. He was a thin man in a dark blue jacket and smelled of a recent cigarette. He glanced at Kellah, nodded, then focused on the crawl through the city and ignored her. She leaned her head against the window and closed her eyes. They'd gotten up at five o'clock to get across town to the agency by seven, to set out for wherever it was they were going. That was never made clear to her.

It was spring break and she planned to spend it in the library on campus, but as usual, Angie nudged her toward the real world. And as usual, the lever that moved Kellah was a plea, "You know this is the most important job I've ever gotten. You know you bring me luck. It's just one day. Please come?"

Kellah smiled to herself. I am such a sucker, she thought. But she had her laptop in her tote bag. If the shoot was too boring, she'd get some work done.

She woke when the car picked up speed. They were well beyond the city center on a road through a ragged commercial area.

"Where are we?" she asked.

"My little short cut," the driver said. "We're almost to the bridge."

"Then what?"

"Don't know. That's foreign territory, so it's all in the GPS."

In another ten minutes, they had gotten through the jammed tollgates and been welcomed to the neighboring state. The GPS directed the driver onto roads of diminishing width and traffic thinned. "In one-quarter mile, turn left," it said.

"I don't see a left turn," the driver said. "You see a left turn?"

She leaned forward and pointed. "It's there. See the sign?" The sign was old and weathered and hung sideways off a frame.

The driver passed by slowly and looked hard at the break in scrub trees. "Hoo-kay." But he missed it.

He drove on until he could make a wide U-turn, came back, and slowed as if doubtful he could fit the wide car into the gap. Kellah thought of offering to get out and guide him, but a loud, long horn blast made her jump. A delivery truck roared up and swerved around them. The limo shuddered.

"Where did that asshole come from?" the driver asked.

The intercom from the back buzzed and one of the voices asked, "Where are we?" The driver glanced in the rearview mirror but didn't answer.

Kellah saw the river straight ahead, as if the road ended in a plunge, but it made a sharp turn to the left just in time.

"I guess this is the place," the driver said. A long two-story brick building rose up ahead of them.

"We aren't alone, anyway," she said.

A small woman wearing black, her silver hair spiked, ran toward them, waving a clipboard. The driver stopped and rolled down his window. "Where the hell have you been?" the woman asked. "Park over there."

The driver waved her off but pulled through the open gate in the heavy chain-link fence that surrounded the building. The yard was full of vehicles, moving vans, limos and shiny black SUVs with dark windows, beat-up older cars and trucks. A caterer had set up a food truck in one corner. A group of men in work clothes stood around it. They watched the limo park and girls get out.

The models headed for the building, urged on by the small woman, but Angie waited for Kellah.

"Should I apologize for getting you into this? I didn't know we'd come to the end of the earth."

Kellah was glad she had downloaded an offline version of her research paper. There was no Wi-Fi here, for sure, and probably no cell signal.

They followed the others across the yard. A wooden platform ran the length of the building. There was one set of steps, centered. A man sat beside them, his legs hanging off the ledge. His eyes were hidden behind mirrored sunglasses, but Kellah sensed that he was watching them approach. He wore a knitted cap, stretched tight. No hair showed under it and she registered a bald, no, a shaved head. Big chest, thick neck. When they got closer, he stood up. He wore heavy boots, work pants, and a hoodie with a logo on it.

"Hi," Angie said as she walked by.

He turned his head to keep his gaze on Angie, then took a

step in her direction, right into Kellah's path. She had to pull up short to move around him. She looked back but got no "sorry" or "excuse me." He didn't seem to see her at all.

The building was old, and whatever it had once been, it was now a big empty space. One end had been converted to a studio for photography. Bright white reflective screens turned the exposed brick interior walls into blank space. In contrast to the minimalism, the set was furnished as for a costume drama, something fit for Marie Antoinette, Kellah thought. Plush chairs and chaise longues in reds, golds, and blues with gilt legs. High concept.

"Can you believe it?" Angie put her arm around Kellah's shoulders and gave her a squeeze.

"Angel, we need you down here, please." The spiky woman with the clipboard took Angie's elbow and led her to the opposite end of the room, screened off by portable panels. A dressing area, Kellah guessed. The woman's words were polite, her voice was all exasperation.

Kellah found a metal chair against the wall and sat down to watch what was going on.

There must have been a hundred people inside, all busy. Some of them—the artsy, techie people—set up electronics on folding tables. Workmen moved banks of lights into place and rolled racks of clothing to the dressing area where production assistants took over.

She heard a piercing whistle, one that would summon a cab from across the park if they were in the city. People fell back, stopped, and turned to face a man in black jeans and a black T-shirt. He stood on something that put him head and shoulders above everyone. The spiky woman appeared beside him, but he gave the orders now.

"First group," he called, and half a dozen models appeared. They wore elaborate dresses and towers of hair. The director posed them in pairs and trios on the set. Photographers snapped. The girls moved as instructed, "Turn. Head back. Look at me. Jump. Body that way. Chin level."

Kellah had seen all of this before, at other shoots. It still fascinated her, the way ordinary young women were transformed into fanciful creatures. When she first met Angie, Angie poured over issues of *Vogue* and *Glamour* and watched old movies, even silent ones, just to see the clothes. She kept notebooks and computer files of images and ideas. She photographed herself and dissected the results. In her head, she was already one of those girls who could be anyone, anything.

And here she was, with a new name, Angel, about to get her own first magazine cover.

Suddenly, the director held up a hand and everybody stopped. The girls relaxed. The photographers plugged cameras into laptops. They stood back while the director looked at the photos just taken. Nothing would happen for a while.

Kellah remembered her own computer, pulled it out, and opened a file. There was a soft cough near her and she looked up.

The big guy from outside stood there, near enough to loom over her. She saw a sheen of sweat on his forehead. He had his hands clasped behind him, his shoulders lifted so his neck disappeared. He was as solid as the brick wall behind him. He still wore his dark glasses, so it was impossible to know what he was focusing on, but he turned his head and swept the room with his gaze.

The director gave orders. The first group of girls trooped back to the dressing area and another group emerged. Once they and the crosscurrents of energy that trailed behind them settled, Kellah tried to focus on her work. The guy was still there. She was certain none of his attention fell on her, but the shadow he cast was suffocating.

Angie came out and glided toward the set. The train of her deep blue dress flowed and flashed with spangles. Her hair was both high and wide, laced with red streamers. She glanced Kellah's way and winked, then offered her hand to the director, who made an elaborate bow over it. Everyone laughed.

The big guy moved. He stepped into Kellah's line of sight now. She got up and stepped back, awkward with the laptop against her chest.

She wanted to watch Angie, but he blocked her view and stood so close she found she couldn't breathe. She eased out the door behind her. It was mid-March. The breeze was chilly, the landscape still wintry. She inhaled, sighed, looked around. The moving vans had a logo on the side, a cartoonish arm flexed to show a bicep, and a name, Big Men Movers. She recognized the lettering. It had been on the guy's sweatshirt. So he was here to work. Why had he gone inside? The rest of the movers sat in their vehicles, motors running, no doubt to stay warm or to smoke or listen to music.

It was well after midday. The sun had begun to lower itself into open space created by the river and the flats it wound through. Kellah saw a glimmer to one side of it, a glimmer Pops had taught her to look for. A sun dog. Then she saw its twin. She knew what caused them, but had long since come up with her own explanation. These were places where the sky of her world wore thin and she got a glimpse of a universe beyond. One for her father, the other for her mother to shine through.

The spiky woman came out onto the platform. Kellah had assumed the director had been the one who whistled before, but no, the sound had come out of this small person. She let loose with another one and the men shut down engines and jogged over, leaving a trail of cigarette butts, paper coffee cups, sandwich wrappers.

"Time for the next set-up," the woman said. The men climbed the stairs and went into the building. Kellah took a deep breath and righted herself before she followed. The models had disappeared. The professional staff moved the lights, reflectors, and technology out of the way so the movers could shift the furniture.

Kellah went to the dressing area and peered around the curtain. Clothing racks stood off to the side. Dresses that had been worn were in a pile on the floor. Wardrobe assistants picked them up, shook them out, wrestled them back into hanging bags. There were a dozen salon chairs with mirrors in front of them, lights over and behind them, each occupied by a model, each model hovered over by hair and makeup people. Kellah picked her way through to where Angie sat. She wore a robe and a hairdresser unwound the red ribbons while someone else wiped the makeup off her face.

"Hi. You looked fabulous." Kellah made eye contact in the mirror.

"Thanks. I lost you, though. Did you leave?"

"I needed some air."

"Meaning you were bored?" Angie grimaced as the hairdresser tugged at her extensions.

"No, I wasn't. I promise." She watched Angie close her eyes to have the false eyelashes peeled off. "Do you remember the man who was outside when we got here? You said hi to him."

"Umm."

Kellah took that for a yes. "I think he's watching you."

Angie's face was naked now, her hair half undone. "Kellah, my life is people watching me." She spoke with exaggerated ennui and Kellah knew it was a put-on. Inside, Angie was the same wide-open girl she'd been at fifteen, but she began to mimic the people around her, cool and detached. She had given Kellah standing permission to tell her whenever she got too full of herself.

Angie shook the hands off of her head for a moment and reached for Kellah's. "My next session is the biggie, so stand where I can see you, OK?"

Angie's biggie was the last session of the afternoon. The set had been stripped back to white with a single chair, a tall black throne, and when Angie came out of the dressing room, she looked like a Renaissance queen in a white dress shot through with silver and gold thread. Her hair was a loose braid wrapped in pearls. Kellah stood up and waved. Angie couldn't wave back because it took both hands to lift the skirt. She mouthed, "weighs a ton," and pretended to stagger. That brought one of the director's helpers to take her by the elbow.

For her first pose, she stood by the chair, in profile, head back, neck a long arc. Kellah held her breath while the cameras fired.

And then, there he was, the guy, almost on top of her again, as if she didn't exist. He was bareheaded now, his cap half in, half out of a hoodie pocket. He pulled his sunglasses off and stared across the room. There was no mistaking it, the light around Angie drew him into her orbit. But Kellah knew all about Angie's planets. She'd watched men come, circle a while, then spin off, for years now. This man was different, dangerous and dark.

"Ape." A man's voice from the door behind them. "We got to load the truck."

The guy shrugged and went back to watching Angie. He had a tattoo on the back of his shaved head. A furious King Kong monster of a gorilla. Eyes red, lips peeled back from fangs, saliva dripping.

She took her phone out of her pocket, found the camera, and took a photo of the tattoo. Ape.

3

MAY 2012

"Nash, you're with me."

Detective Genevieve Nash looked up. Detective Brendan Quick spoke as he passed her desk, on his way to the door. She closed her laptop, grabbed her jacket, and stood up in one motion. Without thinking, she touched her gun, her cellphone, her radio, her equipment belt, her fanny pack. All in place. She glanced at the clock. 10:45 p.m.

"What have we got?" She followed him down the stairs. No waiting for the elevator.

"Missing person."

Their footsteps echoed against concrete walls until they reached the garage, a floor below street level.

Quick clicked the car doors open. "Do you know who Angel is? I guess her real name's Angie Boone." he asked.

Nash slid into the passenger seat. "Sure. Is she the missing person?"

"Her roommate called it in."

He maneuvered the garage's narrow lanes with the concentration she associated with people playing video games, though she doubted he'd like the analogy. He paused at the top of the ramp and turned onto the street. No siren, no blue light.

"My partner's out sick tonight," he said. "It's a good thing you're on duty. It's a young woman who may be missing and a young woman who called. You'll be more help than Bishop, anyway."

"Glad to be useful." She caught his sideways glance. "Where are we going?"

"Parkside."

A high-priced neighborhood, not far from the station. The miss-per and the woman who called it in were both likely white. If Quick thought Nash's age and gender would help, what about her race?

Gen Nash was black. She had been a detective for three months. She'd transferred to the precinct less than twenty-four hours earlier. She knew two things about Quick. As the captain's admin had whispered, he was too good-looking to be a cop. Nash saw dark hair, blue eyes, cheek bones, sharp jawline, but they had no impact on her. Not her type.

The other thing Nash knew about him was that he was a good detective. Smart. A golden boy. Whatever the reason for her being on this call, it needed to go well.

He stopped for a traffic light and she stared straight ahead, determined not to look at him. The light changed, he hit the accelerator. They drove another two blocks and a car pulled out of an on-street parking space ahead of them.

"Our lucky night," Quick said. "That's the building."

It was the kind of street Nash would love to live on, as if she could ever afford it. Human-scaled buildings, no high-rises, just a block from the park. A short street, never widened, so it didn't get through traffic. Some of the buildings were new, infill or replacements for old ones torn down. Others, like the one they headed for, were the real thing—reminders that this was once a fashionable address and had come full circle.

"Is this where you'd expect a hot young model to live?" Quick asked. "This is too old money, isn't it?" He pressed a call button.

"Who is it?" A man's voice came through the speaker.

"Detectives Quick and Nash." The door unlocked with a subdued buzz.

The elevator was a replica of an old one, with exposed gears and cables and a cage door, but Nash saw that the electronics were new. The car rose fast.

When they landed on the fifth floor. The door opened into a foyer rather than a hallway. The entire floor must be one large apartment. A man stood there, waiting for them. He was substantial and paunchy in a way that made her think he was an athlete grown into late middle age. What hair he had left was clipped short.

"I'm Mike Michaels," he said. "ID?"

Michaels's tone was a bit aggressive. Nash had seen it before, the shift of blame for needing to have cops in the house to the cops themselves. Quick was calm, matter of fact, not answering in kind. He let the man study their badges and asked, "How do you relate to this missing person, Mr. Michaels?"

The man's eyebrows rose. "Me? I'm the building manager and I look after the girls, Kellah and Angie."

"Kellah Mace? I spoke with her on the phone."

"She's waiting on you." Michaels stepped aside and they moved forward through a wide arched doorway. The apartment opened out in front of them. The first thing Nash saw was a large abstract painting in soft colors. The furniture—a long low couch, two pairs of chairs on either side of a chrome and glass table—sat on a rug in similar colors. There was a baby grand piano in an alcove. The place was formal, peaceful, and expensive. Quick had asked and now she answered to herself, no, it did not look like someplace a young woman would live.

Michaels led them through to another room, a smaller one much more lived in. A young woman sat in a large upholstered chair that faced the door, her legs curled under her. Her eyes were large and dark under deep bangs.

"These are the detectives, Girly." Michaels went to her side and took up a guardian's post.

"Ms. Mace?" Quick crossed the room and offered his hand. "I'm Detective Quick."

"Thanks for coming so fast." She changed her position so that she sat upright, feet on the floor. She wore loose-fitting clothes that made her look even smaller than she was. Nash saw outward fragility, but she felt her antennae rise, too. The posture, the clothing, the impression they gave, they were not accidental. She glanced at Quick, wondered what he thought.

There was a second chair beside Kellah's and Mike Michaels took it. That left a loveseat for the two detectives to share. Nash felt Quick's brief hesitation and then they both sat.

"Let's start at the beginning, Ms. Mace," Quick said. "I understand the missing woman is your roommate?"

"We both live here." Kellah's voice was low but clear. "We don't share a room."

"Are both your names on the lease?"

"I own the apartment."

He asked her a few more questions. Did she work? A student? At which school? Nash listened while he got information about the woman who'd made the missing person call. It was routine. Kellah Mace answered patiently, as if she understood the preliminaries had to be worked through. Nash used the time to look around.

The room had floor-to-ceiling bookshelves around three walls. They held a lot of books, but also a collection of framed photographs. They were all of the same people, alone or in pairs or the three together—a girl, a woman, a man. The girl, Kellah no doubt, was the center of them all, the glowing focus of the camera. She began as a baby, grew through toddler-hood, the early grades, until the series ended with her as a teenager. That girl wore soccer gear, her foot balanced on a ball, her long hair parted in the middle and pulled back. She had her hands on her hips and a big grin. Her posture said, I just scored the winning goal.

And in another picture, she sat at a grand piano, head down in concentration, the motion of her hands clear, even from a still image.

Nash looked from that girl to the woman who responded to Quick's questions. The focus of the piano player was still there. The joy of the soccer player was not. Where had that girl gone? She tuned back into the questions Quick asked Kellah Mace.

"How long have you known Ms. Boone and how long has she lived here?"

Mike Michaels interrupted. "Hey, Quick, you're wasting time. What about the freaking weirdo she told you about on the phone?"

"Mike." Kellah held up a hand to quiet him. "The detective knows his business." She leaned toward Quick to answer his last question. Nash recorded her body language.

"We met in high school," Kellah said. "A boarding school. After we graduated, I came home to go to college and she moved in with me. She wanted to be a model." She smiled and shrugged, as if to say, we all know what happened next.

"When did you last see her?" Quick asked.

"This afternoon at about two, a little before. We went to brunch at Lacey's Bistro in the next block. We ran into one of Angie's model friends, Vonnie, and her boyfriend. Andrew, I think. They invited us to a party tonight and Angie said we would go. After we ate, she left to go to the gym. I went to the library and came home a few hours later. She never came."

"How would you describe her mood?"

Kellah blinked and looked down. "I told her I didn't want to go to Vonnie's party. Angie thinks I should be more social, so she was a little angry with me when she left."

"Could Angie have gone to the party alone and didn't tell you?"

"Not straight from the gym. She didn't have clothes with her," Kellah said. "Or makeup. She'd have come home first. I found Vonnie's number and called her several times at the party. Angie wasn't ever there." She reached up and swept her bangs to one side. "Detective, is it true you don't investigate missing persons until they've been gone for twenty-four hours?"

"There's no rule," he said. "We have discretion, depending on age, circumstances, the person's normal behavior."

"Angie's a reliable girl," Mike said. "She's not like a lot of them, saying one thing and doing another."

Nash wondered how Quick added things up. Was this a girl who got into a snit with her friend and went to a party by herself? If so, she'd show up sometime before Monday, hungover and sorry. Nothing new there. Or was this a girl who needed to be found fast?

"When did you begin to think Angie could be missing?" she asked.

"I knew it when she wasn't home by seven, even if she did intend to go out later. I started calling her cell and it went to voice mail every time."

"Do you mind if I look at your phone?" Quick asked.

She reached into a pocket and produced it. Mike looked as if he would say something again but closed his mouth with a snap Nash could feel. She wondered if he had experience with the police, or just a general skepticism about being so forthcoming.

Quick scrolled through the call records. Nash wished she knew how to read him, and then thought he'd have to let her know what she should do. She followed the threads of energy in the room. While he focused on the phone, Kellah focused on him.

Suddenly, Quick looked at Nash as if he had just remembered she was there, but he spoke to Kellah. "Ms. Mace, would you allow Detective Nash to see Ms. Boone's room?"

"That's private," Mike said. "Girly—"

Kellah cut him off as she stood. "Of course, if you think it'll help."

Nash rose and followed the young woman down a hallway off the library. They passed a closed door on the right, another on the left, and ended up at the end of the hall, in front of double doors.

"This is Angie's." Kellah turned both knobs and pushed

inward. She turned on the overhead light, then stepped back so the detective could look in. It was a large room with big windows on the opposite wall. The shades were half-open. It would feel airy in the daylight.

"Do you often come into this room?" Nash asked. "Have you been in since you decided Angie's missing?" She took latex gloves out of her fanny pack.

"Decided?" She made the word sound as if it tasted bad. "I went in at about 5:30, but that was before I realized she's missing. And, yes, I go in whenever I want. It's been our habit, ever since we met. No secrets."

"Did you have a specific reason for going in this afternoon?"

"To borrow a dress. The one on the bed."

Nash saw an apricot-colored shift, spaghetti straps, a beaded band at the bottom. It had the sheen of good silk. It would fall to mid-thigh on a six-foot-tall model, knee-length on Kellah. Interesting to think the color would suit them both, but she saw that it would, and then she was embarrassed at the thought that it would look good against her own dark skin, too.

"Where are you going to wear it?"

"I changed my mind about the party. I decided to go with her."

"Why was that?"

"I don't like to make her unhappy."

Nash worked the gloves over her hands. "Does Angie have a gun? Drugs? Needles? Anything else I should know about?"

She turned and faced Kellah, who didn't like the question. "Sorry, but I have to ask."

"There's nothing in her room you need to be afraid of."

Nash studied the room. The dress on the bed was smooth and the bed itself was made. But Kellah could have done that. Somebody left clothes piled on a pair of chairs, shoes kicked off at the edge of the bed, drawers not quite closed.

"OK," Nash said, "from where you stand, does anything look out of place? Anything out of the ordinary, no matter how small, could tell us about her intentions."

"Intentions? You think she disappeared on her own?"

Nash scolded herself, not a smart thing to say to this girl. Kellah Mace had her antennae up, too, and missed nothing. "We have to think of all the possibilities."

Kellah slipped her hands up into the arms of her long tunic. She hardly pretended to look around. "There is nothing out of place, any more than usual."

All right, Nash thought, Angie isn't a neat freak. She would bet Kellah's room was the polar opposite.

"Maybe I'll straighten up for her," Kellah said. "Maybe she'd like to come back to a clean room." For the first time, a trace of emotion showed in her voice.

Nash went to a dresser and looked over its surface, cluttered with scrunchies, nail-polish bottles, and tissues. An octagonal table held books and a vase of mixed cut flowers. There was a desk under one of the windows. It had a tangle of loose wires for electronics spread across it.

"Did she keep a daybook?" Nash asked. "How about a computer?"

"She lived on her phone and her tablet. She had both of them with her today."

Nash pulled out a desk drawer and used her pen to sort through the contents, receipts, unused notepads, a sheet of postage stamps. She moved to a dresser drawer with bras, underwear, scarves, belts, all jumbled together. "Where does she keep papers and letters?"

"I can't remember any. Who would write to her?"

"There must be contracts, work-related things." She paused in her search and faced Kellah.

"I never thought to wonder. Maybe her agent has all of that."

Nash moved to the attached bathroom. It was cluttered, but the fixtures and floors were clean. "Does she take prescription meds?"

"Birth control pills."

The packet lay on the edge of the sink. Five pills were gone from a month's supply. "Does she have a boyfriend?"

"No one serious. But there's usually someone." Kellah's voice trailed off. "People are drawn to Angie."

"Is there a significant other in your life?" She opened the medicine cabinet door. It was almost empty.

"I don't have time."

Nash closed the door. "Thanks for allowing me to look."

They went back down the hall toward the library.

"What is this room?" Nash pointed to one of the closed doors.

"This one is my room. The other one is the guest room."

In her mind, Nash measured the length of the hallway, the depth of Angie's room, and wondered why Kellah, who owned the place, didn't use the biggest bedroom.

"You all right, Girly?" Mike stood up as soon as he saw Kellah. "You want a cup of tea?"

She squeezed his hand as she sat beside him again. Nash,

from behind, caught Quick's eye and shook her head, the tiniest movement she could make. He responded with the smallest nod.

"Ms. Mace," Quick said, "when you called in, you said something about a stalker. What evidence do you have of that?"

"The freaking weirdo," Mike said. "Like I said."

When Kellah began to speak, it was as if she had been waiting for her turn.

"I went with her to a photo shoot about six weeks ago. It was in an old industrial building, a warehouse or something, outside the city. Across the river.

"I'd been to shoots before, but this one was bigger and more complicated. It's going to be huge for Angie's career. Very high fashion. She'll have the magazine cover and a feature article."

Kellah went on to tell them that it had been mid-morning when she noticed this man watching Angie, and that he was one of the workmen who moved furniture around for the different scenes. When the other guys weren't needed, they went outside and hung around the catering truck, but he was always near Angie.

"I know, because I was, too. He tracked her and I tracked him. Angie's big moment was at the end of the day. She came out wearing a dress with a huge skirt. It was white with gold and silver beads. She passed by me and whispered, 'This thing weighs a ton.' She made a face. Once she got by me, the guy stepped right in front of me, I'm pretty sure he snapped a photo or two of her with his cellphone.

"Did you ever speak to him?" Nash asked.

"I did." Kellah looked at Nash as if she had forgotten her. "When everything was over and people were packing up, I went and stood right beside him. When Angie came out, back in her regular clothes, I said, 'Do you know her?' He jumped a foot and mumbled something. I said, 'You've been watching her so much, I thought you must know her.' He hunched up his shoulders and walked off."

"Did he approach her at all?" Quick asked.

"Not that I saw. I told her he was watching her, but she blew it off because it happens all the time. She can hardly walk down the street anymore."

"Can you describe him?"

"I took a picture of him." She reached for her phone, tapped the screen, and held it out so that both Quick and Nash could see it, the back of a man's head, shaved and tattooed. Quick reached out and touched the screen to enlarge the image.

"A gorilla?" he asked.

"Look at its face," Kellah said. "It's full of anger. It's evil."

"How about the man's face? Did you get a picture of it?"

"He was all one color. Pale skin, pale eyes, practically no lips. He's overweight but he still looks like he works out. You can see his neck's thick that way, and his shoulders are broad. It's the tattoo that makes him stand out. I heard somebody call him Ape."

"You're sure he works for the moving company?"

"Oh yes." She pulled the phone back and changed the photo. When she held it out this time, Nash read the words, "Big Men Moving," printed across the back of his T-shirt, red letters on gray fabric. "It's in the city. I saw the address on the trucks."

"So he was a creep that day," Quick said. "But that isn't stalking. Was there anything else?"

Kellah looked at him and met his gaze. Nash sensed a flow of energy between them.

"He showed up here," Mike said. "I was in the lobby and he banged on the door. He had a big bunch of roses, but I know all the delivery guys from the florists in the neighborhood and I'd never seen him before. He said they were for Angel and he was supposed to deliver them in person. He asked which apartment was hers."

"You didn't let him upstairs, did you?" Nash asked.

"Are you kidding? I told him, nobody here by that name. That's when he got belligerent. Said he knew she lives here, gave me a hard time. But he took his roses and left."

"Did you tell Angie?"

"No, but I told Kellah, didn't I, Girly?"

"I showed Mike the photo, but the man was wearing a cap pulled low in back, so he didn't see the tattoo. But when I described him, Mike agreed. It had to have been him."

"I don't understand why you didn't tell Angie," Nash said. "Why not warn her?"

Mike answered. "Kick—sorry, that's my nickname for her—Angie, she has a lot of guys who fall for her. And sometimes she thinks I'm too much the protective kind."

"She says it's an occupational hazard," Kellah said. "There have been men who tried too hard before and she always handles it."

"So why is this time different?" Quick asked.

"This time, she's disappeared."

Quick became all business. He texted the photos to his own phone and Nash's, and asked for contact information for the people Kellah had called that night, Angie's agency, and her father in California. Mike snorted when Quick asked for a recent photo. After all, Angie had one of the most famous faces in the country, maybe the world. Kellah produced one, though, her friend without makeup, her hair pulled back and clipped at the nape of her neck.

The girl next door, Nash thought, pretty but hardly the model whose single name, Angel, was enough to sell anything. Amazing how she transformed.

Quick gave both Kellah and Mike his card. "Here's my cell number. Call it anytime, for any reason. You should try to get some sleep. Don't worry, we'll find her."

"What did you get from Mike Michaels?" Nash asked as they left the building and walked toward the car.

"He's the protective kind, all right." Quick clicked opened the doors. "He told me Kellah's story. Do you remember, five or six years ago, a city bus driver had a heart attack and the bus plowed over the sidewalk? It killed three people. Two of them were Ava and Johnny Mace. Her mother and father."

"Oh my God." She snapped her seat belt closed. "I guess that explains her demeanor."

"What do you mean?"

"Didn't you think she was a little too controlled? And wanted to be in charge? That can be a reaction to trauma, right?"

He adjusted his rearview mirror. "Maybe." Nash thought he sounded unhappy with her analysis but didn't have an argument to make against it. He pulled away from the curb. "Mike explained, he worked for the Maces since before Kellah was born. He seems to see himself as being like a grandfather to her. That's why he calls her Girly. His nickname for Angie,

Kick, is short for Sidekick." He waited for one car to pass and made a U-turn.

"Do we believe Angie really is missing and act on it?" she asked. "Or do we wait to see if she comes home in time for lunch tomorrow?"

"Tomorrow is today," he said. "It's after midnight."

As they turned off the residential street, a late-night bus passed, lit by streetlights, and Nash heard him draw in his breath. The bus was wrapped with Angie's image, the most recent ad she'd done. Her eyes were huge, dark blue as lapis lazuli, with gold flecks, and set like precious stones in metallic gold shadow. Two words, Angel Eyes, floated beneath the image.

"Would you say she's a supermodel?" he asked.

"She goes by one name and that's enough to sell eye shadow." She imagined for a moment what it must be like to have Angie and Kellah enter a room together, tall and petite, blond and dark, a center of attention and a well of reserve.

"We can't lose by doing our job," he said. "If Angie shows up, fine. If not, we're that much ahead. We start by calling this Vonnie and the other people Kellah contacted. They'll still be partying so we can get them tonight. And the dad in California. It's earlier there. First thing in the morning, we get to the boss at Big Men Moving and find out who the freaking weirdo is, talk to him, go from there."

"What about the press and the Internet?"

"It's too soon to go public."

"That's not what I mean. It's going to be on social media in no time."

He glanced at her as if he didn't understand.

"Kellah has already called all of the friends," she said. "If we call them, too, someone is bound to figure out Angie's missing. It'll be out there in five minutes."

"I hate that shit," he said.

"I know, but we've got to let the ups know what's going on and try to get communications involved before it hits Facebook."

"The ups?"

"Sorry." She shook her head. "Our superior officers. That's my internal slang. I didn't mean to say it out loud."

He laughed. "No problem. And I know you're right, but we need to start making things happen and the ups don't work this time of night."

There it was, the click she'd been waiting for. They were going to do this together.

————

Kellah hung up the apricot silk dress and began to pick up the things that were scattered around Angie's room. Then a sense of loss swept over her. She dropped the shoe she held, unable to face the idea of a tidy and empty space. This room vacant, again.

She'd lied to Nash when she said she was in and out of this room all the time. Not even Angie's clutter and scents and laugh could get to the chill that Kellah felt whenever she came in here. It was Angie who came to Kellah's room, just like when they were in school.

She lay down on the bed. A framed photo of Angie sat beside the alarm clock. It was from one of her first jobs, a shampoo commercial. Kellah went with her to the session. Angie's back was bare to the camera, her hair twisted into a loose, gleaming coil that fell between wing-like shoulder blades. In the photo, it looked soft, made the viewer want to touch it, although in that moment it had been sprayed stiff, almost plasticized to get the desired effect. The photographer took a lot of pictures before he finally said, "Thanks, everyone, we're done."

Then Angie turned her head, saw Kellah off the side, out of the glare, and smiled. The camera clicked one more time and that was the photo they selected. A perfect profile, lips tilted in private communication, hair even more glorious in the shift of light. The ad ran with a two-word caption, Angel Hair.

It was enough. Angie became Angel and her agent went from scrambling to find work for a newcomer to coping with a flood of offers.

"Hey, you." Mike spoke from the doorway and brought her out of her fog. "You need to go to bed. Get some sleep, like the detective said."

"What about you?" She got up and crossed the room.

"I'm staying in the extra room, door open. No way I'm leaving you by yourself."

"You don't have to do that. I'll call you if I need you."

"Nope." He hugged her. "Come on."

He held onto her as if somebody might grab her out of the hallway. They got to her door and she gave him a kiss on the cheek. "I'll still call you if I need you."

"Don't you worry, Girly. I'll hear every time you roll over."

When his snore filtered into her room, she crept back to Angie's room. It had been her parents' room. It was where she spent the first night without them. What she remembered now was how cold she'd been that night, and how ever since, something at her core couldn't be warmed.

She picked up Angie's photo and carried it to the window. She rested her forehead against the glass. Five floors below, the garden was entirely dark. Everyone in the building was asleep.

"I'm going to find you."

PART 2

The Three-Year Coma

4

JUNE 2006 – MAY 2009

Kellah went straight home from school. It was the last day, so no rehearsal, no practice, no extra library time. Mike met her in the lobby. His face was a blur, as if someone had erased his features. He put his arms around her and gave her the news.

Neighbors brought food and flowers. Mike told them she was in shock, couldn't see anybody. She went to her parents' room and sat on the window seat. Rectangles of light lay across the lawn below. She tried to remember when Mike had taken down her swing set and playhouse.

"Mims," she whispered. It was her childhood name for her mother. It changed to Mama in kindergarten and Mom in middle school. Now Kellah could only think of her as Mims.

Cousin Irene came from Florida to stay with her. They knew each other. A little. Irene came to the city sometimes to shop, see shows, or go to museums. She cried when she saw Kellah and said, "I can stay as long as you need me."

The following day, Irene took Mike into Mims and Pops's room. They thought Kellah was taking a nap, but she hid in the hall so she could hear what they said.

"We should send Ava's clothes to the charity consignment shop," Irene said. "She wouldn't want her things to just hang there when somebody could use them."

"Too soon for all that, Duchess," Mike said. "My Girly wouldn't like it."

Kellah knew she would have to keep a close eye on Irene. She slept only because she had to after that, and as soon as she woke, she went to open Mims's closet door and run her hand over the dresses, skirts, trousers, the silks, cottons, and wools.

Kellah shivered through the memorial service. Mike's bulk on one side of her was a comfort. Irene's thinness on the other side chilled her.

A lot of people came back to the apartment afterward. They ate and drank and someone began to play *Pictures at an Exhibition* on the piano.

Kellah had been trying to learn the piece. The sheet music was hers. Or did nothing belong to her anymore?

She went through the kitchen and took the back stairs from the fifth floor down to the lobby. They'd once been the servants' routes between floors of the mansion. They were steep and not well lit, but she'd spent a childhood running up and down them. She paused in the lobby. She could go to the garden or she could go out the front door and look for the gap in the universe that Mims and Pops had slipped through.

The elevator bell rang and Mike stepped out. "Jeez, Girly. Where're you going?"

———

Kellah expected a courtroom, like on TV. This room was small, with all the space taken by a long table and chairs on rollers. The guardian ad litem followed her in. "Sit there, dear."

She took the seat at the far left. The dark red upholstery scratched the backs of her knees and she tugged her skirt hem down. The guardian, the lawyer who handled Kellah's parents' estate, another lawyer appointed by the court, and the social worker all settled themselves to her right. Mike was there, too, and he pulled up a chair so that he sat behind her, close enough to touch. She turned and smiled at him.

He looked uncomfortable in a white shirt buttoned to his chin, a tie he probably found on the floor of his closet and his too-tight blue blazer. He winked at her. "We'll get through it, Girly."

A second door into the room opened. Two women came in.

"Good morning," one said. "I'm Judge Wayland's clerk. This is the court reporter. The judge will be here in a moment. She wants to have a good conversation with everyone involved, not be so formal, and that's why she moved us to this conference room."

The court reporter began to set up her equipment. The guardian poured Kellah a glass of water and slid it to her. The lawyers whispered to each other. The clerk opened a laptop, arranged a legal pad and three pens beside it, then set out file folders.

Kellah thought, everybody has a job to do here except me.

She'd been told she didn't have to attend. After all, she was a minor—only fifteen—and would be represented by the court-appointed guardian, the attorneys, a social worker. They were crazy if they thought she'd stay home.

The room was full of sounds she was sure no one else heard.

Papers rustled like far-off thunder. Computer keys thudded like tiny hammers wrapped in cotton. Voices whispered like breezes across water. She looked up. A seal of the state hung on the wall opposite her and Kellah stared at it, stared so hard it disappeared into a haze of faded light. She'd discovered that trick in the last few months. She thought of it as finding a hole in reality, a place where her mind could go when the pressure was too much.

The door opened again. Everyone stood for the judge, a woman in a black robe with a white turtleneck underneath. She smiled at Kellah, gestured for them all to be seated, then took the chair in front of the laptop.

She had gray hair, but her face looked young. She put on a pair of glasses that fit over the end of her nose. "Good morning, everyone. This is a legal proceeding and we will all behave as such, but the court recognizes the presence of the young woman whose future is to be decided, and we will also behave with sensitivity."

The social worker presented her report about Kellah's life, the death of her parents, the lack of relatives. In fact, her only living relative was her mother's cousin, Irene Shaw, who had arrived at Kellah's home after the accident, but had not offered to be the long-term solution to what was to become of Kellah.

Kellah sighed. Was it her fault she didn't have a lot of relatives? Irene was nice. Irene was nice, but live with her? Or Kellah move to Florida? No way.

The estate attorney talked about the money. Investments. Stocks. Real estate. The judge followed along on the computer and made notes on the legal pad. Mims and Pops were rich, so Kellah was rich, too, but now it sounded as if money was as much of a problem as her own existence.

As the judge, the lawyers, and the guardian talked, Kellah heard disapproval in their voices. Apparently, her parents should have made all sorts of complicated arrangements and provisions for both their daughter and the wealth they had left her. There should have been trusts and trustees, boundaries and restrictions, and entanglements. The judge stressed the word "protections" and looked to Kellah when she did, and someone said "grievous oversights."

She wanted to say no, they just didn't plan to die that day.

As the talk dragged on, it became clear without the existence of any of those legal protections, Kellah would inherit all of it and take control of it when she turned eighteen.

Three years. If they could just put her in a coma for three years.

Indeed, the next topic was what to do with her for that length of time. That was why Mike was there. The judge knew he wanted to speak, because she asked, "Is Mr. Michaels present?"

He stood and the judge arranged for people at the table to shift their chairs so that he could move his forward and sit at the corner next to Kellah. The side of his head was to her and she studied the creases in his earlobe and the neck bristles of his fresh haircut.

"I knew Johnny and Ava Mace for more than twenty years, Your Honor. That's when they hired me to take care of the building where they lived. They'd just bought it, hadn't even fixed it up yet. Johnny and me, we didn't mind getting dirty, so when the plumbing in the basement had to get dug up, we dug it. We did it together, made it like a little palace. We got to be like family. I'm the first person they told when Ava found out she was pregnant and I was there when they brought baby Kellah home. I was the first person to hold her. I babysat for her. I walked her to school when they couldn't. If she was sick and they had to go out, I kept her. I have a little apartment on the ground floor, so I'm right there all the time."

He talked on and the judge set the laptop to one side, rested her forearms on the table, and listened. But Kellah knew, no matter how hard the judge paid attention, she wasn't going to make sixty-year-old Michael O. Michaels the guardian of Kellah Mace, no matter how much sense it made to the two of them. Mike had promised it would work out, but even at her young age, she knew better. Poor Mike. He'd be lost without her.

"So here's what I think, Your Honor," Mike said. "There can be a live-in lady to take care of the apartment and help out with female things. But I'll be right there in the building. I can see to it that Kellah gets to and from school safe every day. I'll go to her soccer games and piano recitals, whatever, just like Johnny and Ava would. This way, she doesn't have to lose home and friends and everything, on top of losing them. They trusted me. I think it was because I knew them before they got so swank."

Swank. Kellah drew the word on the shiny surface of the table with her finger. Mims would say, now that's a Mike word, and for weeks everything she liked would be swank.

Kellah traced the word again, and beside it, Mims. Mike cleared his throat and went on talking. Kellah ran her finger over the words she'd formed to erase them both, before anyone saw their ghosts in the high gloss.

When Mike finished, the guardian ad litem addressed the judge again. It seemed that the best thing for Kellah would be boarding school. The Fairbourne School. It had the finest reputation for academics and extracurriculars and educational trips to Europe in the summers. Full sports and music programs, in keeping with Kellah's interests in soccer and piano. Johnny and Ava Mace would surely approve. Because of the circumstances, the school agreed to accept Kellah for the fall term, beginning in two weeks. She could go almost immediately to settle in and get her bearings.

A few days later, the headmistress of Fairbourne School, Ms. Humphries, came to the city for meetings, and arrived at the apartment to pick up her new charge. She was thin and blond. Her gray jacket had a patch on the breast pocket. Gold, blue, green. She held both of Kellah's hands and smiled the sad smile Kellah was accustomed to now. She drank coffee with Irene while Kellah finished packing.

Mike came into her room. He had already cried and promised that he'd keep the building and the apartment just the way they were, for her when she turned eighteen. Now he was brisk.

"Girly, they say it's time for us to get going. Can I take these?" He picked up the suitcases. "I'll come back for that trunk."

He left her door open and she heard the two women talking in the library.

"At least," Irene was saying, "she'll go through life knowing the worst thing has already happened."

"And so young," Ms. Humphries said.

Kellah stepped into the room. They both stood and Irene

moved toward her.

Mike put the suitcases by the elevator and went back for the trunk. "You got rocks in here?" He grunted as he carried it by them.

"Books." And photos and some food, but she didn't have to tell everything.

"What about clothing?" Irene asked. "It doesn't seem like much."

"The girls wear uniforms," Ms. Humphries said. "I'll help her order what she needs."

Kellah didn't care what she wore. She followed Mike.

"Wait," Irene said. "You'll stay in touch? Promise?" She hugged Kellah and shook hands with Ms. Humphries. Kellah looked past her to the big painting on the wall. She didn't want Irene's face to be the last thing she saw of her home as the elevator doors closed.

The train trip took two hours. Ms. Humphries talked about the school, how it was like a family, how welcome Kellah was.

"Will I have a roommate?" Kellah asked.

"No. We thought a single room. Is that all right?"

"Yes." In the last two months, when most of what she wanted was impossible, she wanted only to be left alone. She turned her head, pretended to sleep, then did.

She woke when the train stopped. Her trunk and suitcases sat on the platform when she got off. Ms. Humphries was upset that somebody named Charlie wasn't there to meet them.

"Will you be all right here, dear? I'll go look for him." She walked off with the phone to her ear.

It was a hot day. Pops used to say, country heat and city heat are different. In the city, it pushed against you from all sides. In the country, you pushed through it.

Kellah looked around for a shady place to wait but saw none. The station was a small wooden building that stood by itself at the edge of a little town. It looked like a pretend place. She lifted her ponytail in the hopes of finding a breeze to cool her neck. She heard her name and turned. Ms. Humphries and a man with a cart came toward her.

The van into which Charlie put her things and to which Ms. Humphries escorted her was blue with a medallion on the side. It was the school's symbol, a wreath of gold and green leaves with the silhouette of a tree inside it.

The dorm room was small, furnished with a single bed, a dresser, a chest of drawers, and a desk, with a closet built into the corner. Kellah, Ms. Humphries, and the dorm mother, Ms. Dennis, along with the luggage, filled it.

"May I rearrange the furniture?" Kellah asked.

The two women looked at each other and Ms. Dennis said, "There isn't much that can be done."

"You're right," Kellah said. "It'll be fine."

"I'll help you unpack," Ms. Dennis said.

"If you don't mind, I'd like to do it myself. After I rest a little."

That was a magic word. No one ever objected when she said she wanted to rest.

"You'll both come to my house for dinner tonight," Ms. Humphries said. "Ms. Dennis can show you the way and perhaps give you a little tour of campus." Then they left her.

Kellah dragged her luggage back into the hall. She began to nudge and shove the desk, then the bed, the desk again and the bed, until she rearranged the room to the way she wanted it. She put her clothes away and made the bed. It was positioned along the window wall now, so she could lie on it, propped on pillows, and look out.

She was on the third floor that overlooked the circular drive that connected the dorms, the administrative building, and some of the faculty houses. It made an arc around a grassy swath of ground that Ms. Humphries had called The Green. Footpaths crisscrossed it, and in its center stood a huge tree with benches beneath it. Ms. Humphries said all the old girls loved to come back and sit under the Founder's Oak. Kellah made a pact with herself never to sit under that tree.

She tried to look straight down from her window. The view was blocked because of a ledge, a balcony of sorts, maybe three feet wide. At its outer edge, it was fenced with decorative ironwork. Fancy for jail bars, she thought. She knelt on the bed and tried the window. It was painted shut.

Dinner at Ms. Humphries's house involved baked chicken, green beans, a pear salad, and ice cream. Mr. Humphries was there and talked about the nearby boys' school where he taught. Kellah had grown up in the company of adults and could tell these three were not comfortable with her, but it was OK. It meant they didn't mention her parents, so she could manage to eat, answer their questions, and not have to feel anything.

After they ate, Ms. Dennis led her through one of the class-room buildings, the gym, the library, and along the crest of the hill above the playing fields that stretched to a river.

"You play soccer, don't you?"

"I did." She'd left that behind with old and outgrown things.

The sun had just set and the clouds over the fields showed faded pink. As they walked back to the dorm, Kellah looked up. The ledge outside her room was in the center of the building. It was built to shelter the main floor landing. It extended under just two windows, hers and the room next door.

The next day, Ms. Dennis drove Kellah into town to meet with a psychologist, as ordered by the court. She wanted to re-fuse to go but knew cooperation would work in her favor. She set out to say the right things to the shrink in hopes of bringing it to a quick end.

Back at school, she took inventory of her supplies. She had books, her laptop, telephone, apples, peanut butter, crackers, and chocolate. She decided to come down with the cramps and go to bed. Ms. Dennis checked on her, then brought a heating pad, a pill approved by the school nurse for pain, and luke-warm chicken soup. She went away again without comment on the rearranged room.

———

Just after noon on the day students returned, the circular drive began to fill with cars and people crowded The Green. Kellah watched from her window and listened. Girls squealed loud enough for her to hear them and they hugged as if they'd been apart for years, not two months. Ms. Humphries and teachers who had materialized while Kellah hibernated greeted the girls and parents. Carts overflowed with boxes, crates, and suitcases that somehow had to be gotten upstairs.

Suddenly Kellah saw a girl separate herself from a group. It was as if she stepped out of a hole in the universe and took form then and there. She was tall, slender. Her ponytail flowed from the crown of her head over one shoulder. Sunlight filtered through the big oak's foliage and lit up her pale blond hair. She tilted her head back and raised one hand. Kellah realized the girl was looking right at her. She pulled back from the window and hugged her pillow, caught out.

Dinner and convocation were mandatory, but Kellah didn't go. She ate the last of her apples and chiseled with a nail file at the painted window frame, as she had done off and on for the last few days. It was almost ready to open.

It was fully dark when the girls drifted out of the auditorium and across The Green or around the drive, filtering back to their dorms. Kellah heard singing, but the voices were too low for her to hear the words. A school song. She was going to have to learn a school song.

The front door below her banged open. Footsteps pounded up the stairs and past her room in a storm of chatter and laughter. All along the hall, doors opened and slammed, and in a few moments all was quiet. She should have showered and gotten ready for bed while everybody was out. Now she'd have to face strangers in that shared bathroom, with its rows of sinks, toilet stalls, and half-enclosed showers. Maybe she could wait until after lights-out and sneak down the hall. She leaned back on her study pillow, her room dark because she'd not bothered to turn on the light.

Pa-pop. Pop. Taps on the window beside her head made her jump, and her heart pounded. She backed across the room. There was a shape beyond the glass. Someone on the ledge? A pair of hands gesturing, then a voice, "Open the window."

She found the light switch. The person outside her room was the blond girl from earlier that afternoon.

"I don't know if I can." She was still shaky but made herself go back to the bed, crouch on it, grasp the handles on the window frame and lift. Old wood scraped old wood. She moved aside and the girl came in, long bare legs first, over the sill.

"Hi. I'm Angie. Humps said I should look after you."

"There is a door." Kellah meant to sound unsurprised, or snarky, or something cool, but it came out a whisper.

"That would be a waste of the balcony. Come on." Angie swung her legs back over the sill and disappeared. "Come on," she said again from out of sight.

So the second room on the balcony belonged to this girl, the one who was apparently in charge of her now. Kellah took a deep breath and followed.

Angie, wearing short-shorts and a T-shirt, leaned against the wall of the building, one foot propped on the iron railing. "Do you smoke?" She offered a pack of cigarettes.

"No."

"Neither do I." She put the pack back in her pocket.

"You can if you want." Kellah pressed her rear end against the wall. She was wearing flannel pajama bottoms, too warm for the late August evening, and they clung to the rough bricks. She tried to reach one leg to the rail but was too short to adopt Angie's pose. She sat on the concrete floor and crossed her legs, yoga-style.

"OK, just one." Angie lit up. "Models smoke to stay thin."

"You're a model?"

"I will be." She inhaled and blew a filter of smoke between them. "I heard about your parents. Really sad."

"Thanks." Did everyone here know about the accident? The tang from Angie's match made her eyes water.

"I'm an orphan, too," Angie said. "Sort of. My mom died when I was four. My dad's on his third marriage. He lives in California and has twin babies I've never met. They're already six months old."

Kellah looked up over the trees and saw the moon, fat but not full, lopsided, wobbly. What would it be like to find out Pops was alive and living some other life? "I'm sorry."

They sat quietly for a few minutes. The smoke from the cigarette drifted up and across the moon.

"How did you wind up here?" Angie asked.

"There was a hearing, with a judge and lawyers. I was there but I might as well not have been. They decided."

"It's not so bad," Angie said. "I actually like it here now. When I first came, a year ago, I wasn't so sure, but the girl who had your room then—she was a senior—she showed me how to fit in. If you work it right, you can pretty much do what you want. The last thing Humps wants is to expel anybody, so if you play the game, life is good."

"How do you play the game?"

"Me? Personally? I only smoke out here and I flush the butts." She laughed. "You figure out what they want from you and you give it to them. Everybody's happy."

"Just like that?" Kellah watched while Angie finished her cigarette, ground it out on the concrete, then put it in a metal box that had once been filled with peppermints. "I don't know if I remember how it feels to be happy."

Angie frowned and looked at her, silent for a moment. "Just do what I do. You'll be faking it in no time."

"They're making me see a psychologist."

"I did that for a while. After Dad divorced my first step-mother. Everybody thought I'd have issues, since she was supposed to be the second mother I'd lost."

"Did you have issues?" Kellah liked the way this girl spun things out a little at a time. She liked the way she dipped her head before she answered questions, a gesture that said you-get-me-and-I-get-you.

"Probably. But I was twelve. How would I know? Anyway, even then I was smart enough to figure out how to make the doctor happy, and if the doctor was happy, my dad was happy. They decided I was fine."

"You played the game."

"It's survival, you know?"

Kellah thought about that after she went to bed. She'd come to this place thinking survival meant one thing. Angie made her think it might be something different.

At orientation, Kellah found out that no one was allowed to miss breakfast. The day classes started, she went to the dining hall as late as possible before the eight o'clock bell.

She had to stand back for the flow of girls out of the building, on their way to classrooms. When she got inside, she showed her ID to a woman who scanned it with a hand-held device.

"You're new?" the woman asked. "Earlier tomorrow or you may miss out. I think there's still fruit and a basket of muffins." She pointed to a stainless-steel cart against the back wall.

Cafeteria workers were clearing tables of plates and food scraps. The room echoed from the scrape of chairs across the wooden floor. Kellah grabbed an apple and a muffin wrapped in plastic. Her plan to avoid everyone had worked this time, but she knew the woman would remember her.

She unwrapped the muffin and bit into it—tasted like the plastic—as she headed across the quad.

"Hey, Kellah," someone called. She turned and saw Angie with several other girls coming toward her.

"We saved you a place. Didn't you hear the breakfast bell?" Angie walked on by but turned and smiled at Kellah. "We will see you at lunch."

One of the girls trailing Angie gave Kellah a dirty look. Maybe not everyone would welcome her.

But there was no getting around Angie at mealtime. It wasn't that Angie talked to Kellah much, but she wouldn't let her get away, either. Ms. Humphries stopped by their table at lunch on Thursday.

"Are you girls making Kellah welcome?" she asked. "Make sure she's part of the Fairbourne family." She put her hand on Kellah's shoulder and gave it a squeeze. Without looking up, Kellah knew all these girls were rolling their eyes and that later they'd laugh at her.

Angie tapped on Kellah's window that night but Kellah pretended to be asleep.

The first weekend after classes started was a closed campus weekend. No one could go home or leave school. No visitors, either. There was a girls-only dance party on Friday night. Saturday featured sports and games, then pizza and movies. Kellah couldn't skip out this time. Angie made sure of that.

"It's mandatory and I'm in charge of you," Angie said. "If you get me in trouble with Humps, I will make your life miserable."

But the way she said it let Kellah know, Angie wanted her to go along.

Lights-out came late on Saturday, at midnight. Angie tapped at Kellah's window a few minutes later and Kellah climbed out to join her on the balcony.

"God," Angie said, "didn't you get tired of everybody?"

"Are you kidding?" It shocked Kellah to hear Angie say it. "You're the one everybody loves." Angie had won the dance contests, had a killer serve in volleyball, and nobody laughed at the movie unless she did.

"I know." She drew out the words like a drama queen. "But can't you tell? I'm faking it." She lit a cigarette. "Did you have any fun? I saw you hiding in the corner."

Kellah took a deep breath and decided to let go, to say what she'd been thinking. It was like deciding to jump over the railing, to fly or fall. "Everybody stares at me, like I'm some strange creature. I don't want to just be the girl whose parents died."

Angie turned toward her. "You need a new identity. Like

witness protection or something."

"I'm here, right?"

"Leave it to me. I'll fix it."

Sunday afternoon, after chapel and lunch, was QT, quiet time. Kellah settled into her room with *Jane Eyre*, assigned for English lit and one of her favorites since she was thirteen. She put in her earbuds to listen to the oldies Pops had loaded into an iPod. Cat Stevens. Carole King. Aretha. Then she heard a knock on her door.

Angie and a group of girls stood in the hall. Angie had towels draped over her arm and held one of the plastic pails they all used to carry toiletries to and from the bathroom. She grinned at Kellah.

"Let's go have some fun," Angie said.

"What are you talking about?"

"Meet you down the hall." She turned and led her gang off.

Kellah stopped the music, closed the book, and followed, annoyed and curious.

In the bathroom, Angie stood beside a stool with newspapers spread on the floor around it. "Sit here." The other girls stood to one side and watched.

"Why?" But she obeyed.

"Kellah Mace," Angie said, "take a good look at the girl in the mirror. She isn't you, not anymore. It is time for your real self to be revealed."

Kellah looked at herself. Her eyes were brown like Mims's. Her hair was straight and dark like Pops's. She wore it parted down the middle, shoulder-length, pulled into a low ponytail.

"Take out the scrunchie," Angie said. "Shake your hair loose."

Kellah did as she was told and everyone studied her hair. Angie stepped to the mirror and taped a Xeroxed photo to it.

"Do you know who this is? You, in a former life. Her name was Louise Brooks. She was in silent movies. Silent, like you."

The girls giggled.

The photo was black and white, but Louise Brooks glowed. Her big dark eyes were almost covered by glossy bangs. Her hair was a shiny helmet cut to her jawline, with cee-curls over each cheek. Her chin was curved like a doll's, her complexion creamy.

"She looks just like you," one of the girls said.

"No, she doesn't. Angie just makes you think that," Kellah said.

"That's because Angie knows the truth," Angie said. "Now hold your hair up so I can get this towel around your neck."

"What are you going to do?"

"I'm going to cut your hair."

Kellah went from looking into Louise Brooks's eyes to Angie's, by way of the mirror. Angie brushed her hair straight, then switched to a comb and began to make sections and pin them up. Kellah felt helpless, but also somehow hopeful, as if this was meant to be, and it was good. She convinced herself, it doesn't matter. Hair grows.

Angie had scissors in her hand and began to snip. All the girls inhaled as the first strands fell.

"This haircut is called a shingle," Angie said. "I found a video, how to do it. Tilt your head down."

The scissors were cold against her neck. A curtain of hair

fell over her face and slid to the floor. Kellah sat very still.

When it was over and the photo was gone, she was face to face with herself again. A new self, just as Angie had promised.

Over the next few weeks, the five girls—Linnie, Jude, Zara, Zoe, and Bella—became Kellah's friends as well as Angie's, even if that was only because to hang out with Angie, they had to accept Kellah. She accepted them, too, and always had someone to eat, walk, and study with. When two of them squabbled, she brokered their peace. But it was Angie who mattered in her life. The two of them on the balcony, the two of them talking in the dark.

"Do people tell you your mother is always with you?" Angie asked one night.

"Yes."

"Is she?"

Kellah still didn't smoke, but Angie's lighting up, inhaling, exhaling, set the rhythm for their talks. Slowed things down. Kept them in time, like a metronome for their thoughts.

"The day of the funeral," Kellah said, "the whole apartment was full of flowers. Somehow, a bee got inside and was flying around. Cousin Irene asked Mike to kill it but it got away. Later, it was in my room. It landed on my hand, but I wasn't afraid. It tapped me with its feet, like it was saying hello. Then it flew to the window and buzzed, loud. So I let it out. I was glad Mike hadn't had to smash it because, really, he isn't like that."

"Was the bee your mom?"

"I think so. And I told it, go on, I know you have to go."

"Maybe it'll come back and find you."

"Maybe." She waited until Angie put out her cigarette. "What about you?"

"I can't remember my mom very well. I used to dream about her, but not in years."

"That means they're wrong when they say she's always with you?"

"That's what I think. They're wrong." She put the filter end into the mint tin.

"That's what I think, too."

———

On the first family weekend, Kellah watched the circle from her window until she saw an old gray Saab inch its way through the SUVs and luxury sedans. She ran to Angie's door, knocked and called, "He's here." Then she joined the flow of girls heading down to greet their visitors.

The girls who expected to leave campus with parents or grandparents had to sign out ahead of time. Everybody else had to go to study hall or something the P.E. staff planned.

Kellah was excited because Mike was coming and, for the first time since she'd known her, Angie was down.

"On the first family weekend last year, Dad said he'd be here. He could arrange some business thing in the city and come see me, but at the last minute, he bailed. I spent every single family day playing stinking volleyball with the rest of the losers."

"You can come with me," Kellah said. "Mike won't mind."

"Is he like an uncle? A grandfather?"

"I don't know, but he's all I've got."

They ran downstairs and found Mike under the big oak

tree, looking lost until he saw Kellah.

"Girly." Mike hugged her tight, then held her at arm's length. "Jeez, what'd you do to your hair?"

"Don't you like it? I do." She turned her head side to side and flipped the bangs. She did want him to like it, but Mike was Mike, and he didn't like change. "This is Angie. She is my stylist, so be nice."

Angie didn't wait for acknowledgment. She grabbed his hand in both of hers and pumped it up and down. "She talks about you all the time, Mike."

Kellah saw his expression change from suspicion to pleasure. He grinned his biggest grin. "You must be the sidekick my Girly's been telling me about. You're a long drink of water, I'll say that for you."

"Is that good or bad?" Angie asked.

"It's Mike's idea of a compliment," Kellah said. "Especially for a model."

"I guess it's good I have somebody who can explain what I say," Mike said. "I miss that."

Most of the students got into cars with parents and left campus. The dining hall was open for anyone who didn't have other plans, and that's where Kellah thought Mike would be happiest. They went down the cafeteria line and found a table.

"So, Sidekick," he said to Angie, "where're your folks today?"

"My mother's dead. My dad lives in L.A." She glanced at Kellah. "That's why I'm claiming you. As long as you're coming up anyway, you may as well have two people to visit."

Mike grinned. "You got it." He bumped the fist she held out. "Now, what I want to know is, when're you coming home, Girly? Everybody in the building wants to know if you're OK.

And Lacey tried to send food for you, but I didn't know what the set-up would be. Next time, I'll take her up on it." He had a dish of chicken stew in front of him and looked less than pleased.

"Lacey's is the best," Kellah explained to Angie. "It's a neighborhood place where we used to eat all the time."

"I've never had that," Angie said. "A neighborhood place. I'm jealous."

"It's just that my mother wasn't much of a cook and Pops only made pancakes. Mike makes great chili, right, Mike?"

"And cornbread. Made it for you all the time, didn't I?" He sounded sad.

"So," he said, and she knew he was trying to sound happy again, "how's piano coming along? I got to be sure I know when your first recital will be."

"I've decided not to take piano." Kellah took a bite of pasta, gummy with cheese.

"Girly." He pointed his fork at her. "Are you sure? Are you depressed? I thought the court said you have to see a doctor so you won't get depressed."

"Just because I decide to do different things doesn't mean I'm depressed. And I've been to see the shrink twice now. I'm being good."

"She's reinventing herself," Angie said. "I'm helping."

"I'm not going to do soccer, either," Kellah said. May as well get it all out at once, if this was how he took the news. She wasn't going to tell him that recitals and games without Mims and Pops would be impossible for her. She thought he knew it, but didn't want to say it, either.

By the time they'd shown Mike the campus and their

rooms, he'd shortened Angie's nickname from Sidekick to Kick and made sure she knew how to reach him. "You're my eyes and ears on this one," he said. "You let me know and I'm here in a flash."

That night on the balcony, Angie said, "Maybe you are depressed."

Kellah began to cry, for the first time since the early days of dealing with her loss. Angie put both arms around her and they sat in the dark until the concrete chilled them to shivers.

A few weeks later, on a cold night in late October, when they both wore coats and sat side by side with a blanket over their knees, Kellah asked, "Are you afraid of things?"

"Chem tests." Angie laughed. "I was afraid of the dark when I was little. And stranger-danger. They drilled that into me in preschool."

"I used to be scared in parking decks," Kellah said. "And escalators. I thought they'd suck my feet in at the bottom. I used to have nightmares about being lost in the subway. But I'm not afraid of anything now. It's something I heard Cousin Irene say. She said, I won't have to go the rest of life wondering what the worst thing will be. It's already happened. At first I thought that was like saying I should be glad Mims and Pops died so I could get it over with."

"Bitch." Angie let out a stream of smoke.

"Maybe, but now I don't think so. I think I like not being afraid."

Angie's father sent her a plane ticket to spend Christmas in California. She made him send a second one for Kellah. The two girls spent their days on the beach or shopping, ignored by the stepmother who was infatuated with her two small sons, and by the father who promised Angie big things, gave her his credit card, and then worked the entire time.

Wherever they went, somebody was sure to ask Angie if she was a model or an actress. By the time they flew back to the East Coast, she had begun to reply, "Yes, I am."

At first Kellah scolded her for the lie, but Angie said, "I am a model. You wait and see."

When they talked about what they wanted to do after Fairbourne, Kellah said, "Go to college. Live in the library."

"I can see you doing that. Going where nobody talks, where everybody is just a big brain."

"I'm no smarter than you."

"Get real." Since Christmas, Angie had spent more and more time on the Internet, studying—she called it studying—models, fashion, makeup. She bought all the magazines and brought them to Kellah's room.

"Look, see this girl?" She'd point to a photo. "Now look at this. It's the same girl. Can you believe it?"

Kellah wasn't impressed. Mims taught her, you dressed to respect the people around you, the occasion, and yourself. And you did it fast. Fifteen minutes should do it.

Angie had never been given that kind of advice, Kellah thought and felt a little sorry for her. She hadn't felt sorry for Angie before. She pretended to be interested in fashion and modeling, and when Angie asked, she took photos of her practicing poses and attitudes.

For spring break, she and Angie went with Zoe and her parents to the Bahamas. When she told Mike about the trip, he said, "OK, Girly. You know I miss you like crazy, and I'm keeping the apartment just like it always was. For whenever you're ready."

She didn't like the Bahamas but sent Mike a photo of herself drinking out of a coconut and smiling.

There were school trips to the city for museums and theater. Sometimes Kellah told Mike and sometimes she didn't, because even if he didn't say anything, she knew he was thinking, are you ready yet, Girly?

There could be ghosts at home—Mims's, Pops's, even her own—but they didn't scare her. She didn't like the idea of going there just to visit, then having to leave again. But someday, she'd go there to live again.

Kellah spent her first Fairbourne summer with a group in London. Angie went along and dragged her out to find Carnaby Street. She found vintage stores that sold clothes from the sixties, bought a few things, and took photos of others.

"Maybe I should get my hair cut like Twiggy's," Angie said. "Maybe I should stay here and go to fashion school."

"No." For once, Kellah stood firm. "You will not cut your hair and you will go back to Fairbourne with me."

Mike was at the airport to meet their return flight. He wrapped them both into a hug. "That was the longest summer of my life."

"Are you crying?" Angie asked.

"We missed you, too," Kellah said. "We brought you something." She handed him a package wrapped in Burberry plaid paper.

"Hey, your Pops bought stuff from there." He opened it, careful not to tear the paper. "He had one just like this." He unfolded the scarf, held it in one hand, and felt the soft wool.

"Now he's really crying." Angie took it from him. "Don't get snot on it, Mike." She draped it around his neck. "I helped her pick it out, so now you wear it every day and it'll be like we're hugging you."

"It's August," Kellah said. "Save it for cold weather."

"Girly, when did you get so practical? I like Kick's idea better." He smoothed the end of the scarf over his cotton shirt. "You two coming home with me, maybe?"

"We can't," Kellah said. "As soon as everybody's through customs, we've got to go back to school. There's a van waiting."

"It's been a year." He held out a hand to Kellah. "Don't you want Kick to see it?"

"There just isn't time. I'm sorry, Mike." She took his hand.

"I'm working on her," Angie said. "You know she can't say no to me, not forever anyway."

———

The following year, there was another Christmas in California, a spring break in Florida this time, and summer in Paris, another Fairbourne-organized trip. Angie scribbled notes about street fashion and snapped pictures of women and what they wore, while Kellah worked on her French and went to lectures on the Lost Generation. She told Angie about Zelda

Fitzgerald and Angie launched a search for images of Zelda.

On their last afternoon, they paused on the Pont des Arts to watch the river traffic.

"I really think I might stay," Angie said. "I know I said that last year in London, but this is Paris. And I'm seventeen now."

Kellah felt cold, as she always did when Angie talked about splitting. A tour guide's voice, speaking English, rose from a boat full of tourists passing under them. "I have a better idea. After we graduate, we'll live in the apartment. I'll go to the university, and you'll be able to do whatever you want to do, rent-free."

Angie linked her arm through Kellah's and leaned against her. "For real? I mean, it would be perfect for me, but are you sure that's what you want?"

"I've been thinking about it. It just makes sense." She wasn't sorry, though, that it was still months away.

———

Kellah graduated as class valedictorian, with honors in English and history. Mike cried at commencement, but teased her, too. "Girly, no piano? No soccer?"

He had driven a rental truck rather than his Saab to bring Kellah home this time. He drove both girls and all their belongings back to the city, to the apartment that Kellah, who had turned eighteen in April, now owned outright.

They unloaded the girls' things in the lobby and began to move them up to the apartment, one elevator load at a time. With the first trip, Kellah allowed herself to blank out for a moment. When Mike reached around her to press the doors-open button, she was surprised to see his hand, surprised at the reminder, that this was real. She stepped out into the foyer and stopped to take in the room before them.

She had heard the story so many times. When Mims and Pops bought this rundown old building on a street nobody remembered, people expected them to knock it down and build something new, but Pops said, "We couldn't kill the old girl off." They restored it and created a ground-floor apartment for Mike, who would manage the place, and two apartments each on the second, third, and fourth floors. Pops said people expected it to be a flop, but he knew once they got done, people would be fighting over those apartments, and he was right. He and Mims then bought another building and did it again. "We saved six square blocks," he liked to brag.

But this building was special. They made the fifth floor, once upon a time the attic and storage spaces with tiny bedrooms for servants, into their own home. It belonged to Kellah now.

She moved from the entry into the living room and blinked as if the light that came through the big windows was too bright, even though it was filtered by the same soft translucent drapes she remembered.

"Nothing's changed, Girly," Mike said. "But it's cleaned up one side, down the other. You bet I made sure of that."

"This is like being in a magazine," Angie said. She passed Kellah and did a spin in the open space, slipped off her shoes and wiggled her toes in the thick rug. "We're going to live here?"

Mims had bought the rug not long before she died. It was French, Kellah remembered, and silk, or part silk. It was in soft colors that flowed like those in the big abstract painting over the couch. When the delivery men got it unrolled and left, Mims insisted that she and Kellah take off their shoes and walk across it barefooted.

"This is why I bought it. It feels so good underfoot." And then, Mims laid down on it and made snow angel arms and legs. "Come on, sweetie, it's amazing." They were both lying on the rug, laughing, when Pops came home.

"You two are crazy," he said. Then he took off his shoes and socks. "This is bad. My feet don't want to leave home, ever again."

They ate supper that night sitting on the rug and discussing whether or not they needed furniture anymore.

It all came back, as real as any moment Kellah had lived through since then, and it pinned her to her spot, there on the edge of the rug. If to step on the rug was to step back to that time, she knew she couldn't do it. She could not go through it again, and there was no way to alter what brought her here, now.

"I'll show Kick around," Mike said. "You take your time."

Kellah heard him but the words meant nothing. She heard Angie call her from far away.

"Kellah, where are you?"

She didn't know how much time had gone by. "I'm coming."

She crossed the room, went through the library and down the hall that led to the bedrooms. Her own room was on the left, the door ajar. She didn't go in. The guest room, where she planned for Angie to live, was on the right, but Angie wasn't in there. Then Kellah saw. The double doors at the end of the hall, the doors to Mims and Pops' room, were wide open.

Angie's back was to her. She almost disappeared into Mims's deep closet. She heard or sensed that Angie was there. "Your mom had the best clothes ever. You didn't tell me she was into vintage," she called out. She turned, her face glowing, with a garment on a hanger held like a baby in her arms.

"What are you doing?" Kellah had never been angry with Angie before, and the words came out in a croak from her tight throat.

Angie turned around and her smile melted. "Sorry. Mike said it was OK for me to look around."

"Well, it's not." She went forward and closed the drapes across the wide windows. The room went dark.

"Kellah, you're crying."

Angie's arms were around her and she couldn't push them away. They sat on the floor and Kellah cried herself out. When she stopped, Angie went to the bathroom and came back with tissues. Kellah found her breath, stood up, and let the light back in.

"I was an idiot to come in," Angie said. "I'm really sorry."

"I didn't think about her things still being here. I should have, but…" She drew a deep, ragged breath and turned around. "Listen, you should have this room. And if you want some of the clothes, that's OK, too." To give it away was to keep control.

"No, no. This ought to be your room."

Kellah closed her eyes, shook her head. "I can't. Seriously. It's yours."

Later, Kellah took Angie into the back garden, the lawn bordered by trees and shrubbery all surrounded by a high wall. "I lay under that tree and read. Pops taught me to kick a soccer ball here." She walked into the middle of the space and looked up at the windows on the top floor. "Mims watched us."

"It's so quiet back here," Angie said. "It's like being in a secret place." She sat on the grass, her arms straight out behind her, propping her up, her legs stretched out in front of her. "Can we tan back here?"

"I had a kiddie pool once. Maybe we should get one."

"Yeah, we will." Angie jumped up and did a cartwheel. "We're home."

They went down the block to Lacey's Bistro. Lacey, ruddy-cheeked, red hair hidden under a ball cap, came out of the kitchen and hugged Kellah for long seconds. She smelled like every good thing to eat from Kellah's childhood.

"I am so glad you're back, sweetie. I was afraid you'd forgotten about me."

"How could I forget? I need some of your spinach lasagna." Kellah stepped out of the embrace. "This is Angie. She's going to live in the apartment with me until she gets to be too famous."

"Oh, stop." Angie shook Lacey's hand. "I've been hearing about you and this place for a long time."

"And Mike told me about you. You're a model?"

"Yep, the world just doesn't know it yet."

"She only eats salads," Kellah said.

"Not tonight," Angie said. "We're celebrating. Bring on the pasta tonight."

PART 3

What Rises, What Falls

5

Albert went back to the warehouse the following day. The gates were locked and he could see the heavy chains on the double doors. So getting in was the first thing. He drove to a small town nearby and found a hardware store where he bought bolt cutters and a pry bar.

It was easy once he cut a hole in the fence. He found a hidden door under the loading dock. It was unlocked, just for him. Maybe he was the one with the devil's own luck. He went into the black basement, found steps, and climbed to the main floor. The windows were covered now but he had a flashlight. It was so vast and empty, it was hard to remember what it had been like just twenty-four hours before. He walked around inside and listened to the echoes. Angel saying "hi." That stupid woman with the hair who whistled like they were all dogs who had to come running. The man who stood above everybody and gave orders. The way Angel had to do what they said. They treated her like a thing. Painted her. Dressed her. Posed her. He was the only one who saw the real Angel under it all. He made a plan.

It took weeks to get everything ready. He brought in the stuff he needed and built a frame to tack canvas on, to make a little room out of one corner, a space he could clean so it would be OK to bring her there. He brought in a blow-up mattress, brand new sheets and pillows, a table, two chairs, LED lanterns, water jugs, protein bars, duct tape, a toilet contraption that used a big bucket, garbage bags, and kitty litter.

Then he focused on Angel. He found out where she lived from the Internet and he watched for her outside her building. He tried to figure out which apartment in the building she lived in. Then he had the idea to take her roses. That would get him inside. He'd been in places like it, and he knew there would be a list of residents or names on the security call box. But the old stupid guy had seen him and threw him out.

Sometimes a black car picked her up early in the morning and brought her home at the end of the day.

Sometimes she went out again at night, by herself or with a short girl he paid no attention to except that she was there. They'd get in a black car like the one that picked her up in the mornings.

Sometimes she came out of her house and headed for the subway. That made him nervous. He never rode it himself, because he saw creeps down there and it was dirty, and he hated to think of her underground. He settled himself with the knowledge that his chance was coming.

It was a Saturday. She ate lunch at a restaurant, at a sidewalk table. She'd talked to three other people, the short girl who'd walked there with her, and a tall skinny black girl who showed up with a white guy. They laughed and touched Angel on the arm or the hand. As if they cared. It all looked fake to him. More people using Angel. Lying to her. Making her fake, too.

Then she left and walked away by herself, toward the park. He knew she took the same path a lot. It was easy to be at the other end, where she would come out. When he was a little kid, he'd learned something nobody else seemed to know. Even in the city, there are empty spaces. There are moments when a person is all alone on a street or in a shadow. When things can happen and nobody sees. It had been true when he was the little boy who ran away from home and hid in the bushes by the playground. That was the moment he needed with Angel, and here it was.

6

Angie's dad was too busy to attend graduation, but he flew the girls to California. Kellah planned to start at the university in the fall and would have taken summer school courses before then, but Angie wouldn't let her. "Absolutely not. You are going with me. You are going to buy a bikini and lie on the beach. You are going to go dancing."

Besides, Angie wanted to get her portfolio together, so her father had his secretary schedule appointments with the best makeup artist and photographer in L.A. Kellah went along and watched from the background as her friend was transformed over and over with clothes, makeup, hairstyles. It mystified her why her smart, strong friend was so willing to let herself be consumed in make-believe, yet she couldn't look away. She wondered if heart surgeons were more serious and focused than this photographer and his minions.

When they fell back into the limo, Angie squeezed her tight.

"Did you hear him? He thinks I'm going to be huge." She laughed and collapsed against the seatback.

"You loved it, didn't you?"

"Sure. It's like my life is a movie or something." She faced the window for a moment and then turned back to Kellah.

"You don't get it, do you? That's OK. Just knock some sense into me when you need to."

Mike had had Mims and Pops's bedroom furnishings moved into storage and the girls went shopping to turn it into Angie's space.

"You're sure?" Angie asked.

"For the hundredth time, I'm sure. If you're going to be famous, you need a big room."

"No, I don't. I really don't."

"Then do it for me. You'd fill that tiny guest room closet in no time and move out. Then what would I do?"

Kellah found that she could still register for the second summer session and took an advanced French course. Every day, Angie put on skinny black pants, a natural linen jacket over a white T-shirt, pulled her hair into a high ponytail and went from agency to agency, carrying a portfolio of photos with her. By Labor Day, she had representation.

They fell into a routine, up early and out of the apartment, to what Kellah thought of as their separate worlds. But evenings during the week, they were home with takeout from Lacey's and talk about their days.

Angie went to parties on weekends. "It's work, I swear," she said.

"Right, and you hate every minute."

"Come with me and you'll see."

Sometimes, Kellah let herself be persuaded. She let Angie

dress her in black, with red lipstick and lots of mascara. She got her share of attention at the parties, but most of the time she just watched her friend move through the room the way she'd moved through high school. Later, they laughed about the pretension on display.

"Seriously," Angie said, "don't let me drink the Kool-Aid."

Those were the moments when Kellah worried. Would she lose Angie to that world?

"You'll be in it, but not of it," she told her.

"That sounds right."

For a while, Kellah went out with a grad student who chatted her up in the library. And Angie had a long line of admirers. By unspoken agreement, and to spare Mike from having to work overtime as their protector, they didn't bring men home. It amused Kellah that Angie didn't sleep with the men she went out with.

"Who knew you'd be a prude?"

"I see what goes on," she said. "It's not pretty."

When Kellah tired of her grad student, she changed her study habits and he faded away.

Angie began to get commercial work and she dragged Kellah along whenever she could. "Tell them you're my personal assistant," she said. "They all have at least three."

And then, overnight it seemed, Angie's face was everywhere. She was Angel, known by the one name, and the paparazzi began to follow her.

"I smile and wave and ignore," she said. She got a second cellphone for Kellah, Mike, her father and her agent to use.

When it was hacked, she purchased another one with a different number. "Don't worry. Nothing's forever. Besides, I'm still
just your sidekick."

7

The promise she had made to Angie, to find her, settled Kellah's nerves. She went to bed, her phone under her pillow, and dozed. At 6:30, she was up. She dressed and tiptoed past the guest room where Mike was still snoring. If she took the elevator, there was a chance that the bell would wake him, or that she'd run into another early-rising tenant heading out, so she went down the back stairs.

She wasn't usually on the street at this hour on a Sunday morning. It was daylight, but sunless. The air was damp and a slightly moldy scent rose from the pavement. Parkside never saw heavy traffic, so city sounds were in the distance. The few dog-walkers and joggers, the lone people in search of newspapers and coffee, were all intent on their own purposes. She began to walk south.

The streetscape changed and there were no more shops or apartment houses with small green patches tucked between them. The buildings were commercial, then industrial, some of them deserted, boarded up and fenced off. Everything around her had a shut-down gloom to it. She kept walking until she finally reached the address that was her goal.

When she stood in front of it, she called the number she'd stored in her phone. As it rang, she realized how unlikely it was that anyone would be there.

"Come on," she whispered, and it worked.

"Big Men Movers." A man's abrupt voice.

"Hi. Good morning. Are you inside the building on lower Third?"

"What? Who is this?"

"I'd like to talk with someone in charge," she said.

"Lady, I'm the only one here. And I own the place, so how can I help you?"

"I'm outside, in front of the building. Would you come out and talk with me?" What if he said no? She hadn't thought about failure until now.

"What's this about?" He sounded more curious than annoyed.

"My friend is missing and I believe one of Big Men's employees may know where she is. I need to find out who he is, so I can ask him."

His sigh was throaty, a grumble. "What the hell. OK, I'll come out."

In a moment, a door in the brick façade opened and a heavyset man walked through it. He had on work pants and a gray and red T-shirt with the logo like the one Ape had worn. He saw her, took the narrow steps to the ground, and covered the distance between them.

"You're out here by yourself?" He looked up and down the street. "Where are the cops who called?"

She was surprised at that, but pressed on. "Do you know a man with a shaved head and a tattoo of a gorilla?" She touched the back of her own head.

Before he answered, she heard a sound and looked up the street. A car turned the corner and drove toward them. It stopped and Detectives Quick and Nash got out.

"Ms. Mace," Quick said, "what are you doing here?"

"Are you Mr. Biggers?" Nash asked the man. "I'm Detective Nash. I called you."

"Yeah, I've been waiting on you. I got what you asked me for."

"Do you have an office or someplace where we can talk, sir?" Nash asked.

"You got to go down the alley. I'll meet you there." He turned and walked back toward the building.

"How did you get here?" Quick asked and Kellah looked him in the eye. His lips pressed into a thin line. He was angry, but she was not going to be intimidated.

"I walked. I want to find Angie, and this man may know something."

"We know," Quick said. "That's why we're here. You've put yourself in danger and you're interfering with our inquiry."

Kellah glanced at him to gauge whether he was angry or just surprised. Nash looked at him, too, with an odd twist to her mouth.

"You can't stay out here by yourself," he said. "Come with us. Stay where I can see you and don't say anything."

He headed for the alley that ran beside the building. Kellah followed and Nash walked behind her. Biggers already stood on a landing, holding a security door open with his hip.

"My office is in here," he said. They followed him to a small room crowded with a large desk and wall-to-wall file cabinets.

"I can get more chairs." He didn't move, though, maybe in hopes that they didn't plan to stay long enough to sit.

"I'll help you." Nash went with him down the hall.

"What did you say to him?" Quick asked.

Kellah looked down this time, afraid that if she challenged him, he'd make her leave after all and she wanted to know everything Biggers told them. "I said my friend is missing. I asked if he knows the man with the tattoo."

"Those questions give him a lot of information. What if he's involved? It's not good for Angie, or for you."

It's true, she thought. She had told him a lot without being aware of it. But she wasn't going to acknowledge to Quick that she'd done the wrong thing.

Biggers carried in two plastic chairs and Nash brought one. They managed to squeeze them in and everyone sat, Kellah hemmed into a corner with Quick to her left and a filing cabinet to her right.

"So?" Biggers asked.

"As I told you on the phone," Nash leaned toward him, "we want to identify one of your employees." She held out her phone and Kellah guessed she showed him the photo of Ape.

Biggers squinted at the phone, then looked up at the ceiling and sighed. "Albert Darwin. What's he done?"

"We need to talk to him. Can you give us his address, phone numbers?"

The man yanked open a file drawer and pulled out a folder. "He's my wife's cousin's kid. That's the only reason I hired him. If he's in trouble with the law, that's the end of it, no matter how much his mom cries."

He turned a sheet of paper around so Nash could see it.

She took a photo of it, then took out a notebook and wrote something.

"Do you have your employees fingerprinted? Run background checks?" Nash asked him.

"Yeah, but not him. I try to keep peace at home, you know? When he comes around, looking for work, I find something. It's not like he's a regular." He was nervous. It showed in his voice.

"This address," Nash said, "is it his? Or his mom's?"

"That's Jackie's. His mom. He lives there most of the time."

"Most? If you had to guess, when he's not at his mom's, where would he go?"

Biggers sat back. "Look, my wife and Jackie will be pissed at me, but I don't owe him anything. I've got to take care of my business, right? If people think one of my guys is some nutcase, there goes my business, right? His dad had a restaurant not far from here. It shut down a few years before he died, but Jackie still owns the building. She thinks the neighborhood will go upscale one day and she'll be able to sell it for millions. I've always thought, when Ape—I mean Albert—disappears for a while, he might have a crib there."

"Ape," Kellah said. "I heard someone call him that." She caught the glance Nash shot her, the you-were-told-to-be-quiet glance.

"The address?" Quick asked.

"On Borman, between Third and Fourth, the north side. I think the name's still on the window. Darwin's Good Eats."

Quick stood up. "I think that's all we need, Mr. Biggers. Thanks for your cooperation."

"She said something about a missing girl." Biggers nodded

toward Kellah. "You think he's got something to do with that?"

"There is one more thing," Quick said, as if he hadn't heard the question. "If you hear anything about Albert, call us. In the meantime, don't tell your wife or Jackie or him about this meeting. If you do, I could interpret it as interference with a police investigation, and I could arrest you for that."

"Yeah, yeah. Like I said, I don't owe him anything. I've got my business to take care of."

The plastic chairs had to be moved before they could leave the office. This time, Nash led the way. Quick touched Kellah's elbow and gestured for her to go ahead of him. Biggers let them out and locked the door behind them.

Quick opened the back door of the car and held it for Kellah. She got in. He closed it and stepped away to talk to Nash.

Kellah knew they thought she'd been foolish to come to Big Men Movers. In truth, she'd given no thought to the fact that it was Sunday morning and it was unlikely anyone would be at work. Or that there could be any danger to her. With Angie missing, days of the week and time didn't seem important. Nor did she feel any fear. No one, not even Mike, could understand what it meant to her.

But she'd learned something important. She'd learned that Quick and Nash believed her about Angie. They'd all been lucky to find Mr. Biggers.

She didn't remember Nash's first name. Quick's was Brendan. She'd seen how he talked to Biggers, quiet and professional with his threat. When he showed he was angry at her, it felt different, with the edge of something personal, a connection. He cared.

Nash walked away and made a phone call. Quick got into

the driver's seat and turned to look at Kellah. His face was stony.

"I'm sorry," she said. "I know you're mad, but Angie means everything to me and I thought—or I guess I didn't think." She looked away, and then back at him. His eyes were blue, paler than Angie's, and had fine lines around them, making him look tired. "Please find her."

"It's what we do." His voice was softer than she expected.

Nash got into the car, glanced at Quick and then at Kellah.

"Did you get through to the captain?" Quick asked.

"We're set," she said. "As soon as we can get there."

"Ms. Mace, we've got to take you home before we do anything else. That costs us valuable time. Your interference stops now, understand?"

Quick escorted Kellah into her building. He knew she'd gotten to him and he knew he had to shake it off. He'd let Nash deal with her from now on.

Mike Michaels came out of a door into the lobby. "Jeez, Girly. Where you been?" He put his arms around her and glared at Quick. "You know what I've been thinking?"

"I'm sorry, Mike." Her voice was muffled by his body. She freed herself. "I'll explain it all. Detective Quick just brought me home."

"Where she's going to stay, correct?" Quick said. "Listen, Kellah, Angie might show up, or call you. You need to be here for her." He nodded once to the other man. "Michaels, can you keep an eye on her?"

"I'm not letting her out of my sight." Mike gave her a little shake, released her, and jabbed the elevator button. The door opened and closed on them.

8

Quick took a moment to watch the brass dial show its ascent to the fifth floor. Then he trotted out of the building, got into the driver's seat of the idling car, and made a wide U-turn.

"I hope you got the point across," Nash said.

"What do you think?"

"Sorry, but she's a wild card. She's pretty and feminine and throws off a crazy reckless vibe."

Quick's silent concentration on driving raised a shield between them. Nash hoped she hadn't burned too much good will with her comments about Kellah. She was apparently one of those women men like Mike Michaels and now Quick just had to defend. Nash worked hard to avoid being seen that way and couldn't help wanting to tell those women to shape up. They might get what they want, but there was a price to be paid, and not just by them.

They headed back to the southern part of the city and located Darwin's Good Eats's address. A dingy sign hung over the door. Quick drove past it, maintaining the speed limit, and Nash checked it out.

"The windows are papered over," she said. "The door's blocked with trash and junk."

They had passed into the next block, where two black vans were parked.

"There's the team." He pulled up beside one and Nash lowered her window. The team leader, an experienced SWAT officer, got out of his van.

"Got the search warrant." He leaned in to hand the document to Quick. "No signs of life inside. We're going in the back door."

"OK," Quick said. "You know there could be a hostage in there, right?"

"We got it." The man waved a hand and the vans emptied. His people obviously knew where to go, what to do.

Quick turned around, drove back toward the restaurant and parked across from it. Nash looked up at the buildings around it, storefronts with what could be offices or apartments on the upper floors. A few windows had air conditioners hanging out of them. They all had a Sunday-morning blankness to them.

"It'll be a while before Darwin's mom makes her millions in this neighborhood," Nash said. She checked her watch. It wasn't yet 9:30 and that was a good thing. She hoped that whoever lived in these dim-looking places would stay put a while longer. Just as she thought it, the door in the building nearest her opened and a disheveled man stumbled out. He looked right at her and, as if he could read her thoughts, he turned, disappeared back inside, and pulled the door shut behind him.

Two cops jogged past and took up posts on either side of the restaurant's front door.

"Get down," Quick said. He lowered his head and body so they were below the car windows. Nash unlatched her seat belt and followed his example. She heard a thump-thump, muffled and distant. A flash-bang. Did that mean they had found somebody inside? Her heart pumped against her ribs and she felt a rush of adrenalin. Quick raised himself up and turned his head. She did the same in time to see the restaurant door open from the inside. The two cops kicked junk aside so they could go in, guns drawn.

They moved at the same time, out of the car, across the street, and into the building. It was dark. The smell of mold, ancient rancid grease, and old bodily fluids, was strong. Somebody ripped paper off a window to let in some light. The place was empty. The carpet was gray with thick dust, undisturbed except where the cops had walked. The bar across the back looked like plywood, cheap and disintegrating.

"There's nothing up here." The team leader met them as they moved toward the kitchen. "My guys are securing the basement now."

It was as empty as the upstairs.

"Biggers guessed wrong," Quick said. "There's no crib here."

"You got a Plan B?" the leader asked.

"As a matter of fact," Quick said. He turned toward the door and Nash ran to keep up.

9

MAY 2012

Albert was tired. Angel needed rest, too. "I'll come back," he said. "Then we'll go away and be together forever."

He took the big flashlight and made his way down the metal steps to the basement. His backpack made it a tight squeeze. He crossed the space, stepped outside and made sure the door closed behind him. The door was under the loading dock. When he stepped out from under its cover, the sun hit him in the eyes. It froze him. Had there been night, or just the dark space inside the warehouse?

He crossed the yard to the gap he'd cut in the fence. He looked up and back to the building where he'd first seen Angel, where he left her now. It stunned him to think he could leave her and come back and she'd be there. Safe. And she'd have realized, they would be together from now on.

He pushed through to the other side of the fence and dragged the big old tire he used to mark the spot into place. His feet felt like they weighed fifty pounds each. He trudged through the overgrown field to where he'd left the van behind a few skinny trees. It alarmed him to see how big it looked, how white, but he calmed himself. In the weeks after the photo shoot, he'd come here many times and there was never anybody around.

Once he and the other workers from Big Men packed up furniture, racks of clothing, cases of cosmetics, lights, and junk, once all the photographers and the girls and people who did things he didn't understand got into their black cars and left, this was his private world. Those people had existed only to bring him and Angel together, and then they had vanished.

He climbed into the van and set the pack down on the floor. He wanted a shower and clean clothes, some sleep. He had a motel room rented, just ten minutes away, but he had to compose himself before he could drive. He stretched out on the front seat. It was cramped but the discomfort calmed him. He thought back over what had happened since he first saw Angel, when she spoke to him, that single day when his life began.

He rolled to his side on the van seat. Even though Angel didn't love him yet, everything had gone well. Better than he had imagined. His plans were perfect. Details he had not thought about in advance fell his way. The devil's own luck, his dad would say. But it exhausted him.

His legs began to cramp and woke him. If he'd slept, he didn't know. He pulled himself up, got himself behind the wheel, found the keys under the seat and started the motor. He drove past the warehouse and thought about her. He'd had to get a little rough, but it would be OK. When he came back, he'd be kind to her, bring food and water. He'd take care of her. Then she would understand and she'd love him.

He had stayed at the motel a few times while he got the warehouse ready. The first time he registered, a woman who made him think of Bitch Mom watched him fill out the card, took his money, and gave him a key. After that, it was a young guy who looked like a Muslim. Now, as he drove in, both of them stood outside the office and watched him go by. He looked at the clock on the dashboard. It was 8:30. Did it matter that they'd seen him? Would they think he'd been gone all night, or would they think he'd been out to get breakfast? He realized that from then on, he needed to be unseen, unrecognized.

The room was tidy, the way he'd left it. The thread he'd closed in the bathroom door was in place. That helped, but his nerves were still bad. He put the pack on the bed and reached in for the plastic bag. Angel's hair was tumbled and tangled. Later, he would straighten it strand by strand. The thought made him sick with happiness. He held the bag to his chest for a moment before sliding it back into its hiding place, along with the knife and his money.

He went to the bathroom and saw in the mirror that his clothes—jeans and a T-shirt that was too big even for him— were grimy and stained. Sweat, blood, dirt from the warehouse floor. He had cleaned and cleaned the area he'd screened off, made it tolerable, but the place was too big and too filthy to get as clean as it should be for Angel. He'd explained and apologized, promised that she wouldn't be there long. "Only until…" He started to say, until you love me, but her eyes got big and dark and she started to cry, so he stopped talking and did what he needed to do. The knife had been enough most of the time, but at the end, he'd had to get a little rough. That was when he explained about purifying her. She didn't understand. He'd make it up to her. Give her whatever she wanted, once they got out of there.

He stayed in the shower a long time. He thought about the things she'd said to him, that she didn't recognize him or the place, at least not at first. Then she began to remember, so it must have been all the junk people had filled her head with. He dressed in clean jeans and a shirt that fit better. The old clothes he stuffed into a trash bag. He'd get rid of them. He had a cooler with a carton of milk, some sliced cheese and ham, and a bunch of grapes. The ice had melted, but the water was still cool. He had a loaf of bread and packets of mustard. He made a sandwich and ate it. Then he stretched out on the bed and fell asleep.

Somebody banged on the door. "Housekeeping. You staying another night, you got to go to the office and pay."

"Yeah," he called. He heard the housekeeper and her cart move down the sidewalk to another room. He was groggy, but this time from dense sleep. He rolled over and looked at his phone. Damn. It was mid-afternoon, after two o'clock. He had to get back to Angel.

He left the cooler and food behind, except for the grapes because Angel would like them, took the bag of dirty clothes, the duffel that held clean ones, his knife case, and the backpack, and went to the van and drove toward the warehouse. His nerves were calm now. He was in control of his life as never before. And Angel would be happy to see him. He would talk to her about the future.

———

Nash and Quick found Jackie Darwin drinking from a coffee mug and shaking with anger. Quick went straight upstairs to find the officers who went through her son's room.

"Ms. Darwin," Nash said, "I'm Detective Nash. May I ask you a few questions?"

Jackie stared at her and for a moment Nash expected an expletive, maybe racial. The thought was there, she could tell. The woman was pushing sixty, wiry, with hair dyed too dark for her complexion.

"I don't give a fuck who you are. If you people damage my property, I'll sue. Albert isn't here. You got no reason to disrupt my life like this."

Nash took a seat at the kitchen table and waited.

"OK." Jackie drained her mug and sighed. "What do you want?"

"Where is your son, Ms. Darwin?"

"I don't know." She rested her forearms across the table and gripped her hands together.

"Can you give me a list of his friends?"

"No."

"Have you ever heard him speak of a woman named Angie Boone? Or Angel?"

That seemed to stir something. She glanced up at Nash and then blinked. "He doesn't know any girls. Why?"

Quick came into the kitchen. He put a file folder down on the table and opened it. It was full of photos, all of Angie, printed from websites or cut out of magazines. "Do you recognize her, Ms. Darwin?"

"She's just some girl. Looks like a whore. Anybody can have pictures of her."

"And your son does. We found these in his room. Do you know where his computer is, ma'am?"

She didn't answer. She stared at her hands and Nash sensed she was shifting from anger to worry. It wasn't the time to hassle her about lying.

"Ms. Darwin," she said, "if it's on the premises, we will find it. It'll be much better for you and your property if you tell us."

She sighed again, unclenched her fists and flexed her fingers. "If he doesn't take it with him, he locks it in an old trunk in the basement."

"Do you think it's there now?"

Jackie shrugged, and looked up, her eyes tight. "You'll just have to look, won't you?"

They did not find a computer but took the photographs and a few things that would yield DNA. They also took a case of knives of different sizes and materials, including a vicious-looking long blade hidden in the closet. Jackie denied knowledge of them, said her son would never hurt a fly.

On the ride back to the station, Nash began to feel the effects of a long night, two shifts without a nap in between. Quick drove without speaking but also without the intensity she'd seen before. There was a heaviness about him, a slackening of energy that matched her own. She wanted to stay awake, so she flipped again through the photos. Three of them showed Angie in an elaborate ball gown with a full skirt that had to be supported by some internal structure. It was beaded in gold and silver.

"What did Kellah say about a heavy dress Angie wore at the shoot? I bet this is it." She held the three pictures up so that he could take a glance while stopped at a light. "These aren't professional. He snapped them himself. Probably on his phone."

"OK." Quick's tone encouraged her to think a step further. The thought came slowly.

"You know where I think he'd take her?" She turned toward him. "He'd take her to the place where he met her. That big empty warehouse."

He nodded and held out his hand, palm up, for her to slap. "Call Biggers and get the address of that warehouse."

It took Biggers a minute or two to find it and read it off to her. She scribbled it down, ended the call, and began to pull up a map on her phone. "This is a problem. It's across the river. In a different state."

"Let's go convince the captain this is going to be worth the trouble."

———

Kellah leaned back into the soft nest of Angie's bed and closed her eyes. She clutched a pillow to her chest and breathed in Angie's scent and energy. Her grief was dry. Brendan Quick had promised to find Angie, but how could he when he knew nothing about her? Kellah was the one who should find her, who should know where she was. Just know.

She picked up the framed photo of Angie again. Angie mocked herself for keeping it by her bed, said, I'm such a diva. You'd better keep me in line.

But Kellah understood, it was a talisman, a good luck piece, and even though no one else knew, it showed the bond between the two of them. She touched Angie's face, touched the smile, and wished she could go back to that moment. Go back. With the phrase, something clicked inside her.

She dropped the picture and ran to her room to change back into the clothes she'd worn that morning. Then she ran to the kitchen, where Mike was making soup for their lunch.

"You ready to eat?" he asked.

"I know where she is," she said. "Get the car."

"Are you crazy, Girly? Remember what Quick said." Then he asked questions. "Where is this place? How do you know?"

"We're wasting time. Come with me, or I go alone. I've got the extra car keys."

He sighed. "I can't let you do that. Give me a few minutes."

When they headed down the street toward the garage, he carried a canvas tote with a zippered top. It was heavy and he shifted it from hand to hand.

"What's in that?" she asked.

"We might need tools. You never know."

It took longer to reach the warehouse than she remembered, but when she had gone there before it had been early morning, with light traffic and a driver. Now, Mike made fits and starts between red lights until they got through the toll-gates, across the bridge, and beyond the first circle of suburbs.

"So you remember where to turn, right?" he asked.

"I'll know it when I see it." But her heart rate was fast and shallow. She hoped some power outside herself would give her a sign. Then, there it was, the old sign, faded and rusted, its frame crooked so that it didn't face the road anymore. The limo driver had missed it on the morning of the shoot, cursed, made a U-turn to go back, and a delivery truck had come at them, horn blaring. Later, Angie had laughed. "My big break and I almost get smooshed in a car before I get there."

"Turn left." Kellah gripped Mike's arm and pointed.

"You sure, Girly?"

The road into the property was rutted and the pavement broken into a jigsaw puzzle. Mike drove slowly but the suspension on his old car did little to smooth the ride. He made a sharp turn at the river and there they were, in front of the old brick building. She knew it was the right place, but it felt different. The fence was more imposing than she remembered. On the day of the shoot, the gate was open wide, with vehicles parked all around the inner yard. The tall, narrow, arched windows had been open. Now they were covered with sheets of plywood.

Kellah began to get her bearings. The caterer's truck had parked where Mike stopped the car. And the water beyond them wasn't the river. It was a canal that must have served an industrial purpose at some point.

"I don't see a way in," Mike said.

She got out of the car and went to the gate, but it was secured with a massive U-shaped bar and lock.

"I got a crowbar, but it won't dent that setup," Mike said.

"There has to be a way. You go left, I'll go right. Check every inch."

She made her way along the fence, shaking it with her hands or leaning into it. It was wobbly from age, but didn't give enough to allow her to get in. She rounded the corner into a field overgrown with weeds. Under the weeds, the ground was littered with paper, bottles, scrap metal—a dumping ground bordered by trees on the far side. She slowed to watch her footing but still tripped and fell over something large. When she sat up, she saw it was an old tire, a big one. How had she missed something that large, even in a knee-high thicket? It was tight up against the fence. She leaned in and saw that some of the links in the chain were loose. She pressed and a section gave a little, then a little more.

"Mike," she called. "I found it."

He was opposite her on the far side and lugged his canvas bag so it took a while for him to get to her. She managed to shove the crude flap in the fence open by a few feet before he got there. It dragged against the ground and marks in the dirt showed it had been opened before, more than once, though if she had not stumbled on the tire, she could have missed the signs. She felt calm, clear in her mind what had to happen next.

"Now, let's take a minute." Mike let the bag drop and leaned over, his hands on his knees to catch deeper breaths. "If he's in there, it could be dangerous."

"He's not here. He uses the tire to hold the fence in place. The only way to do that is from the outside." She kicked at the fence until the gap was wide enough to step through and ran across the yard toward the building. She heard Mike grunt and swear behind her, heard his heavy steps. She climbed the steps to the platform that ran the length of the structure. There were three double doors spaced along it, each locked with heavy hardware. She put her ear against the middle one and heard nothing.

"Angie, it's me. We've come to get you." She slammed both fists against the door, and then went to the others. They were equally silent, unmoving, but she called to Angie each time. She stood for a moment, her eyes closed.

"Down here, Girly." Mike's voice was muffled and distant.

She looked back but he'd disappeared. She went down the steps and met him coming from under the platform.

"I found a way in," he said. She followed him into the dim

space, tall enough for her to stand upright, but requiring him to stoop.

The door was at the bottom of a narrow well. He put his weight into it. She followed him into darkness that smelled like dirt and damp. Then a cone of light spread out in front of her, played across and up.

"Got one for you, too." Mike handed her a flashlight.

"You're great." She turned it on and their beams crossed each other.

"One of us has to be thinking straight." He played his light up the wall around the door, found a panel of switches and tried them, but they were dead.

Kellah stepped into the interior, saw a hard-packed earthen floor, steel posts, and a low ceiling tracked with heavy beams. Then she saw a flight of metal stairs on the far wall. "Mike, over there."

They climbed and emerged into a vast space. It had been a dreamscape on the day of the photo shoot, a romantic break from reality, furnished with brocades, tapestries, and peopled by beautiful young women in impossible garments. Now it was stripped and hollow, almost as dark as the basement. The only light filtered in around the edges of the plywood over the windows.

"Do you hear something?" As she said it, she began to walk. The beam of her flashlight led her. She wasn't sure if she moved front to back, or back to front, along or across the axis. Then her light caught something, an odd vertical line where none should be. She went to it and touched it. It was coarse fabric tacked to wooden slats, a screen of some kind.

"Oh, God." She stepped around it and went down on her

knees beside Angie, slumped in a chair. She dropped her flashlight so she could hug her friend. She felt flesh and realized Angie was naked, that she was bound to the wooden chair, and her head was covered. "Mike. Come quick."

"Here, hold this." Mike handed her his flashlight and took over. "The bastard wrapped her head in tape." He motioned to Kellah to shine the light. She had to hold it with both hands to steady herself.

"There's gauze under here," Mike said. "I think we can cut it off. My sweet Kick, what's he done to you?"

"Is she breathing?"

"Yeah."

Kellah watched him work the knife, then tug, work the knife, tug a little more. He grunted with the effort. She held her own breath until he had peeled the mask off Angie.

"She's taped to the chair," Kellah said.

"Yeah." He sat back and looked. "If we try to pull it off, we'll take her skin off. We need help."

Kellah found her phone in her pocket. "There's no signal."

"OK. I'll try from outside." He reached into the bag and took out a water bottle. "You stay here. Talk to her. Get some water in her." He reached into the bag one more time. "You know how to shoot this?" He held out a gun.

"No, I don't." But she didn't hesitate to take it.

"Flip this. It's the safety. Point it and squeeze the trigger. If that Ape comes back, shoot him." He took the phone from her and headed for the stairs.

She laid the gun beside her, put her hands on Angie's cheeks and lifted her head, wanting a sign of recognition, a glimmer of spirit.

"It's me, Angie. You knew I'd come, didn't you?"

Only then did she realize. The long blond hair was gone. She held her friend's chin in one hand and ran the other over her scalp—bare, bristled, and scabbed where someone had hacked at it.

––––––––––

Nash kept quiet while Quick stood, his head down, his hands linked behind him, and they both listened to the captain. Did they know how hard it was to get a search warrant in another state? On a hunch? Their first one, about the restaurant building, had come up empty. Did they want to put their necks—his neck—on the line based on nothing?

Nash was surprised when Quick told the captain about the warehouse and didn't attribute the idea to her. And he'd argued it with more conviction than she thought was in him. She had to bite her lip and keep quiet. She told herself, he was the lead so right or wrong, he'd get credit or blame. And maybe he was thinking, the captain was more likely to agree with the proven golden boy—white golden boy—than a black newcomer, female. Maybe that was true, but it was hard to be passive while the men argued back and forth.

The captain had a TV behind his desk, always on the news channel, always muted. Nash focused on it. A cut from the studio to a live feed caught her eye. A reporter stood in front of a place that looked familiar. Then she knew. It was Kellah Mace's apartment house. A reporter talked to a tall, thin black woman. The closed captions read, "In front of Angel Boone's house, talking with her friend, Vonnie Stewart. Vonnie, you may have been the last person to see Angel before she apparently disappeared yesterday. What can you tell us?"

"Sir." Nash stepped forward and pointed. Both men looked first at her, then at the TV. "They've got the story."

"Hell." The captain swiveled his chair so that his back was to the detectives. "How? You two didn't—"

"No sir," they said in unison.

"It could have been Kellah Mace," Nash said and saw Quick's jaw clench; he wanted to deny that. "But we called this Vonnie Stewart and all Angie's other friends. They probably talked to each other, figured out that something is wrong. It doesn't take much for word to spread."

Just then, Quick's cellphone rang. He looked at the screen and answered. "Kellah?" He looked at Nash and shook his head. "Mike, what's up?"

The captain frowned and crossed his arms.

"It's Mike Michaels, a friend of Angie's," Nash said to the captain. "Maybe he has news."

Quick's mouth opened as he listened. Nash read puzzlement, then anger. "What do you mean you found her?" Then, "Wait, hold on."

He put the phone on speaker and held it out. Mike was saying, "…Kellah's idea, the warehouse where Ape met her. So we came and she's here. She's bad, Detective, we got to have some help."

"Is that enough for a warrant?" Quick asked. The captain's face turned red.

Nash eased the phone out of his hand and spoke to Mike. "We'll call local law enforcement and they'll be there fast. Are you armed?"

"I got a crowbar, a knife, and a gun. Licensed."

"Don't have any of it on you or near you when they get there. They don't know who the bad guy is, or isn't. Tell Kellah. You both stand aside, you cooperate."

When she hung up, the two men had gotten past their pissing match. "I've got it," the captain said. "I'll have it all worked out by the time you get there."

Quick moved the car through traffic, quiet except for his curses at drivers who didn't move out of the way fast enough, even with the siren and blue lights. They cut across the outer ring of the city and took the bridge. Then his thunderous mood broke.

"What kind of idiots were we, not to figure this out hours ago? It's so obvious."

"No. We started with the most obvious places, then started working our way out," Nash replied.

"I'm going to punch Mike Michaels in the face. He should have stopped her."

He's crazed, Nash thought. Is he blaming me for not figuring it out earlier? Blaming Mike and Kellah for getting there faster? They found Angie. She's alive. Isn't that the point?

But she felt for Quick. She liked him and he was hurting. Exactly why he was so upset, she wasn't sure.

They found the turnoff that went to the warehouse. An ambulance, blaring and flashing, passed them going the other way on the narrow access road. They both turned to look at its taillights and then at each other.

The gate had been broken open, and the yard around the warehouse was full of cars marked and unmarked, two fire trucks, another emergency medical van, and an old Saab. Nash saw Kellah sitting in the open back of the van, a blanket over her shoulders. An EMT hovered over her. On the far side of the yard, Mike and a couple of uniformed officers hunched, hands on knees, looking at the ground at the base of the fence.

Quick parked and got out. "You go talk to Michaels." He walked straight toward Kellah.

"Quick," Nash said, "be careful."

He turned and glared at her. He didn't like her words, but she hadn't expected him to. She just had to say something to let him know his frame of mind was obvious. She headed for the group of men by the fence.

For the next half hour, she listened to Mike's story, made sure the sheriff's department had adequate crime-scene techs, and made arrangements to take Kellah's and Mike's statements at the local sheriff's office. She kept looking toward Quick, thinking he would join her. Kellah was getting care and he needed to attend to police work, but he stayed near her. It wasn't until she and Mike walked back toward the emergency vehicles that he broke away from the young woman.

"I bet you want to cuss me out," Mike said when the three of them met halfway between the building and the fence.

"You should have had better sense," Quick said. "This could have been a bad scene."

"I didn't believe it, when she said she knew where Kick—Angie—was."

"But you came armed."

Nash stepped in. "The SOC guys are in the building, so we can't go in. Kellah's OK, Mike, so the sheriff will transport the two of you to their station."

She went to Kellah. "I'm glad you're all right, and Angie, too. We'll need your statement when we get to the sheriff's office."

"I told Brendan everything." Her voice was low, as if her throat hurt.

Brendan, Nash thought. First names now. "We need to record your statement, and the local cops need to hear it, too, since we're in their territory."

"Where is he?" Kellah looked past her. She might have been a child looking for her protector, but there was something off. Nash didn't see dependency behind Kellah's big dark eyes. She saw someone who was determined to be in charge.

––––––––––

A firetruck, all lights and sirens, came up behind Albert on the highway. He pulled over, and as it passed him, he felt the van sway in its wake. Then he saw in his rearview mirror that an ambulance was right behind it. The turnoff for the warehouse was in sight, and once the ambulance passed, he sped up, anxious to reach it, to be out of the dangerous world that made him small. Then he felt a cold spike through his guts. The firetruck and ambulance turned into the drive he headed for. Two cop cars came from the other direction and made the same turn at high speed.

Why? They couldn't know about Angel. That was impossible. There had to be another reason. It was a mistake. Something was on fire nearby and they got the directions wrong. But what if they found her by accident? They'd take her back to her old life. She was in danger, and he didn't know how to help her.

He looked at his hands. They tightened on the steering wheel and refused to make the turn. He had to keep going. The road in front of him went back to the city. He had to go back home some time. It was in the plan. Get more money, more clothes. The knives he didn't carry with him. But all of that he intended to do after Angel realized she was meant to be with him, trusted him, and then they'd go away together. So, he thought, plans change, right? He'd adapt. He'd survive.

Traffic on the bridge was light and it took less time than usual to get to his home neighborhood. With luck, Bitch Mom wouldn't be home. He'd get his stuff and go back to the warehouse. The law would be gone. He'd take Angel and they'd go off the grid. Off the grid. It was something his dad used to say, cussing the IRS when he lost his restaurant, cussing Albert's mom when she screamed at him, cussing the neighbors who called the cops when their fights ended up in the front yard, cussing Albert for existing. "A man can't live like this. I'm going off the grid."

He never did. He was diagnosed with cancer and died in four months. But Albert would do it. Just to show the old man.

But when he drove down the block, he got another shock. A gray car with dark windows sat in front of his house. It had permanent license plates. It didn't belong, and he saw the shape of a man in the driver's seat. So it wasn't an accident, back at the warehouse. They were after him. But why? How did they know about him and Angel? His thoughts shattered into little pieces.

Once again, he kept going. At the end of the block, he turned left, down the alley. He could park there and walk back, but two men he'd never seen before sat in lawn chairs in the yard next door. The woman who lived there never liked him, had called him a dirty brat once.

He thought about the money he had with him. More than $3,000. There was more than that hidden under the floor of his closet. He wanted it, but he never worried about money. It was something he could get anywhere. But Angel. He knew she was lost to him now. It hurt more than anything because it was his fault and he didn't understand. How had it happened?

———

The procession of cars, one with Kellah, one with Mike, a deputy in the Saab, and Quick and Nash last, pulled up in front of the public safety center in the nearest town. Since Kellah and Mike had touched Angie, the chair and the tape that bound her, they had to be fingerprinted and swabbed for DNA. Quick and Nash were escorted to an interview room to wait.

"Just like home," he said. There was a table attached to the wall. Chairs attached to the floor. The video camera mounted in a corner and the audio recorder on the table were turned off.

"How long have you been awake?" Quick sat down, folded his arms on the table and rested his head.

"I don't want to think about it." Nash stretched her back.

"Anybody wondering where you are?"

"It's my mother's birthday today. My sister is giving a party later. They won't miss me until then. How about you?"

"Nobody." He looked up. "You're going to be a good detective."

"Going to be?" She laughed and sat on the table, her back against the wall.

"OK, you are. You had the right instinct today about where to look for Angie. That's not something they can teach you."

"Thanks. But the civilians beat us to it."

He shook his head to show it didn't matter. "I made a decision on the way over here. I've been admitted to law school. I've known for months, of course, but until today, I wasn't sure what I'd do. Now I am. I'm going."

"Law school? Going nights?"

"No. Full time. I'd appreciate it if you don't tell anybody until I have a chance to tell the captain."

Someone knocked on the door and a deputy came in with a box that held two sodas, two bottles of water, and two wrapped sandwiches. "Your interviewees ought to be down in a few minutes." Then he was gone.

"So they heard my prayers," Nash said. "Turkey, or turkey?" She held out the sandwiches.

"Turkey." He laughed, took one, opened a water bottle, and drank half of it. "You heard me, right?"

"About school? I heard you. But I have to say, it sounds like it's a sudden decision. Maybe you just need to take a little time off." She unwrapped her food, suddenly didn't want it, but knew she needed to eat. She pinched off a corner of the dry whole wheat bread.

"It's not as sudden as it sounds. I mean, I had to take the LSAT and fill out the applications. It's time for a change."

"But are you sure today's the day to make that decision?"

"Why? Because I haven't slept and I'm strung out on a case?"

"Something like that." She continued to pick at the sandwich. "I don't know you very well, but it seems like this one has touched a nerve."

"My last case was a murder-suicide. Before that, elder

abuse. Before that, a store clerk shot when a robbery went bad."

She nodded. "That's the job."

"So why does every case feel like the worst one yet? Why do I dread the next one because I know it'll be the new worst one? Today, Angel's safe. I didn't do my job, but it turned out OK and nobody died. A good time to quit."

There was another knock on the door. The deputy who'd brought them food stood there, Mike Michaels beside him.

"We've put Ms. Mace in Room B," he said. "With the Feds. You can sit in."

"I'll take her," Nash said. Quick looked at her and she repeated it. "I'll take her."

"OK. Mike and I will keep each other company."

"Try not to punch him in the face." She was glad to hear him laugh as she followed the deputy.

———

Back at their precinct, the captain listened while Quick told him what the cops across the river had found when they got to the warehouse.

"This was no spur-of-the-moment thing," Quick said. "Albert Darwin had everything planned. He could have kept her there indefinitely."

"Any chance he'll go back?"

"The first guys there broke down the front gate and tore up the yard with their trucks. If he does drive in, there's no way he'll miss it. But the sheriff is going to have somebody watching the area for a while, just in case. They've been in touch with the property owner, too, but it's unlikely he knew anything about all this."

"Where's Angel now?"

"Still in the hospital. She's got security."

He was less worried about her now than he was Kellah. That's why he was angry with her for disobeying him. Mike, he saw now, was no match for her when she made her mind up and she seemed to have no sense of how reckless she'd been. After she and Mike had given their statements at the sheriff's headquarters, they headed for the hospital, but Quick had a moment to say to her, "Be careful. You could be in danger from Ape, too. He knows where you live."

"I'm not afraid," she'd said. "I'm never afraid."

Then Mike had blustered about taking care of her, about his crowbar, knife, and gun. He wanted that gun back, by the way. A deputy had taken it. Quick told Mike he'd have a word with the sheriff, and then he'd watched the two of them drive off in the Saab. No fear, he thought, and that's the problem.

Nash came into the captain's office and snapped him back to the present. "Here's a copy of the interview with Kellah." She handed the captain a thumb drive. "The FBI made it clear, I was there as a spectator. Agent Welch had her go back over everything from yesterday, how she happened to figure out where Angie was. Was that just luck, or did she maybe know something about it? Welch pushed her on every detail. She kept her cool."

"What was he going for?" the captain asked. "Did he think she was involved in the kidnapping?"

"You'd have to rule that out, right?" Nash said.

"You would, yes." The captain turned the thumb drive over between his fingers. "Here's what I want to say to you both. You were right on with this hunch of yours. I know it hurts to be right and not get credit, but if Kellah and Michaels had stayed home like they should have, you would have saved that girl's life. So good work."

"Nash figured it out," Quick said.

"I'm not looking for credit." She sounded testy. Tired, he thought. We're both too tired. And coming down from the adrenaline.

"Let me say it again," the captain said. "I know." He stressed the pronoun "I," and cleared his throat. "As of now, the FBI is in charge of the search for Ape. And our friends across the river have the crime scene. When Angie can tell us when and how and where he grabbed her, the city DA can charge Ape with kidnapping, et cetera."

"So we're out of it," Quick said. "Nash and me." He was disappointed. And relieved. He thought again about his decision to quit.

"You both need to go home. Get some sleep. I don't want to see either of you for thirty-six hours." The captain stood up and offered his hand.

10

The captain said they weren't fit to drive and told a sergeant to arrange for both of them to get rides home. Quick waited with Nash until she'd gotten into a car and it had pulled away. Then he waved off the other driver and began to walk. He lived only a few blocks from Kellah's neighborhood, so it was a short detour to go by 100 Parkview.

It was late Sunday afternoon by now, and the streets were in shadow and quiet. He walked by Lacey's, the cafe where Kellah and Angie had had brunch and parted company. He hadn't recognized the name, but when he saw the storefront, he knew he'd eaten here once before himself. It seemed to be part of the women's lives. They could have been in the restaurant when he was there. Suppose he'd happened in the day before? The women would have caught his eye, no doubt. Maybe he'd have noticed something the civilians didn't, something that would have kept Angie safe. He shook it off.

Kellah's house was a block beyond. As he got closer, he saw things that were out of place. Two men stood together in the doorway of a closed fruit market opposite the house. They wore black from head to toe.

"Guys." He flipped open his ID. "What's up?"

"Hey, man," one of them said. "We're cool. We're waiting to see if Angel comes home tonight." He held out a camera with a long lens. "You heard? She was kidnapped, but got rescued."

"She's my girl," the other man said. "You see my picture of her in *The Daily*? The Club Madrid photo? Five hundred bucks."

"How did you hear about the kidnapping?" he asked.

"We don't reveal sources," one of them said.

"The Internet?" Quick asked. "TV? What?"

"I got a text," the other man said. "Just don't ask who from. I don't reveal sources, either."

"Let me guess. Somebody at a party last night?"

"It's a two-way street, man. Lots of people want the attention, you know?"

You shits, Quick thought. He turned to look across at the house. The sidewalk had become a makeshift shrine. Flowers, balloons, teddy bears. Enlargements of Angie's photo, the Angel Hair one, taped to the iron railing. She's not dead, he thought, but apparently her fans felt a need to express something. It was creepy. There ought to be security here. Unless the paparazzi could be called security, but they'd let a crime happen right in front of them and post the video. He'd call the captain.

A car came down the street, going slow. Mike Michaels' Saab. It went past the house, past him, and he saw the back of Kellah's head. The photographers took no interest in the old car. He didn't want to alert them, so he moved slowly and headed in the direction Mike was driving. He saw the Saab go into a monthly rental parking garage.

Quick waited by the gate until they came out. Mike's arm

was wrapped around Kellah and they both walked with their heads down. Quick didn't want to startle them so he spoke as softly as he could and still be heard.

"Hi, you two."

Mike swung himself between them before he saw who it was. "What are you doing here?"

"I'm on my way home and just wanted to be sure everything is OK here. I didn't expect to see you."

"It's not OK," Mike said. "Have you seen the house? How the hell do people know what's going on?"

"It's all over the Internet." Quick watched Kellah's face. She looked fragile, but he no longer took her to be weak.

"Come on." She tugged Mike's arm. "Let's just go home."

"There are photographers watching the building," Quick said. "They're waiting for Angie."

"I wanted to bring her home tonight. Thank goodness the doctors said no."

"Is there a back way in?"

"It's my house. I'm going in the front door."

Mike sighed. "No use arguing."

"I'll walk with you," Quick said. She nodded.

As they reached the steps, the men across the street came to life and so did their cameras.

"Hey, Kellah," one called. "Where's Angel?"

"Does she know people are praying for her?" the other called. "Come on, Kellah, talk to us."

She didn't flinch, didn't even acknowledge her name, just went to the door and entered a key code to unlock it. The entrance hall was dark except for a light from the elevator.

"Want me to sleep upstairs again tonight?" Mike asked.

"No. You need to sleep in your own bed. I'll be all right." She raised on her toes and kissed his cheek. "You know we love you, right?"

He put an arm around her and kissed the top of her head. When he let go, he looked at Quick. "Detective, see you out?"

"I want to talk to Brendan," Kellah said. "If you have time?"

Mike's eyebrows pulled down and together. "I'll call you in a little while, Girly. Just to be sure."

When he'd gone into his apartment, she asked again, "Do you have time?"

"You're dead on your feet. So am I, to tell the truth. We could talk tomorrow."

"Please, come up for a few minutes."

They rode the elevator to the fifth floor. This time, she led him through the living room, a formal dining room, into the kitchen. He would have expected stainless steel and granite, but it was small and old-fashioned, like his grandmother's kitchen.

"I need to eat something. What if I scramble some eggs?" She opened the refrigerator and began to take things out.

"How was Angie?" He eased into a chair at a small wooden table.

"IV fluids. IV drugs of some kind, so she was sleeping. They did a rape kit. I wanted to be with her, but apparently that's not allowed. When they said she couldn't go home, I said I'd stay all night, or until she wakes up. I want to be the first person she sees, but Mike, the traitor, dragged me out."

"Did she talk to you at all?"

"Not a word." She broke eggs into a bowl and whisked them. "Why did you really come here tonight?"

"I'm off the case. I just don't feel done with it."

"Off the case? Why?"

"The Feds take over the hunt for Darwin, since he took her across state lines. If he kidnapped her in the city, the DAs will sort out who brings what charges. There's nothing more for Nash and me to do."

When he said that, he understood. He had failed to keep his promise to her and he wanted the last twenty-four hours back, to do it again and get it right.

"But you're the one I trust." She set a pan on a burner and turned on the flame. "The FBI agent was awful."

"Nash said he questioned you pretty hard."

She poured the eggs into the pan. "It felt like I was supposed to break down and admit I hired Ape to do something to my friend. Or he's my lover and we worked together. It was stupid." She put two slices of bread into the toaster. "Nash thought it was stupid, too, I could tell."

"I know."

"So who do I talk to, to keep you working on it?"

"Nobody. It's settled."

There were her brown eyes again, deep under the fringe of her glossy hair. She turned away, back to the stove.

"Would you get plates out of that cabinet?" She pointed, in control again. "Mike says you're mad at us. You don't act mad."

"Not mad. Furious, and mostly at him. He should have stopped you." He found the plates, put two on the table. "I'm known to get quieter, not louder, when I'm pissed off."

"Don't blame poor Mike. I would have gone, with or without him."

"Nash figured we needed to go to the warehouse. We would have gotten there."

She didn't answer. She served the eggs from the pan to the plates, added toast, butter, a jar of jam to the table and turned her back to him.

"You were reckless," he said. "After I told you specifically not to do so, you put yourself in danger. And Mike." He was tired and it was hard to keep his voice steady. Maybe he should just leave before he lost it.

"Sit," she said. "Eat." She took her own chair and waited until he followed suit. "When my parents died, Cousin Irene said that it was the worst thing that ever would happen to me. If that's true, then what have I got to be afraid of? There's no other danger. Except losing someone else."

When he could trust his voice, he said, "I spend my life being present for other people's worst things."

She put her fork down, reached across the table, but did not touch him. "Not tonight."

When they'd finished their food, she walked him to the elevator.

"If you are off the case, we can be friends. You can care and we can talk." Her phone rang. She answered it. "Mike, go to sleep."

The elevator door opened and Quick stepped on. His last glimpse of her was in profile, her head tilted away, her dark hair a veil over her face.

———

Gen Nash opened the door to her apartment, went in, and stumbled to the couch. She sank into it and closed her eyes. She felt sleep all around her, like a well she could fall into. Its gravity pulled at her. But she forced herself upright again. She had to shower and eat something. She could just make it to her mother's birthday party. If she missed it, she'd be in deep trouble with both her mom and her sister. She passed her phone, the landline, and saw the slow blinking light that meant messages. After the shower.

She got out clean towels and let the water run hot. She assessed herself as being about a five on the cleanliness scale of one to ten, but she tried to live like an eight. She kept her space clear of clutter, the bed made, the dishes washed if not put away. It was important to her when she came home exhausted like this. She looked in the mirror that was already fogging up and said, "Thank you, Gen."

When she was wrapped in her thick terry cloth robe and had slices of bread in the toaster, she dealt with the telephone. There were missed calls and she scrolled through them. Her mother, twice, at not-too-frequent intervals. Finally, third time, she left a message. "So, you'll call when you can." It was the last line of a longer speech and she imagined what her mother might have said to herself to lead up to it. She smiled.

The second message was from a man. "Genevieve, hi. This is Paul Bayard. We met at Scottie's softball game. I wonder if you're free for coffee or a drink sometime soon. I go away for a few days on Tuesday, so maybe when I get back? Hope so. Talk soon."

A different kind of smile stretched across her lips. This man was nice, and nice-looking. A friend of her friend Scottie's, so probably not a bad guy. They had met when Scottie's softball team played for its league championship two weeks earlier. They sat near each other in the bleachers. When he heard her cheer for their mutual friend, he moved closer and introduced himself. She thought, I've got to tell Scottie not to give this number out, and then reconsidered. It was OK this once.

She smeared peanut butter on the toast and poured a glass of milk. I should do this guy a favor and not call him back, she thought. I've got no right to pretend I have a life. She saved the message.

It came as a surprise, how quickly he got out of the city, off the grid. He stopped at a no-name burger joint that looked like a place he'd see on old sit-coms late at night. Dim, dull, checkered floors, windows scratched and fogged. The lighting made the three people inside look yellow. He didn't want to stay there any longer than he had to, so ordered his food to go and ate it in the van. The trash can in the parking lot already overflowed so he tossed his paper bag and napkins out the window and drove off.

Darkness caught him on a narrow unlit road, with nothing but trees on either side, forever. It ate up his headlights and when something crossed the road in front of him, he hit the brakes hard. He stopped right where he was and leaned over the steering wheel until his heart calmed down. He drove on, slow, his eyes sweeping for anything else that might come at him. He passed a dirt road off to the right, reversed, and pulled in. It was narrow, more like a driveway than a road. There was a gate across it, maybe twelve feet in. Plenty of room for the van, and he thought the gate being closed probably meant nobody used the road much. He got out, stretched his back, took a leak, and drank some water. The woods weren't just dark, they were loud. Louder than the sirens and horns he was used to. Animals, he guessed. Maybe dangerous.

He slapped himself on the cheek, hard enough to sting. It was no time to let fear sneak in. He took a few deep breaths. His body was tired, his brain tireder. He had a mattress in the back of the van, so he could sleep right there. But the mattress smelled like Angel because he'd put her there while they drove to the warehouse. He felt like crying. He reached into the backpack and found the plastic bag with her hair inside. Even in the dark, it glowed. He didn't want to take it out because he couldn't risk losing a strand, but he put his hand into the bag and let the hair run over his fingers.

He woke when the van got hot from the sun. He remembered the grapes he'd meant for Angel and ate them. He was still hungry but told himself not to be a wuss. Just drive.

The longer he drove, the more he let in the thoughts he'd pushed down the day before. Questions looped in his head. He heard her name over and over, Angel, Angel, Angel.

The sun came straight at him. When he stopped for gas, he picked out a pair of sunglasses. At the counter, he asked the stupid woman who took money if there was Wi-Fi.

She stared at him and he tried to smile but couldn't. "The town library has computers," she said.

He paid for the sunglasses, but not for the packs of crackers or can of soda in his pocket, and drove on. There was a roadside picnic table and he pulled over. He had his phone and Angel's in his backpack. Hers was unlocked. He'd found that out when he first asked her for it, after he got her into the van. "You need to always lock this," he'd told her. "You need to be more careful."

He pressed the button. Not much signal, but maybe enough.

He went to a news website and there it all was: Model and aspiring actress, Angie Boone, known to millions as Angel, kidnapped by a stalker identified as Albert the Ape Darwin.

Albert the Ape. He almost threw the phone against a tree. Nobody called him that. Sometimes just Ape and that was OK. It meant he was powerful and fierce. He'd even gotten his tattoo because of that. But it didn't mean he was an ape, an animal.

He dug a thumbnail into the palm of his other hand until it hurt, calmed down, and looked back at the screen. There was his photo from his driver's license. It was old because he had never bothered to renew the license after the first or second time. His face was like a pudgy kid's. There was another photo, this one of the back of his head, his gorilla tattoo. Where had that come from?

There were photos of two city detectives. One a white man, the other a black woman. They were stupid, though, because they weren't the ones who found Angel. Some girl named Kellah Mace did. He enlarged this Kellah's face. He had seen her with Angel. She had big eyes and a little face, like one of those animals he'd seen on TV. A lemur, that's what it was called. The stupid detectives were off the case. It was up to the FBI now. Anyone who knew Albert the Ape's whereabouts should call an 800 number. Assume he is armed and dangerous. Angel was in the hospital, under guard.

Under guard. If he were there, she'd be safe. He'd left her safe. It was Kellah the lemur who had her locked up.

He had his back to the road but heard a car approach, slow,

then go by. Time to move on. He opened the phone, took out the memory card and the battery, and tossed it into the trash can.

Back on the road, he had time to think. No mention of his van, and that was good, but he'd steal a new license plate first chance he got, at the next crossroads hick town, maybe trade the van for a car in a day or two, just to be safe. In the meantime, he could sleep in it if he had to.

He reminded himself, his plan had been perfect. This Kellah—how could he have known about her? The FBI could fuck itself. He was off the grid.

PART 4

Odd and Even

11

Brendan Quick walked across campus toward the student bookstore. He wanted to act as if he belonged on the brick walkways, but in his second week of law school, he didn't yet feel that. No one around him, not the other students in his classes, not the professors, could sense the world the way he did, the way a cop did. The world would move them in his direction, he was sure. It would rough them up, wear them down. He wished he could smooth some of his own edges and regain their ease.

"Yo, on your left, man." A young guy, an undergrad most likely, passed him on a skateboard, so close Brendan felt the breeze of his wake. That was the other thing: they took their space here for granted. The university was in the city, but it was an oasis of old oak trees and buildings with gargoyle downspouts. He had completed his criminal justice degree in a school for commuter students, one with no attention given to architecture or landscape, just get the degree and get on with life. He envied the kid on the skateboard.

A woman reached the door of the store just as he did. He grabbed the handle, opened it for her and stepped back. She stopped suddenly, looking up at him, and he froze. Kellah

Mace. Her mouth opened in surprise. She smiled and tossed her head so that her bangs cleared her eyes.

"Brendan," she said. "What are you doing here?"

"Long story." He smiled back. "You?"

Someone came out of the store and turned sideways to squeeze by them. He extended a hand to draw Kellah out of the way.

"Just started my senior year. Want a cup of coffee?" Kellah said.

"Sure. Where?"

"Follow me." She went inside and down the narrow aisles between displays of merchandise with the school logo. In the far corner, there was a coffee bar with a few tables.

"My treat," she said. "What would you like?"

"Just brewed coffee, black."

"That's how I take mine, too. Get us a table, by the window if you can." She handed him the messenger bag she'd worn across her body.

He found a table, put her bag under one seat and his own canvas and leather satchel under the other. He watched her at the counter. Her hair was the same, shiny, black, short to set off her delicate face. She wore a short black leather jacket over a long gray top with red stripes. Her black leggings were tucked into red suede ankle boots.

Maybe she wasn't as tiny as he remembered, maybe not as fragile.

"Here you go." She carried two full cups. "I told them not to bother with the lids. Hope that's all right." She put down two large paper cups with waffled cardboard holders.

"Good. I hate sipping out of those things."

"So. Tell me the long story."

He tried the drink, but it was too hot. "Now that I think about it, it isn't that long. I'm in law school."

"Really? Does that mean you aren't a detective anymore?"

"That's what it means."

She shook her head. "Is that why you haven't called? I thought you might follow up, even if you weren't on the case anymore."

"I had some leave saved up, so I went to Florida to visit my sister for a while."

She shook her head again, as if this didn't adequately answer her question, and studied the surface of her coffee.

"How is Angie?" he asked. "I read about her in the papers, but I know not to believe most of that stuff."

"Have you read that she hasn't been seen in public since she was kidnapped? That part's true. She has panic attacks if she thinks about going out."

"Hard on you both."

She nodded and raised her eyes to look at him. "I do the best I can."

"I wasn't suggesting ... you obviously care a lot about her."

"In her own way she saved my life, then she reinvented me." Now she smiled.

"You'll have to explain that." He smiled back.

"When I got to the boarding school where I met her, they put me in a third-floor room. The window was painted shut and I spent days chipping out the paint with a nail file. I was doing it so I could jump if I decided to, but it turned out, it was so Angie could climb into my room."

"How did she do that?"

"Hers was right next to mine and we shared a ledge. We called it the balcony. It was about this wide," she held her hands three feet apart, "and we spent hours on it."

"Were you ever serious about jumping?"

"I don't think so, but I didn't feel I had control over anything, so the idea that I could if I wanted felt good for a while. Until Angie."

"The reinvention?"

"You're a good listener. Or is that from being a cop?" She touched the wing of hair that curved over her cheek. "Angie loved old movies, vintage fashion, things like that. She'd seen a picture of an actress, Louise Brooks, and she thought I looked like her, so she cut my hair to match Louise's."

"I don't know Louise Brooks, but it looks good on you."

"I'll tell Angie you approve." Her voice had a teasing note now. Before he could speak again, her cellphone buzzed with a text. She took it out of her jacket pocket and glanced at the screen. "That's her. She wants me to bring lasagna home for supper."

"Is that good or bad?"

"Exactly my question. She quit smoking, finally. She's eating a lot, so Mike is happy. He always thought she was too skinny, didn't understand why those model girls all had to be nothing but gristle. His words. But what worries me is, she says she'll never work again, so her weight doesn't matter."

"Has she had any counseling? There are some good support groups for trauma survivors."

"I've suggested it, but that means going out. I found a shrink who makes house calls, but Angie wouldn't see her." She picked up the cup and drank. "All I can think to do is wait.

Hair grows back, right? In another month, hers should be long enough to cover the scars he left on her scalp. In the meantime, I supply the lasagna."

She moved her chair back and picked up her bag. "The problem is, she won't talk to me about that day. I have no idea what happened to her." Her voice cracked. "Sorry, but I need to go. I let you off too easily. Next time, you have to tell me about you and law school."

He sat until she'd had time to leave the building, but had no interest in the coffee without her. Her senior year. So how old? Twenty-one? Twenty-two? He was thirty-four. He still didn't really know what her relationship to Angie was, friend or something else? It made no sense for him to be so attracted to her, but— He couldn't finish the sentence, even to himself.

The next day, he had to attend a study session that ran late. If she had gone for coffee, she had left by the time he got there. The following day, he found her at the same table, this time with a heavy white china mug in front of her, whipped cream piled on top.

"That's not coffee, black." He didn't wait for her to ask him to sit.

"It's Friday. I treat myself to a mocha on Fridays. You'll have to get your own." Her smile was the easiest he'd seen from her.

He came back with his usual, also in a mug. "How have you been?"

"No. We're not talking about me today. How have you been?"

"All summer, I tried to psych myself up to be back in the classroom, but I had no idea. Maybe it's because I'm such an old man."

"You're not old and you've done harder things."

"There's a guy in my study group who calls me 'sir.' I'd like to smack him around."

"He's just jealous. Have mercy on him."

"It isn't easy." He watched her eat the cream with a spoon. This isn't easy either, he thought.

"Do you plan to be a prosecutor?" she asked.

"Everybody assumes that, but I don't know. I think I'd rather hang out with a better class of people."

"White-collar crime, then. Clean and bloodless." She stirred the rest of the cream into the mocha and sipped it.

He laughed. "I've known mobsters who considered themselves clean and bloodless because they had other people to do the messy part."

"That night, after we found Angie, when you met Mike and me outside my house, you said you were on your way home. Do you live near there?"

"Not too far. I can see the park from my building's roof, if I hold my neck just right."

"So it's walking distance from here, too?"

He wondered if she was aware of how he might string those questions together.

"I told Angie I'd be late this evening," she said, "if you'd like to spend a little time with me."

He lay on his side, she on her back, both under a light sheet. He put his hand on the flat of her stomach. She didn't open her eyes, but she sighed. Be careful, he told himself. It's only sex.

But already, it wasn't, not for him. Her breathing became light and regular and he thought she was asleep. Then she sighed and turned her head to look at him.

"It's time for me to turn into a pumpkin."

"I'll walk you home," he said.

"No, I'll get a cab." She dressed and took a comb out of her bag. He watched her run it through her hair in front of his mirror. She caught his reflected gaze and smiled.

"Does she know where you are tonight?" he asked.

"No." She turned around and sat beside him on the edge of the bed. "I don't think I can tell her, not yet. She's very fragile."

"And you're very protective." He resisted the impulse to hold her. "Do you have plans for the weekend? Can I see you tomorrow or Sunday?"

"It isn't that easy, Brendan. I'm sorry. But I'll look for you in the coffee shop Monday."

He saw her into a cab and watched the taillights until out of sight. It was still early on a Friday night. There was a bar a block away where there'd be a ballgame on TV, muted, and somebody to talk to if he wanted to talk. It was chilly for September and he went back upstairs to get a jacket. He hadn't noticed before, but while he had been in the bathroom, Kellah made the bed. She's not coming back, was his first thought, and then, maybe she was never here.

But despite his doubts, he found her at the table by the window on Monday afternoon. After that, they saw each other on campus almost every day and went to his apartment on Fridays. She stayed longer sometimes, and he ordered takeout.

She left a toothbrush and some makeup in the bathroom, and a silk robe in his closet. The robe still had the sales tags on it when she brought it in, and he understood she didn't want to bring one from home. Would Angie know if something she wore was gone? He didn't ask again if Angie knew she was seeing him, and gradually Kellah began to tell him more about how things were.

All these months later, there were still people with cameras lingering around the entrance to the house. Mike ran them off but one guy got into a shoving match with him. They both threatened to call the cops, but she managed to calm them down. A photo hit the Internet, a woman in a long coat, her face obscured by a floppy hat, identified as Angel, but wasn't. Angie saw it and had a crying jag. She knew Angie was drinking. A lot. Kellah found an empty vodka bottle and asked a local liquor-store owner not to deliver anymore, but how did you go to every store in the city?

Kellah received secret phone calls from Angie's father, who knew only how to throw money at the problem. When he talked to Angie, he told her, get a grip, move on, look to the future.

"That sets her back for two days, so I take her phone, and tell him she's asleep."

So far Angie had said very little to Kellah about what happened at the warehouse. "She told me, she gave the FBI everything she remembered, and now she wants to forget. But she can't."

Kellah and Brendan talked about other things, too, law school, her honors thesis, her graduate school plans, how his parents split up when he was a kid, then both died. "Orphans of the storm." She kissed him.

He told his sister about Kellah and when she asked how they'd met, he told her, "On a case, then we happened to run into each other after I started school." When his sister figured out the age difference, she said, "Be careful." Gen Nash had cautioned him about Kellah months earlier. He wondered when he'd become so transparent.

"You know I'm in love with you." He said it over coffee, on a Tuesday in early December. She set her cup down and took his hand.

"You don't have to feel the same way," he said, suddenly afraid.

"I love you, too, Brendan. You are the only person I can talk to about Angie."

"What about us?" he said. "There's an us here, too."

She pulled her hand back. "I have something to tell you. Angie's dad wants us to fly to California for Christmas, maybe stay a while."

"Stay? For how long? What about school?"

"All I have to do next semester is finish my honors thesis. I can do that from anywhere."

"But you wouldn't leave the city. Your house. Mike."

"It's not forever, but Angie isn't getting better. I have to try something. You know I'd do anything for her."

"Yeah, I know." He thought back to the day Kellah had found Angie. When he and Nash got to the warehouse, he had gone straight to her. He expected shock, maybe tears, maybe acknowledgment of how foolish she'd been, but she'd looked at him as she was now. Defiant.

"When do you leave?" he asked.

"The twentieth."

"What happens between now and then? Do we carry on like nothing is changing?"

"I haven't made any promises. I haven't said anything that isn't true, including when I just said I love you, too. You have been my oasis."

"And now you move on."

"It isn't forever," she said again. "Unless that's what you want."

He got up and left.

He stayed away for a day, but then counted the days until she left for California and went back to her.

Brendan visited his sister for Christmas. He played Jenga with his niece and nephew and jogged on the beach with his brother-in-law. Stayed up late by himself, and slept in. He thought of Kellah and Angie, also on a beach, in southern California. He texted on Christmas day, "Merry, merry. Hope you are happy and A is better. Miss you."

She texted back, "Thanks. Thinking of you, too."

She texted him at 11:50 p.m., his time, on New Year's Eve. "Kiss at midnight."

He answered, "Back at you." Then there was silence.

He enrolled for a class that met at four o'clock on Mondays, Wednesdays, and Fridays so he wouldn't be tempted to go to the coffee shop, to look for some trace he and Kellah had left behind. The third week of January, it snowed all night, and instead of walking to campus in the morning, he caught a bus. It let him off at an entrance to campus he never used and he joined the crowd of people in their puffed-up winter coats, jostling to pass under the arched gate. The snow stopped, so once he had space, he paused and shoved his hood back. He saw a woman do the same, fifty feet away. She slid her hood back with both hands and shook her head to bring every hair back into place. There was no doubt. This was not a girl who resembled her—a mistake he'd made a couple of times—and this was not a vision. It was Kellah. Why hadn't she called him to let him know she was back? The truth hit him. She'd never left the city. Only him.

She slipped the strap of her messenger bag across her body and walked toward the library without looking around.

PART 5

Off the Grid

12

The first couple of weeks he was out of the city, those photos of him were everywhere online and on TV. It scared him at first, but when he got a grip, he came up with a plan to change his looks. Lose the weight. No fries, no shakes, no beers. Get into shape. Push-ups, squats, burpees. Ditch the baggy jeans, the XXL T-shirt. Wear chinos and button-downs. Quit shaving his head so that the hair would grow to cover the tattoo. That was too bad, but he knew it was there and touched it when he needed to remember. Couldn't go to a barber, so he tried to trim his hair himself, looking at his neck backward with two mirrors. It was easier to let it grow out enough for a ponytail, even though he'd always thought ponytails looked douchy on guys. He wore a hat all the time until then. By the time he could pull the ends together and loop a rubber band around them, the rest of the plan had worked. He looked at himself and thought, nobody would call him a douchy loser, not anymore.

He liked to look in the mirror now. He liked to see how his face had changed. His eyes looked bigger and his nose straighter. When Bitch Mom got drunk, she told him he was fat and no girl would ever look at him twice. If she passed him on the street now, she wouldn't even know him.

He moved around a lot. In any town where he spent a few days, some woman, maybe more than one, came on to him. They looked at him sideways, smiled, licked their lips. But he had no time, no interest. He would be true to Angel until he could rescue her again. The idea kept him going.

He had downloaded dozens of her selfies from the memory card on her phone. He put together a slide show of Angel looking at him, only him. He went through it every day, maybe changed up a few pictures, and then looked again at the Angel Hair photo—the one that showed him that she needed him. In that one, she gazed off to the side, looking at someone out of sight. He closed his eyes and knew, he was that person. When she saw him, she stood up and walked straight to him. He held a robe to wrap her in, to protect her from all other eyes. The other people disappeared.

The other pictures from magazines and billboards—Angel Eyes, Angel Skin, Angel Lips—he didn't like them but he understood. People made her do those things. He had saved her from all that. Since their night in the warehouse, she'd never been photographed, exposed like that again. Even though he couldn't be with her, he'd done that for her. And he planned to go back for her, just like he'd promised. He just needed to find the right time.

Sometimes he took her hair out of the plastic bag. He smoothed it out and tied it like a ponytail, so he could comb it, braid it. Sometimes he went to sleep with it across his pillow.

He got birthday cards and Valentine's cards and Christmas cards for her and saved them all in his backpack, but the date he really celebrated was the anniversary of their one night. Year one, year two, year three, year four. To my sweetheart, my soul mate, my beloved, my dear wife.

He moved around, state to state, small town to small town. When he needed money, he worked some crap job or found something to steal and sell. And just like Mr. Murphey had told him, there was always somebody who needed to get a computer fixed. Easy money, and it gave him time to think about Mr. Murphey.

Mr. M had lived around the corner and fixed laptops out of his dining room. Bitch Mom gave Albert fifty dollars and her laptop and told him to take them to the man. Albert was about fifteen.

"So you're Jackie's kid," Mr. M said. Albert thought it was a stupid thing to say, so he gave him four tens and said that was all Mom had given him. Mr. M just looked at him and waited. In a minute, Albert took out the fifth bill and laid it on the table.

"You want to stay?" Mr. M asked. "It could take two, three hours. I'll show you what I do." Albert looked around and saw six or eight laptops, some open, some not, sitting around the room.

"Sure. I'll stay."

Mr. M talked the whole time, that time and later when Albert kept going back to learn from him, and he said the same things over and over, but he never cussed and he never yelled.

"Good," he said when he let Albert reset a computer. "You learn quick."

If Mrs. M came home while Albert was there, Mr. M called her Doll and she called him Murph.

"You learn this," Mr. M told Albert, "and you can always pick up easy money. You know why? Because people are afraid of their own computers. I mean, why don't they say to themselves, 'What's the worst thing that can happen if I hit the reset button?' Of course, if they did that, we'd be out of work, right?"

He taught Albert, get fifty dollars up front and two hundred when it's done. "And you know what? These things practically fix themselves."

He taught Albert and hired him to be his assistant. He made him come on time and do what he promised. When somebody came to pick up a fixed computer, he paid Albert on the spot and said, "Living the dream."

Half of what Mr. M said, Albert was still trying to figure out. But when he thought about living the dream, he heard Bitch Mom's voice. "You're dreaming." It's what she said when Dad said, "I got to get off the grid." She said it like dreaming was a cuss word, like it was the worst put-down she could think of. That's when Albert stopped thinking about Mr. M and, whatever he was doing, looked at Angel's picture again to calm himself.

Money was no big thing, anyway. He didn't know why people thought it was hard to get money. He swapped vehicles every month or so, stayed in motels, once bought a tent and a sleeping bag, but he hated camping. Too dirty.

He used the Internet in coffee shops so he could keep up. He was afraid he'd miss something about Angel, but after a while, there were no more pictures, no more stories about her being locked up. The world forgot, but he didn't. There was no more news about him, either.

Then he saw a headline, "Mother of fugitive in Angel kidnapping dead at 56." Bitch Mom was dead. Served her right. But he wished she had known before she died how wrong she'd been. About him.

In all that time, more than four years, he never cheated on Angel and he kept a vigil, always looking for news about her.

But when he saw her face in an ad for a new TV show, it gave him a jolt. It took a moment to understand. The show was about cold cases and it focused on Angel because it was just a couple of months before the fifth anniversary of what they called her kidnapping. It talked about how the city detectives—there were their faces and names again—and the FBI and the sheriff from across the river—how all of them were stupid. How Angie Boone was no longer seen in public and her friend, Kellah Mace, the girl who looked like a lemur, had started this thing called the Angel Foundation to work with crime victims and survivors.

"Where is Albert the Ape now?" the reporter asked. It ended with Albert's old face filling the TV, with an 800 number for people to call if they knew his whereabouts. The old fat boy's face. The shaved head. The tattoo.

He got up and looked in the mirror. That face, it was gone. Nobody who saw him now would ever think, that's the guy. It wasn't easy for him to recognize himself. He had changed everything. All for Angel.

The following day he saw the new girl. It was by accident. He went into a coffee shop and some woman at a high table had her laptop opened so he saw it when he turned from the counter. The new girl's picture on the screen looked straightaway into his eyes. He felt it all the way to his gut.

He turned on his own computer and pulled up a website he

used to visit, back when he was on it all the time, after Angel. It was gossip, snark, movie stars, criminals, and it disgusted him, but he guessed right. There she was. Dorrie Auburn.

He found a video of her singing. He plugged his earbuds into the jack. Her voice started out low and sad, then it rose, high and clear. Something about perfect love. It was her big number from the musical she was starring in. It had made her famous.

The night before, she'd won an award for acting and singing. She stood on a stage, hugged a little statue, and cried. More video: She wore a long dress with a slit up the side and she posed on a red carpet with a guy who put his hand on her hip, like he owned her. They kissed, but when she turned to face Albert, her expression changed. Help me, her eyes said.

Later that night, she got out of a limo with her legs wide and everybody could see she wasn't wearing underwear. That was the headline. It was a big joke on the Internet, a scandal. She was drunk and maybe on drugs. But he saw, it wasn't her fault. Those people around her, they used her, made her do this shit. He thought about Angel and he knew she'd expect him to do the right thing.

He went back to the moment in the red-carpet video when Dorrie pleaded with him. He took a screen shot and erased everything around her. Where Angel's hair was silvery blond, long and straight, Dorrie's was gold, thick and wavy. If he handled it, it would curl around his fingers, cling to his wrist.

PART 6

The Devil's Own Luck

13

He started his trip a few days later. It had been more than four years since he left the city. He counted the months off by tapping the steering wheel. Four years and ten months. The city would all be the same, but he was completely different. He'd move through it like an invisible man.

He got there at rush hour. Traffic was worse than he remembered and he inched along, smelling exhaust, feeling the vibration of all the engines around him, and getting a little sick to his stomach. He remembered that feeling. It felt like home.

He found a parking lot for the car and started to walk.

What he knew about Dorrie was simple. She was in this play and that meant she was at the theater every night. He found it in the middle of the theater district taking up five or six city blocks. He tried to buy a ticket, but the snot-face in the booth said people got them months in advance, told him to go online.

Albert went to a restaurant across the street and sat at a table by the window in the bar. He ordered a steak and a bottle of beer. The steak arrived under a silver dome and the beer with a frosted glass. The waiter poured it like he'd gone to school to learn how.

"When does that show across the street let out?" he asked the waiter.

"Ten-thirty. Shall I bring your check, sir?"

So this guy wanted him out? Albert picked up the steak knife, held it in his fist and ran his thumb along the edge. "Bring me another beer."

The waiter stepped back after he brought the second bottle, no glass this time, and left Albert alone.

By 10:15, cabs and long black cars lined the street. Albert guessed that the shows in all the theaters ended at the same time. The bar began to fill up. Albert pocketed the knife and made his way out against the inflow of laughing, happy people. He walked away from the bar in case the waiter noticed he'd left without paying and stopped a few doors down. He still had a good view of the wide glass and gold doors of Dorrie's theater. The way people came out—many of them smiling, doing stupid little dance steps, bumping together—made him nervous. He didn't know about plays. Did the actors come out the front door, or where? For all he knew, they lived in the place.

The street was jammed with cars not moving. Horns blew, loud and crude in his ears. Idiots. Like that helped.

Then he noticed an alley beside the building. He crossed the street between fenders, stepped on and over bumpers so close they almost touched. A man yelled at him. So many people, so much noise. He felt sick to his stomach again.

The alley was narrow and smelled damp, but it was sheltered from the street noise and his gut settled. A small group of people stood around a black metal door in the windowless brick wall of the building. The only light was right over them and they looked like human bugs attracted to it. They were there for a reason, but he didn't know what. Then he saw a small sign, Stage Door. He put his right hand in his pocket, felt the handle of the steak knife, rubbed his fingernail over the groove where the blade fit, and waited in a shadow.

Two men and a girl came out of the theater and there was a lot of chatter and happy talk, all phony sounding. But from what he heard, he knew they were actors and these people wanted their autographs. Then he heard Dorrie's name.

"We know, Dorrie's the one you really want." The girl said it and laughed just so somebody else would say, "No, no, you're great, too."

"She'll be out soon," one of the men said. "She'll sign anything you've got." Then everybody laughed like he'd said something dirty. Albert's skin got hot. What if he showed this guy the knife, or sliced him as he walked by? But he didn't. The three actors passed him without a glance.

The next time the door opened, the crowd cheered. "Dorrie, we love you." "Dorrie, don't let them get you down."

"Me? Never." There she was. Taller than he expected, and thinner. A lot like Angel. Her gold hair was loose on her shoulders and she wore a blue dress that sparkled as she moved under the light. She was nice to these people, took her time, but said sorry, no photos. "You know what happened the last time, right?" And she pretended to pull her skirt up. A joke, but Albert didn't think it was funny.

Some jerk held up a cellphone anyway and she ducked, turned her head. "Really, no, please."

Albert saw how much she needed him. Why didn't she just turn around and see him?

For now, all he could do was blend into the group of

autograph seekers on their way out to the street, and then linger for her. She walked by him and went straight to one of the black cars. The driver had the door open for her and she disappeared behind dark windows. Traffic moved now, slow enough that Albert walked beside the car to the end of the block, where it turned right. He followed it for another block, when it accelerated through a yellow light and was gone.

He drove around until he found a cheap hotel for the night. He went to sleep imagining himself as her driver in that car. Where they'd be by now.

The hotel had Wi-Fi and, slow as it was, it took him only a few minutes the next morning to locate where Dorrie lived, almost. A few weeks before the award thing, before the no-underwear thing, one of the newspapers had done an article about her. It didn't give her address, but the story said where she stopped for coffee on her way to work and had a photo of her in front of a flower shop where it said she shopped all the time. Blossom Truly was its stupid name. That would get him to her block.

The next morning, he talked to a guy who worked at a parking lot, asked if he knew anybody who bought and sold vehicles. Sure, the guy said. Albert said he needed a panel van so he could start up a delivery business, but it was all off the books, right? Sure, the guy knew what he meant, and he could help him, no problem. By the end of the day, he was rid of the mid-sized sedan with plates he'd swapped out in a bus station parking lot two states away. He drove his new van out to the airport area and checked into a motel.

During the time he was off the grid, Albert had watched satellite images of places on his computer. He looked at the city anytime he wanted to, the street where he'd lived, his dad's boarded-up restaurant, Big Men Moving, the alley where he'd parked and waited for Angel. And he looked at the house she lived in. It was one of those old places that had been a mansion before somebody turned it into apartments, and it had a back-yard with a high fence surrounding it. He guessed that even if Angel could leave her apartment, there would be guards inside the front door, where he'd talked to the old guy the time he'd tried to take her flowers. Even if she went out the back door, she'd be inside this fence. Kellah Mace kept her prisoner there. He switched to street view and zoomed in on the building, window by window. Was she there, looking out, wondering where he'd gone?

After looking at the mansion, he'd look at the satellite view of the warehouse. He looked at it a lot. He'd read that the photos were updated only once or twice a year, but he was sure that was a lie. He was certain there were people who could see anything, anytime. If they looked.

Right now, if they looked, they could see his van, first hidden in all the traffic at the bridge, then in the lines at the toll-booths, and on that highway past all the suburbs. But he was invisible and they were stupid.

There was less and less traffic the farther he went and, eventually, he saw the turnoff to the warehouse. A chain stretched across the entrance and a Keep Out sign dangled from it. That was new. He edged the van forward until it popped the chain. The pavement had been crumbling five years earlier. Now it was powder under his tires. He saw the gap in the trees ahead and made the left turn that put the building in front of him, the canal to his right.

He had studied the warehouse many times while he was off the grid, zoomed in on it with street view, so that he knew the fence still stood and had yellow tape strung around it. Crime Scene. Do Not Enter. In fragments now, but still there. He pulled off a strip and wrapped it around his fist while he studied a dingy white sign with heavy black lettering. Property Under Surveillance, it said. It featured a picture that was meant to look like a camera. He looked around but didn't see any. Maybe it meant the satellite. That was funny. He tilted his head back and looked into the sky. Idiots. He gave the watchers the middle finger.

He went to the fence, pressed his hands against it, and rested his weight on it. It sagged but held. He closed his eyes. Angel. This was the place where he'd had her and lost her. He felt tight inside, like everything in him was expanding—the way he'd read the universe was expanding—and would come busting out of his skin. It was how he had felt that day when he saw police cars turn off the main road to come here. He held tighter to the fence, rested against it, and waited for the pain to pass, so he could get on with what he had to do.

He grabbed his backpack with the flashlight and a few tools. The field on the far side of the property was even more overgrown than before. Little trees, knee-high, so close together they grabbed his legs, tripped him twice. Despite the stumbles, he knew exactly where to go, knew like it was yesterday, where he'd cut the fence. That old tire he'd used to mark the spot, it was gone, and somebody had wired the sections together, but his utility knife took care of that. His secret door reopened for him. No need to worry about closing the gap after he went in. No need to think anybody but him would ever come here again. Well, except Dorrie. She'd come.

He stood still a minute and looked at the building, big, dark, silent. His place. He crossed the weedy and pitted gravel lot, then ducked under the loading dock. His door was there, with a padlock on it this time, but the lock was a lightweight. He smashed it with the butt of his knife until it popped. He was in.

He'd heard people say they felt like they lived in a dream, but he'd never known what they meant until now. What did he hear? Was it Angel breathing? If he called out, "I'm back, just like I promised," would she appear and hold out her arms?

He slapped himself in the face. It was now. Angel was gone. Dorrie waited for him. He had work to do. He got out the flashlight and moved into the space.

By the time he was back in the van, his insides were quiet. His brain still buzzed, but that was because he was happy.

He stopped at a convenience store on his way back to the city. He bought a bottle of water, a protein bar, and an energy drink. In his head, he had his list of things to do, supplies to buy, how to make everything perfect. After that, he would find where Dorrie lived and begin his vigil.

Over the next week, he bought the things he and she would need. It was like going back in time, like getting ready for Angel. He bought the supplies at different stores scattered around the city and suburbs. Two inflatable mattresses, a sleeping bag for Dorrie, then separately a new one for himself, a cooler, two camping lanterns with LED lights, four five-gallon water jugs, a cooler, two plastic buckets, a tarp, a folding chair, and rolls of duct tape. He perused pawnshops until he found the perfect knife to add to his collection, a slim switchblade with a pearlized handle that fit his hand as if made for it. He knew all these stores had surveillance cameras. He wore different hats, sometimes with his ponytail tucked up, sometimes with his hair down over his collar, and changed sunglasses for every stop, rotated through his three jackets and five button-front shirts so no two cameras captured the same image.

Every time he set out to check something off his list, he felt the power being invisible gave him. He thought about himself as the little boy who'd had to fade out of sight to survive, and he smiled.

His reward for each act of genius was to allow himself to look at Dorrie. It had taken him only a day to find her building. It was a high-rise. The glass front was smoky dark so he got glimpses of the inside only if he happened to walk by as someone came out or went in. Marble, metal, cold, closed-down. The people were the same. They never looked at him, and that suited him fine. He hated them from behind his own black glass. He had to keep moving because there were always two doormen on duty. Big guys who opened and held doors when somebody went in or out, who looked up and down the sidewalk, who seemed always to be on guard, but they weren't so smart. He walked by, swung around, walked by again, crossed the street and lingered, watched the door for a while, and they never marked him.

Dorrie came out at about ten o'clock every morning and got into a black car at the curb. One morning, two women stopped Dorrie to get an autograph. He had timed his stroll so that he passed within two feet of her and saw how she smiled and laughed for them. Then, she must have felt the pull of him because she turned her head and included him in the smile. His heart pounded and he had to lock his hands together behind him to keep from grabbing her then and there.

Some nights, she came straight home after the theater. He knew that because it was eleven, eleven-thirty, when she got there, no time to have stopped in between. He was on her street and watched her slide from car to doorway, duck past the security guy who waited for her, and vanish into the building. If he hadn't known it was her—known by her height, her slimness, her gold hair that flashed in the light for a fraction of a second and left an afterburn on his vision—it could have been anybody.

Other nights, she did not return until the wee hours and she wasn't alone then. Some guy—he couldn't tell if it was the same one, maybe the asshole who had his hand on her hip in the red-carpet video—got out of the car with her and they leaned on each other like drunks. There were often photographers who seemed to come out of nowhere to take photos. Dorrie yelled at them and called them names until a security guy came out to help her and her friend get inside. She shouldn't act like that, Albert thought, but it wasn't her fault. She didn't have anybody she could trust, so she got in trouble.

The warehouse was ready now, everything in place. The

van was ready. Backseat taken out, mattress on the floor, tape so he could secure her until she understood what was going on. It would happen too fast for him to have time to explain, so just like with Angel, he'd have to be a little rough at first. It'd be OK once he explained. He just had to be patient and watchful.

14

One night, a black car came fast down the street and braked hard in front of Dorrie's building. A second car came in hot behind it and the driver stopped at an angle to block the three motorcycles that chased them. The riders left their bikes in the middle of the street and ran toward the first car, cameras flashing and clicking. Albert ran, too. He got around both cars as the two doormen barreled out of the building. They yelled at the photographers to get away and one of them held a baseball bat over his head. Before the door closed behind them, Albert was inside the building.

He looked out and saw that Dorrie's driver, the guy with her, and the two people—another man and a girl—from the second car had lifted her out of her seat. They carried her across the sidewalk. She was barefoot, in a short dress that rode up on her thighs. At first, he thought she was unconscious, but then saw her eyes open and her mouth move. One of the photographers got in front of her and the doorman jammed him hard in the shoulder with the head of the bat. He went down.

The people around Dorrie pulled her and shoved her, almost dropped her. Albert heard nothing through the thick glass, but he knew by the way their mouths moved, they were screaming and shouting. He, on the other hand, felt calm, in control.

It was he who held the door open for the people who carried her, he who pressed the elevator call button and said, "What floor?" as he got on with them. A guy reached past him and pressed a number. Fourteen.

"Put me down," Dorrie said. Her voice was thick.

"You can't go on like this." The other girl was crying.

"I know, I know," Dorrie whispered. She was on her feet now, leaning against the wall. "I know." Then she looked down. "Shit. Those were brand new shoes." And she began to giggle.

The elevator door opened and Albert held it for the four of them. He waited inside the elevator and watched them until they stopped at an apartment door. The guy he'd seen with Dorrie fumbled with a keypad, and they disappeared inside. He stepped into the hallway and looked around. There was an alcove with a mirror, a big vase of fake flowers, a table with a cloth over it. The cloth hung to the floor. He crawled into the space and sat with his knees under his chin. It was tight, barely big enough for him to squeeze in, but he figured he wouldn't be there long. It smelled dusty and he was disgusted that nobody had bothered to vacuum under it.

He heard voices and pulled the table cloth away from the wall enough to see three people come out of Dorrie's apartment. The girl was still crying and she said something he couldn't make out. One guy had his arm around her and kissed the side of her head. The other guy, the one Albert had seen with Dorrie before, walked ahead of them. When he stopped at the elevator, he punched the wall with his fist. "I'm done," he said. "It's over." Then they were gone.

Albert stayed put. Those people weren't her friends, or they wouldn't have left her at a time like that. But I'm here, he thought. It was so easy, too. He'd just seen the opportunity and taken it. That felt good. Felt right.

He crawled out, brushed the dirt off his clothes, and stretched his legs. The hallway was silent except for far-off whirs and hums. It was sweet to think how many hundreds of people were asleep in this building and he alone was awake.

It both did and did not surprise him when the door to her apartment opened for him. The stupid guy hadn't locked it, hadn't set the alarm, if there was one. Maybe not, because the whole building was so safe, right?

There was a light on in a room beyond the one he had walked into, so he went toward it. A bathroom. A puddle of black, sparkly cloth lay on the floor. Dorrie's dress. A second doorway took him into the bedroom. It was dark. He opened the bathroom door wider to let light in. He could see her, Dorrie, her shape under a blanket. His breath pumped his ribs in and out. His pulse pounded in his neck. He held onto the doorframe for a moment until other things in the room became clearer. There was a chair by a desk. He slid along the wall and sat down to wait for her to wake up.

Off and on she snored, rolled and tossed, went quiet again. It had been the same when his old man finally got through the meanness of one of his drunks and passed out on the couch. Albert watched him sometimes and Bitch Mom stood behind him and whispered, "Ought to kill him now. What if I dropped a cigarette on him? They'd think he'd burned himself up." Albert had waited and hoped, but she was drunk, too, and stumbled off to her own bed.

There was a window in Dorrie's room and dim morning light began to come in. The way she moved began to change, from heavy to easier, from dream-driven to waking. He expected she'd scream when she saw him, and she did, but he stood by the bed and his hand stifled the noise.

"Shh. Dorrie, it's me."

The skin around her eyes was blackened from smeared makeup, but that made the blue irises look bluer. He let up on the pressure and ran his thumb over her cheek. She pulled away and twisted her head so he bore down again. Not to hurt her, just to make her listen.

"You know who I am," he said. "I'm the one you've been waiting for."

Her phone rang. It was deep in the bed, under the covers, and she reached for it but he pinned her shoulder down and held her until it stopped. Then he felt around, found it, and put it in his pocket. The laptop on her desk dinged with email. He let her go but held up his hand like a stop sign. "Stay there." He went to the computer, turned it over, and popped the battery out. She disobeyed, ran at him, pounded on his back and called him names.

"You son of a bitch. Get out of here, you fucker."

"What's wrong with you?" he said, but it was like her ears were shut down. He held both her wrists in one of his hands, produced the pearl-handled knife and popped the blade open. "You know I don't want to hurt you."

"OK," she said. She stepped back and went soft. "You can let me go. I'll be good."

He wanted to believe her so he let go. She ran for the door. He grabbed her around the waist and pulled her down, and it wasn't until then he realized she was almost naked. When those people put her to bed, they'd left her thong panties on and some little top that was twisted around so that her breasts showed. He lay on top of her, the knife somehow between them but harmless.

"Do it and get out," she said.

For a moment, he didn't know what she meant, then it came to him like he'd been stabbed. She thought he wanted sex.

"I'm here to help you," he said. "I wouldn't do anything bad to you."

"Then get off me." Her voice was harsh and he flinched.

"If I do," he said, "you have to act right."

She nodded, just once, and he let her up. She shook herself and looked wild, with her hair all over her face. "You need to leave. Go now and I won't call the cops."

"Not without you. I'm here to rescue you. Don't you get that?"

She pulled her hair back with both hands. "Are you crazy?"

Bitch Mom's voice. He shook the thought off. "You should get dressed. We'll leave later, when it's safe." He held the knife at his side but didn't feel its power now. She wasn't afraid of it. She wasn't like he had expected, not at all.

"I want a shower," she said. "Then I'll get dressed. I want to eat. If that's not OK with you, you can get fucked."

He hadn't felt this weak in a long time. Since he was a kid hiding in the bushes at the park. Since the old man grabbed him by the hair and threw him against a wall. He reached up to feel his own ponytail, loosened in the fight.

She straightened her shoulders and stared him in the eye.

Then she went to the bathroom and slammed the door. He heard her pee, flush the toilet, and start the water in the shower. He remembered, there was another exit into the rest of the apartment. He opened the door.

"This has to stay open," he said.

She shrugged and he thought she mocked him by being naked in front of him. He stayed where he was until she got into the shower with its glass door, shampooed her hair, rinsed it, stepped out, and wrapped up in towels, one around her body, one around her head. She pushed by him and opened dresser drawers.

She put on underwear, a bra, tight black pants, a black T-shirt, and pink flip-flops. With her hair wet and slicked back, she looked like a little girl, sweet, the way she should be. She went to the kitchen and he followed. She drank two glasses of water, ate yogurt and a banana, standing the whole time. He thought she'd offer him food, but she didn't. He took a banana and poured himself a glass of orange juice. Before he drank it, he studied the label on the bottle.

"This has too many sugars," he said. She started to laugh, but he could tell it wasn't a real laugh. Her forehead had a deep crease he'd never seen before.

"You break into my house. You sit in my bedroom while I sleep. You attack me. You watch me take a shower. You say you come to rescue me. From what, orange juice?"

"No. From them. From all those people who make you do bad things."

She pulled out a chair, sat down, and rubbed the sides of her head. "Jesus, the hangover just hit. I guess waking up to you postponed it."

"You wouldn't do that, get drunk like that, if they didn't make you."

"You think? I'm not sure they'd agree with that. Can you make coffee?"

He shook his head. "Caffeine is poison."

"I'm being held captive by the food police." She laughed again. It sounded worse this time. "If I go back to bed and wake up again, will you be gone?"

"I told you, we'll leave together when it's safe. But you can sleep till then if you want to."

She went to the bedroom and lay down in her clothes. He sat in the chair again. Her back was to him, but he was sure that she was awake.

"People will be looking for me," she said. He didn't answer.

He let her lie there, sleep, get up again, eat, even watch TV, to pass the time. He didn't speak to her anymore, even when she asked questions. He knew she wasn't ready to accept what he had to say. He'd wait till they got to the warehouse.

It was twenty-four hours after he first got into her apartment that he dared step out into the hall. The building was as quiet and dead as it had been after those people carried her in. When he decided it was time to go, he twisted a plastic bag into a rope and tied her hands behind her. Then he picked her up, held her off the floor, shook her hard, threw her down and stood over her with fists. "I need you to be afraid," he said. "Are you afraid?"

This time, she nodded. The look in her eyes now, the way she flinched when he reached for her again, made him think she'd begun to weaken. He'd explain later why he had to do it this way, and she'd understand. She'd thank him.

He made her go down the stairs because he couldn't risk the elevator. They went all the way to the basement, into the underground parking for the building, and out a side door that wasn't alarmed from the inside. The alley was lined with dumpsters. Trash smelled like trash anywhere, even where rich people lived.

Albert stopped at the street and looked up and down. A car went by. Then the street was empty. The van was in a parking lot in the same block and Dorrie walked beside him until they got to it. Then she tried to run, but it was her last gasp. He got her in, onto the mattress fastened to the tie-down hooks he'd installed. "Lie still," he said. "You're safe now."

She would be ready to listen, once they got to the warehouse.

The drive took forty-five minutes and he was nervous for every one of them. When they got there, he opened the door of the van and the scent of her poured out. The sweet perfume from her hair, skin lotion. Skin. He pulled her out and she started again. She struggled, she sweat, and that lotion rose like oil to the surface. He licked it off her neck—a mistake—and she tried to bite his ear.

"Don't do that," he said. "What's wrong with you?"

He forced her down, turned her over, sat on her back and pressed her face into the dirt until she stopped kicking. Her ribs went in and out against his knees when she breathed.

"I keep telling you, I'm the one you've been waiting for."

"You're insane," she said.

"They've poisoned your mind," he said, "but I forgive you."

She got still and quiet again, so he stood up. "You going to walk, or do I have to drag you?" He lifted her by her bound wrists and turned her in the direction of the fence. She nodded, just once, and moved her feet, bare now, as he pulled her along.

Through the gap in the gate, across the yard, he did drag her when she moved too slow. She balked at going under the loading dock, but he wrenched her arm so she had to stoop and he could propel her all the way to the low door, into the basement of the warehouse. When he let go, she fell. He shut the door, got his flashlight out of his pocket, and reached for her.

This time her teeth sank into his arm. He hit her on the head with the flashlight. She rolled to her side and didn't move, but he knew she was faking.

One more time, he got her on her feet, across the basement, and up the steps to the main floor. She stumbled and went limp against him.

"You need to help me," he said. "I got it all set up for you." He'd rebuilt the little room in the corner, just like he'd prepared it for Angel.

When he finally got her there, he let her down onto the wooden chair. She didn't respond, just let her head droop, loose and floppy.

"Dorrie." He knelt beside her. "You're messing everything up," he said. "Why can't you act right?"

She didn't move. He was sweating. He was dirty. It was her fault. She wasn't like Angel at all. He taped her legs to the chair, then her body. Finally, he opened his knife. His hand shook but he had to do this so he'd know later that it was real. He had a plastic bag there, waiting.

He cut off her hair, the blade right against her scalp. Even the hair seemed to fight him. It didn't want to go in the bag, but he forced it, zipped the bag shut, and tucked it into his shirt.

He crossed the yard toward the fence. He recognized the darkness he walked through, thick with exhaustion. He'd known it before, after Angel. But then, there'd been light, too. When he left Angel, he'd had more hope than at any other time in his life.

But Dorrie, she fought him with her mind the entire time, and there was no light.

The scent of her had dissipated. He crawled into the back of the van, lay there, and covered his face with his hands. Had he been wrong about Dorrie? Maybe she wasn't worth saving. He'd have to get some sleep, something to eat, and think about it.

15

Kellah sat at her computer and edited the grant application a new staff member had written. It wasn't bad, but the woman didn't yet have the Angel Foundation in her DNA, so Kellah needed to work on it. She knew she had to learn to let go, to trust the people to whom she delegated, but she couldn't rest easy until she had added her touches.

Her personal cellphone rang. If it was Angie, she'd take it. The last few weeks had been hard. Every anniversary of the kidnapping caused a flare-up of Angie's anxiety and depression, and this time, the fifth anniversary, a TV show that examined unsolved crimes did a segment on Ape, Angie, and even Kellah and the Angel Foundation. The producer asked Kellah for an interview, as well as access to Angie. He got neither.

Once the show aired, other news outlets and Internet sites picked up the story. It was almost as ubiquitous as it was when it happened. Kellah warned Angie but it was impossible to protect her. The nightmares came back full force. Photographers camped out at the apartment building and followed Kellah to her office.

She glanced at the phone. It wasn't Angie but when Kellah saw the name of the caller, she answered anyway.

"Detective Nash?"

"Hello, Kellah. I know this is out of the blue, but there's something you need to know."

Kellah pivoted her chair so that she faced the window, looked into space. "Is it Ape? Have you found him?"

The beat of silence flattened any hope that this was the call she waited for. Then Nash answered. "It is about him, but not what I want to be able to tell you. Can we meet?"

"Of course." She pinched the bridge of her nose. "When? Where?"

"Here, if you don't mind. I'm at headquarters downtown now. I can send a car for you."

"It's that serious?" She tried to sound light, but again Nash was silent. "I'll get a cab."

She saved her edits, packed her laptop and both cellphones, and told her surprised personal assistant she wasn't sure when she'd be back.

Since Kellah had set up the Angel Foundation to help victims and survivors of crime, she'd become familiar with police precinct buildings and courthouses all over the city, but she didn't often go to headquarters downtown. It was an old building, from a time when public structures were designed to impress and impose. It housed administrators now, kept in use because of its symbolism and history, and she thought, because it struck awe in the citizens who climbed the imposing marble steps and crossed the wide stone landing to the public entrance.

In the lobby, a raised desk dominated the space. The officer who frowned down at her now looked as if he'd come with the original furnishings.

"I'm Kellah Mace, here to see Detective Nash."

"That's Assistant Chief Detective Nash." He reached for a telephone. "Somebody will come down."

She stepped back to wait and in a moment, not just somebody but Nash herself stepped out of the elevator. She had not changed in five years.

"Thanks for coming." She offered Kellah her hand.

"It's been a long time. Congratulations on your promotion."

"It comes with an office. That's the best part." She motioned Kellah into the elevator and pressed the button for the fifth floor.

"And thanks for your donations to the foundation," Kellah said.

Nash smiled. "It's a good thing you're doing. A hard thing, too."

Nash's office was small, but at a corner so it had light from two windows. The wall Kellah faced when she walked in had a shelf with framed photos of Nash in dress uniform with the police chief and the mayor, certificates with seals that Kellah assumed were commendations, and a shadowbox with a medal mounted on black fabric. She paused to look more closely.

"My mother set this up," Nash said, "It's a little embarrassing, but she came to the ceremony and charmed my boss into letting her arrange the display. Technically, it's against regulations."

"Is this her? I see the resemblance." In one photo, an older woman stood to one side of Nash. She looked at the camera with the kind of ownership friends and family have at graduation or promotion parties. The police chief in full dress uniform was shaking Nash's hand. "She's proud. That's nice."

Kellah called on corporate executives to ask for donations and was used to admiring similar displays of their climb up a ladder. She told herself this was like one of those appointments. Be calm, assured, smile. Whatever Nash had to tell her, how bad could it be?

"I'd be happy to stash it all in a box under my desk," Nash said. "Please, sit down."

Kellah took the offered chair. "Tell me why I'm here."

Nash nodded and looked her in the eye. "I wanted you to hear it from me, before the news breaks. There is a dead girl, and Ape is responsible."

Kellah gripped her hands in her lap and tried to keep her breath even. "Who is the girl?"

"Dorrie Auburn. The actress."

"But she … Oh God. It's like Angie all over again, isn't it?" She felt cold with shock.

"It is. Point for point."

Kellah looked down. "Tell me."

"She was at the same place, the warehouse. Taped to a wooden chair. Her hair cut off."

"Oh God," Kellah said again. She looked at Nash and saw sympathy in her dark eyes. Even though she'd delivered the news in few words, her manner was gentle.

"I'm sorry," Nash said. "I know it's not something you want to relive, but it's going to be out there very soon."

"I've never stopped living it." She hadn't meant to say that. Her life was helping Angie, helping other people. She never talked about or thought about herself, so why had she said that?

"Of course you haven't," Nash said. "I didn't mean that you had." She broke their shared gaze. "Can I get you something? Water?"

"I'm OK. I'd like to hear everything. He killed her?"

Nash took a deep breath and sighed. "He didn't shoot her or stab her or strangle her. What he did was, he left her."

"The way he left Angie. How long was she there?"

"We're piecing it together. It seems that no one saw her or talked to her for at least two weeks."

"But she's famous. She's in the media all the time. How could she just disappear?"

"The last time she was in the news, maybe you remember, she was photographed falling-down drunk at a gala. Her boyfriend and two other friends carried her out to the car and took her home. The paparazzi followed them. Her friends tried to keep her out of sight, but there was a fight of some sort on the street in front of her building. Somebody got pictures, sold them to a tabloid, and it was on its website in a couple of hours. When she didn't answer the friends' calls the next day, they thought she was too hungover or too embarrassed. They thought she'd get in touch when she was ready."

"They were not her friends." Kellah was angry on Dorrie's behalf. "What about her family?"

"It was her mother who finally called me two days ago. A few months ago, Dorrie was photographed flashing the world. Getting out of a limo, no underwear. Maybe you remember." Nash continued, telling Kellah that Dorrie's mother wanted her to go into rehab then, but Dorrie told her to get out of her life. They didn't speak for a while and even when they reconnected, things were strained. So with the last incident, the fight in the street, Ms. Auburn thought Dorrie was too embarrassed or stubborn to get in touch.

"I've talked to Dorrie's agent. He said she'd begun to tell him she might need help, so he thought—hoped—she'd gone somewhere to dry out. The producer of her play was fed up already so he quietly went with her understudy. Everybody in her life thought she was either on a real bender or had gone to a clinic and wanted it kept quiet. Her mother finally couldn't stand the silence any longer and started to call people. When she realized no one knew really where Dorrie was, she called the police.

"It got routed to me because everyone knows I have a special interest in missing girls. Who she was, her looks, everything, set all my alarms off. I talked to the sheriff who was involved in Angie's case and he took a chance on my gut feeling that somebody needed to check the warehouse. That's how she was found."

Kellah forced herself to exhale to a slow count of six, forced her shoulders to relax. "Are you sure it was Ape?"

"We're waiting for DNA, but the fingerprints are enough. At the warehouse and in her apartment. He probably kidnapped her in her own home." She shook her head. "I've always known he'd surface. Guys like him don't quit. At least this time, I can stay involved. I want this guy, for Dorrie and Angie and because he will do it again."

"How long before this becomes public?"

"Our communications officer is working with Dorrie's agent to put together a press release. Her mother and other family members are flying in this afternoon. That's the other reason I wanted to talk with you. Could the foundation offer them services?"

"Of course. Anything they need. I'll do it myself."

"I don't expect that. It would be very close to home for you. You have a staff, don't you?"

Kellah didn't remember an empathetic side to Nash. She remembered a lack of trust—no, an outright distrust from the detective—directed at her five years earlier. Had it softened, or did the need for the foundation override it for a while? She smiled. "Thank you. I'll be fine, and I do have staff to help if I need it. How can I reach Dorrie's mother?"

Nash offered her a sheet of paper with the information. "Her name is Ann Auburn. Her husband is retired on disability, but he is making the trip with Ann's elderly mother and two sons. They are younger than Dorrie. Ann will have her hands full."

Kellah read their names. Ann's phone number and email address were highlighted. "The foundation has connections with hotels. I can probably get a suite comped, and I'll be sure it is equipped for a wheelchair. Who is meeting them at the airport?"

"I am," Nash said. "There will be security for them, and I think you should get security for Angie."

"You think Ape's still in the city? Before, he just vanished. Why would he stay now?"

"It's my gut again, Kellah."

Kellah's panic was slow, rising from deep inside. It was what she'd felt when she first knew Angie was missing. She stared at the window behind Nash. She saw herself outside, a small figure in the dark. A voice whispered, the worst thing has already happened. But had it?

"Kellah?" Nash had come around her desk and put a hand on Kellah's shoulder. "Are you OK?"

"Sorry. I'm fine." She stood and picked up her bags. "I have to get to Angie. I want her to hear this from me."

The garden behind the apartment building was Angie's refuge. Ivy and old rose bushes climbed the twelve-foot walls. Perennials softened its base. Everyone who lived in the building had access to it, but the other residents respected Angie's privacy.

Kellah found her there, in a lounge chair in the late afternoon sun. Angie's small dog, Guffy, lay beside her and raised his head as Kellah crossed the lawn. He barked once then wiggled a greeting. Angie sat and pulled her knees up so that Kellah could sit down.

"What time is it?" Angie asked. "Are you home early?"

"I need to talk to you." Kellah rubbed Guffy's ear and he leaned into it. She knew she needed to come out with it, the way Nash had. Get the shock over with. "There was a missing girl. Kidnapped. The police found her yesterday. Dead."

She told the whole story, as she learned it from Nash. As she talked, Angie wrapped her arms around her knees and tucked her face into the shell she created. Kellah kept her voice steady and calm, but the depth of anger that fueled her was a surprise. When she stopped, Angie stayed as she was and didn't move. Kellah reached for her and she turned her head away.

"Angie." Kellah blinked, surprised to hear her own voice raw and demanding. When Angie looked up, her eyes showed astonishment. Neither of them was acquainted with a Kellah who was this insistent.

"Angie," Kellah said, "it's time."

16

Brendan Quick stayed at the office until 6:30 to sort out the trust language to present to members of a contentious family. He liked this part of legal work well enough. There were rules. There were details. He brought order to bitter squalls of private chaos. He enjoyed the knowledge that no matter how people screamed at each other across the conference table, the consequences were of little importance outside the rooms they inhabited. It kept his domestic situation skills honed. Apoplectic in-your-face patriarchs didn't scare him. Once in a while, he got to play his ace: I've seen people gutted over a lot less money than you've got.

The partners appreciated his negotiating skills and, he suspected, liked the idea of having a former detective as an associate. One called him the enforcer. Another wanted advice about security for his vacation home. A third, a woman, asked about what kind of gun she could carry in her purse. He was tired of all that after his first week and expected that he'd wake up bored with the work one day, too.

The last few weeks had raised some memories that made him antsy, aware of ghosts that trailed him, just out of his peripheral vision. When the fifth anniversary of Angie Boone's kidnapping approached, the media had decided it deserved to be rehashed. At the time, a high-profile crime reporter had labeled Quick and Nash as failures for being the last people to reach the crime scene. Now she reminded the public that if they'd been faster to respond, Ape Darwin might be in prison now, rather than still at large. Brendan was sure people at work, lawyers, paralegals, receptionists, and clients most of all, gave him side-eye glances and wondered how incompetent he was. But most of all, worst of all, reliving the events made him think about Kellah.

He shut down his computer. It was Friday night. He needed a workout, something to eat, a ball game on TV.

The sidewalk was crowded. He fell into the flow of people who were indifferent to his state of mind. His gym was down a quieter street and he made the turn just as his phone rang. He looked at the screen and stopped so short a woman behind him walked into his back.

"Hang up and walk." She pushed by him.

He stepped into a doorway to answer. "Kellah?"

"Hi. I was afraid you had changed your number."

He pressed his fingers against his other ear to shut out sounds other than her voice.

"I'm fine, thanks," she said.

Did she think he'd asked, or was she chiding him for not? "Sorry, I'm on the street and it's noisy." What he might say to someone he spoke to daily.

"I'd like to talk with you. I have a favor to ask."

A favor. Had he heard her right?

"I'm at home," she said. "Is there any chance you could come by? I won't keep you long, if you have plans for the evening."

How many times had he awoken in the wee hours to ponder what he'd say if she ever called, wanted to see him? He didn't want to ask himself that question now. If he did, good sense might prevail. He might say no. "I can spare a few minutes. And I'm not far away."

It was only the third time he'd been inside this building, taken this elevator, and stepped into the foyer of her apartment, yet he felt like he was returning to a well-known place.

Kellah met him, her hands extended for him to take and hold a moment. She smiled and he felt his grin open up, ignoring the signal from his brain to be cool.

"Thanks for coming." She held his hands and stepped back to appraise him. "Nice suit."

"Thanks. I dress better now." He took the moment to gaze at her. Her hair was cut the same way. It shone, as it always had. Her eyes were dark as ink under long bangs. Her skin was smooth as ivory. She wore black pants and a silk top, white with red and blue flowers.

She squeezed his hands and released them. "But I see you, the real you."

Just like that, she had him off balance, on the verge of a fall.

The living room looked the way he remembered. Large abstract paintings. A vast Persian rug. Blond leather upholstery. Chrome.

"I really am glad to see you," she said and looked past him. "Here's Angie."

He turned and saw her. Tall, as he would have expected. Her silver blond hair, once famously long, was short and close to her head. She'd gained weight since the Angel days and wore oversized clothes of no particular style, but she was still a woman who'd draw stares.

"I'm glad to meet you at last." Her voice was hushed but she smiled and extended a hand. He took it.

Kellah touched her arm. "You're OK?"

"Why not?" Angie smiled at Brendan. "It does seem like we should have met before, doesn't it?"

"My partner and I tried very hard. We didn't miss by much."

"I know. I've heard."

"Angie, did you put the lasagna in the oven? And, can you stay for dinner, Brendan?" She led the way through the living room into the library, where Angie sank down into a large soft chair.

Brendan remembered this room, too. He and Nash had talked to Kellah and Mike there, the night Angie disappeared. It seemed more cluttered than before, shoes kicked off beside a chair, books left face down on the floor, electronic chargers, and earbuds scattered on a table.

"I'll be right back," Kellah said. She went in the direction of the kitchen.

"Take off your jacket, if you want," Angie said. Brendan had taken his tie off in the cab and was glad to shed the jacket as well. He folded it over the back of a chair and sat down on the loveseat.

"I hoped you'd come," Angie said.

"It was a surprise to me to get her phone call. I hadn't heard from her in a long time."

"I know about you two. She told me this afternoon. Back then, she thought I wouldn't understand, so she kept it quiet until now." She pressed the palms of her hands together and dropped them into her lap. "Poor Kellah had to get away from me once in a while. For a long time, I did everything I could not to think about what happened to me. I went crazy so I wouldn't have to. I self-medicated. I broke all my mirrors. I had panic attacks so I didn't have to leave the house, whatever it took."

"You make it sound like you chose those things."

"This much." She held up a hand and measured the tiniest space between thumb and forefinger. "It was the last tiny bit of control I had."

Angie shifted in her chair and continued. "You know, until he explained it to me, I didn't know that parading around in fancy clothes and makeup was bad. It was all because other people made me do those things. He came to save me from all of them."

She sounded breezy, la-di-da. He heard the pain.

"That's what he told you?" Brendan asked. "You know he lied."

"I know to say I didn't deserve what happened. And sometimes I can believe that." She looked in the direction of the kitchen door. "Kellah wants me to be tired of the person I've become, so I can be fearless like she is. I don't tell her, but I still have the nightmares."

Brendan wondered why she confided in him, what role she played in his being there.

Kellah reappeared with a tray of cheese, crackers, a slice of paté, and grapes. She put it down on a low table, went to a cabinet and brought out a bottle of red wine, a corkscrew, and two glasses she held upside down by the stems. Brendan rose and took the glasses from her. It was an awkward transfer and their fingers touched. It was light and passing, but he felt the sensation go up his arm and across his chest.

"If you'll do this," she said, "I'll get the tea." She went back to the kitchen and Brendan opened the wine. Her coming and going felt orchestrated to give him and Angie time to talk, but not too much time. Kellah in charge, he thought. He poured a glass and offered it to Angie.

"No thanks," she said. "The tea is for me. Oolong. It's good for your complexion, reduces inflammation. Besides, I don't drink anymore."

Brendan heard sounds from the living room, a man's voice. He stood as Mike Michaels came in and put a small dog down on the floor. It stopped to give the stranger a warning growl, then ran to Angie, jumped into her lap, and posed on her knee like a lion.

"Meet Guffy, my protector." She laughed.

"What the heck?" Mike asked. "Detective Quick, what are you doing here?" He smiled and limped across the room.

Kellah came in with another tray that held a ceramic teapot, a mug, and a small milk pitcher. It went on the ottoman at Angie's side.

"You're just in time," she said to Mike. "I'll get you a beer. And he's not a detective any longer."

"Yeah?" Mike offered his hand to Brendan. "Good to see you, whatever."

"Thanks, Mike." He thought he should answer the question of what he was doing here, but didn't know what to say. "How are you doing?"

"Good. Good. Kellah made me retire, but I still keep an eye

on things. Including my girls here."

"And he has a lady friend," Angie said. "Bonnie Leland. She lives on the second floor. She's lovely."

"Hey, Kick," Mike said. "He doesn't want to hear about that." But he grinned like a teenager.

Kellah reappeared, open beer bottle in hand. "Did you tell them, Angie?"

"Not yet."

Kellah gave Mike his drink and faced the two men. "We need your help, Brendan. Yours, too, Mike. Albert Darwin is back."

"That fucker." Mike ground out the words.

Brendan froze for a moment. The air in the room shimmered. He stared at Kellah, who handed Mike his drink and sat for the first time, near enough to Angie to touch her hand before Kellah went on.

"Genevieve Nash called me today," she said. While she explained what she had heard from Nash, Brendan studied her face. It was calm, though her voice wavered when she told how and where Dorrie died. She looked to Angie, and he followed the gaze. He assumed Angie had already heard it, had steeled herself against hearing it again, and against new nightmares. She studied the top of the dog's head and massaged his ribs with both hands. Her chest rose and fell in quick, shallow breaths.

"The fucker," Mike said again. Kellah looked at him and paused. He coughed. "Sorry, Girlie."

She turned back to Brendan. "We always knew he'd come back, didn't we?"

He felt there was a trap for him in that question. "Did you

ask Gen Nash that? I doubt she's surprised."

"That's true. She isn't. And she thinks he's still around, even now. He feels safe because he can go back into hiding anytime. He's proved he's good at hiding."

Brendan nodded. "Yeah, he's proved to himself he's the smartest guy in the world."

"We have to prove he's wrong." Kellah focused on him as she took a sip of her wine. Brendan remembered how, when they were lovers, she had a way of pulling the edges of the world in until it held only the two of them. He had to stay out of that trap this time.

"Kellah." He leaned forward. "You put yourself in real danger before. If Ape had been there when you and Mike went into the warehouse, you could all have died. You have to let Nash do her job this time."

"But it was my fault," Angie broke in. "I owe it to everybody to help now."

Kellah reached for her hand, but she kept them both on the small dog that raised his head when she spoke.

"None of it was your fault, Angie," Brendan said. "Trust me. I was a cop for a long time and there was nothing you could or should have done differently."

She shook her head. "Maybe not, but I existed. I still exist. He told me, we are meant to be together. He promised me he'd come back, and now he has. If I put myself out there, he'll come out of hiding. Then Nash can catch him."

"Is that the plan? To use her as bait?" He turned to Kellah. "What are you thinking?"

"Girly," Mike said, "I got to go with Quick on this one."

"You see why we need you both," she said.

"Not happening," Brendan said. "Not unless…" He stopped to think. What kind of ultimatum would make any kind of impression on Kellah?

"Unless what?"

"You tell Nash. If she agrees, and if you have a police escort everywhere you go—either one of you—I'll go along with it."

"All right," Kellah said. "I'll talk to her tomorrow. There is going to be a public announcement about Dorrie and I'll be there."

"I'll come with you."

The way she smiled let him know this was exactly what she intended all along.

17

JUNE 2017

Officer Cam Rush got the call from her sergeant just after her shift started. At the request of Assistant Chief Detective Nash, Rush was to do foot patrol that day in a five-block area in the East Edge district. She was to be the eyes and ears for anything, anybody, out of the ordinary.

"That's not much to go on, Sarge."

"It's all I got."

Genevieve Nash was who Rush wanted to be, and if this was a chance to get the assistant chief detective's attention, Rush was all over it. She walked the perimeter first, then began to cover the blocks in a systematic pattern. The neighborhood was one of small bungalows, with narrow front porches and grassy patches for yards, each with a fence to set it apart from its neighbor. She speculated that before long, money would find this area and it would go upscale. These little houses would be replaced with boxy stacks of co-op apartments.

On her second pass, she saw an older woman sitting in a glider on a porch.

"I can't remember the last time I saw a beat cop on this street," the woman called. Rush stopped by the gate.

"Yes, ma'am. Have you lived here a long time?"

"We bought this house forty years ago. What are you doing here?" The woman sounded like it was her job to know what went on.

"You look like someone who keeps an eye on the neighborhood. Have you seen anything unusual in the last few days?"

"Like what?"

"Anything you'd find odd," Rush said. "Or anybody."

The woman crossed her arms and looked both ways, up and down the street. "I saw a man yesterday. I saw him twice in about twenty minutes, out my kitchen window. Other side of the house, facing the alley. But he must've gone around the block because he was walking in the same direction both times he went by."

"You didn't know him?"

"I almost did. Like I should have, but not quite. If you know what I mean."

Rush didn't, but she nodded. "Did he do anything besides walk by?"

"He stopped and stared at that house." She pointed to the white vinyl-sided house next door. It had a plastic tricycle on the porch. "Young couple lives there, two little girls. It's nice to have good neighbors after all these years. The people who used to live there? I called the cops on them myself two or three times, and that was way before their son turned out to be a psychopath."

"A psychopath?" It wasn't a word she expected.

"That's what they said. You ever hear of Albert Darwin? He lived here."

"The kidnapper? Here? Wow." Rush whistled. "You must have known him."

"He was always a weird kid. Anytime a neighborhood cat went missing, I suspected he was behind it. I said they ought to lock him up. So I wasn't surprised."

"Do you remember when you saw Albert last? I mean, it's been five years since he kidnapped Angie Boone."

"Sure. I told the police, it was that day. Early in the morning. He left the house, drove off in his van that used to block the alley. I never saw him again. That van. Gives me the creeps to think what went on inside it."

"Could the guy you saw yesterday be him?"

"Albert was fat. Shaved his head. But maybe, if he changed a lot." She sounded skeptical but also as if this was a new idea, both intriguing and scary. "Five years, a lot can change, you know?"

"Can I give you my card?" Rush asked. "You call me if you see the guy again." She opened the gate, went up the woman's sidewalk, and handed her the card.

"You think it's him?" She studied the card.

"I can't say, ma'am, but you call me."

Rush went back to her route, but the name the woman had said stuck with her. She'd been in college in the city when Angel Boone disappeared and was found before anybody knew she was gone, which didn't keep it from being a big deal. It had creeped Rush and her friends out. They started going out in groups, with a designated non-drinker to keep an eye on them all. They memorized the photos of Albert Darwin, joked about not going out with any guy who had a gorilla tattooed on the back of his head.

As Rush paused at the entrance to the alley behind the block of houses and looked down it, she saw a man's back. He walked away from a green Forester, an old one, parked between rows of trash cans. She couldn't tell whether the car was connected to him, but she noted it. He reached the side street and turned right. She reversed herself, made a left and then another left so if he circled the block, she would cross paths with him.

Sure enough, he walked toward her. The lady on the porch had gone inside. Too bad, Rush thought. She'd like to know if this was the man she'd almost but not quite recognized, who might or might not be a psychopath. She had to admit he looked nothing like the Albert Darwin she remembered from photos. He was muscular, not fat. He wore a baseball cap, but she could see long hair underneath it, pulled back behind his ears, maybe into a ponytail. He wore mirrored sunglasses, a white shirt untucked over khaki pants, and black athletic shoes. Because of the glasses, she couldn't tell where his eyes focused, but as the two of them closed the gap, his head never moved the way it would if he was about to acknowledge her presence. In fact, his neck looked like it was a metal rod welded to his shoulders.

He didn't look down, either, until she spoke. "Sir, you stepped on some gum."

He twitched at the sound of her voice and looked down at his feet. When he lifted the right one, strings of pink stretched between it and the sidewalk. "Shit." Then he bent over, yanked off both shoes and began to walk away from her, walking fast as if he wanted to run.

Sarge wanted her to notice out-of-the-ordinary, she thought. I can give him that. But did it mean anything? She got to the corner in time to see the Forester disappear.

She called the station and gave her sergeant a report. He

told her to come back in. She'd just gotten to her car when she got the call. There had been a shoplifting reported at a shoe store three blocks away. She responded and found a cranky owner waiting for her.

"Strangest thing ever," he said. "This dude comes in, in his stocking feet. He's carrying a pair of shoes. He says he wants to try on new ones. They have to be black. I had to ask, what's wrong with the ones he's got? He shows me there's gum stuck to one. I tell him, I can clean that off for you, but he says, no, they're ruined. He's a little agitated, so I do what he asks. I bring out three pairs. He tries them on, then he asks if I have one more brand and I go in back to get it. When I come out, he's taken off with the Nikes. And a new pair of socks."

"Describe him."

"Black cap, white shirt, khakis. Never took his sunglasses off. That should have tipped me. It's not that bright in here."

Rush asked him for several plastic shopping bags and used her pen to pick up the empty shoebox, the plastic bag the new socks had been in, and both the shoes and socks left behind. She agreed it was beyond crazy and made no promises about catching the thief. Outside, she called her sergeant again and he told her, good work.

It was early afternoon. Kellah and Quick wore visitors' tags so they could join the official group assembled at the downtown police headquarters for an announcement. The department often used the wide landing at the top of the marble steps for press conferences.

Kellah took a place near the wall where she'd be

inconspicuous. Brendan stood beside her. "Big crowd," he whispered.

The previous evening, the police department had notified the media that a woman's body had been found, that she was believed to be a resident of the city, apparently kidnapped and taken across the river, and that further information would be available at this briefing.

That had been enough to get the attention of the twenty-four-hour news channels, all of the newspapers, tabloids, crime bloggers, and national TV networks. Speculative stories, whether based on leaks or imagination, guessed at parallels to Angel's disappearance. Headline after headline read, "Is Albert the Ape back?"

Now, several hundred people gathered on the broad front steps, most of them with cameras and recorders ready. Others, just curious, crowded the sidewalk below and the street was closed off, except for the news trucks.

The Auburn family was secure in the hotel Kellah had arranged, and she'd told them not to turn on the TV or radio, not to go online, not to buy a paper. Nash had security in place for them. Kellah worried about Angie, too, but trusted Mike to watch over her.

Motion to her left caught Kellah's attention. Genevieve Nash came out of the building and went to the far side of the door. They had texted each other earlier and planned to talk after the announcement. Two uniformed officers followed Nash and flanked her. Other cops were already stationed down the flight of steps that fell away from the wide landing. They wore conspicuous sidearms and faced out and down.

The spokesperson, a captain in dress uniform, stepped up

to the cluster of microphones at the lectern. "Good morning. It is with a heavy heart that I have come to confirm what many of you have reported. The body of a young woman was found the day before yesterday in a warehouse across the river. She has been positively identified as the actress, Dorrie Auburn."

The crowd reacted with a stunned groan. In spite of all the speculation, nobody had guessed the identity of the dead person. Reporters began to yell questions, demand details. The captain held up her hands and waited until they quieted.

"The medical examiner's report will not be available for some time, but preliminary indications are that Ms. Auburn suffered from dehydration and exposure. She had defensive wounds that indicate a struggle. A blow to the head may have contributed to her demise. But we won't have definitive answers until the M.E.'s office has finished its work.

"However, fingerprints and other forensic evidence have already confirmed that Albert Darwin, sometimes called Ape, was at the scene. Also, Ms. Auburn was held captive at the warehouse used in the Angie Boone kidnapping five years ago."

Kellah held her breath, hoping the captain didn't provide further details. In an early-morning call with Nash, Kellah argued for sparing the family the pain of seeing the media dwell on how awful the scene had been, how long it had taken to find Dorrie. Nash had agreed.

"There are details about the crime only Darwin would know. We won't make those public. Will you make a statement, Kellah? You can help plant some stuff we hope he'll pick up on."

"Now," the captain said, "Kellah Mace, executive director of the Angel Foundation, has a statement."

Kellah stepped forward. "You all know that Angie Boone was the inspiration for the Angel Foundation that serves crime victims and their families. It is with Angie's permission that I tell you that she is devastated and extends her sympathies to the Auburn family. The foundation has offered its services to them and I have two requests to make of the media and the public. First, please respect their privacy and allow them to grieve with dignity. They have full confidence in all of the law enforcement agencies involved to bring Albert Darwin to justice. That includes the city police and Assistant Chief Detective Genevieve Nash, who is in charge of the kidnapping investigation.

"Second, if anyone within the sound of my voice, which is to say, given Dorrie's fame, anyone anywhere, has information that will help Assistant Chief Detective Nash find this man, please come forward."

Kellah turned away and let the questions yelled for her deflect off her back. "Will Angel be at the funeral?" "Is Angel getting protection?" "When will we hear from the Auburns?"

She wondered if the reporters and bloggers felt any twinge of responsibility. They had started the five-year anniversary stories—rehashed details, rerun the leaked crime scene photos and reports on Angie's condition, reminded their audiences that the city police force had failed and even the FBI had let the case go cold, that Ape Darwin was still out there. People who had never spoken to Angie made free to analyze her agoraphobia, her self-medication, her emotional collapse.

The captain began to take questions, most of which she answered with, "We do not comment on rumors, we do not have additional information, we will keep you updated."

Finally, she said, "That's all for today. My office will email further information."

When it was over, Kellah accepted Brendan's words, "good job," with a nod. Her phone vibrated. It was a text from Nash, who stood twenty feet away. "Officer will escort you to my office. I will be there in ten."

Kellah sat in the chair she'd used the day before. Brendan studied the display of photos and awards.

"Does it make you wish you'd stayed?" she asked.

He laughed. "I have flashbacks, but no regrets."

When Nash came in, a tall young woman in uniform followed her.

"Hi, Quick," Nash said. "Welcome back." Her smile was genuine as she shook his hand, but Kellah knew she wanted to ask why he was there.

"Brendan is providing legal services to the foundation," Kellah said. "He'll keep anything we say confidential." They had not discussed any such role for him and she saw that the muscles around his eyes gave the small lie away. He controlled his face again, but she was sure Nash saw his reaction.

"Let me make introductions," Nash said. "Kellah Mace, Brendan Quick, this is Officer Cam Rush. Rush, there's a folding chair behind the door."

They settled.

"Rush has had an interesting morning," Nash said. "I want her to tell you the story."

Rush took off her cap and when Kellah looked at her, her cheeks flushed. Poor thing, Kellah thought. That complexion can't be fun when you're a cop trying to exercise authority. The woman, who might be Kellah's own age plus or minus a year, was a strawberry blonde and had blue eyes. She pinned her hair up and back in a severe twist, but strands worked loose around her face.

Rush began to explain about a foot patrol she'd done. Kellah kept looking to Nash, who appeared to know what was coming. Finally, Rush said the words "psychopath" and "Albert Darwin."

"You saw him?" Kellah asked.

"Let's look at the video," Nash said. She turned her computer screen so Kellah could view it. "She wore a camera."

The perspective of the video disoriented Kellah for a few seconds. It was as if she wore the camera herself, as if it rose and fell with her own motion. Then she saw a man come into the scene. While the camera focused directly on him, he stared past it into the distance. He had to have deliberately ignored Rush, pretended she didn't exist, to stare so straight ahead. As he moved just beyond the camera, it swung around and Kellah heard Rush's voice. "Sir, you stepped on some gum."

The man stopped, looked down, then at her, his face crumpled with fury. He pulled off his athletic shoes and began to walk away, fast.

Kellah felt gooseflesh up and down her arms. Her diaphragm seized so she couldn't breathe for a moment.

Then Rush began to talk about a shoplifter in a shoe store.

"The shoes and socks he left behind may give us DNA," Nash said, "but even without that, he left fingerprints on the shoebox and sock wrapper. That was Albert Darwin."

They sat quiet for a moment and then Kellah asked Nash,

"Is that why you sent her there? To look for him?"

"Something I didn't tell you yesterday. There was an anonymous call three nights ago, on my personal voicemail. The caller said, 'Why isn't anybody looking for Dorrie? You're stupider now than you were five years ago.' He sounded angry, furious. I had no idea what it meant, though. This was a few hours before I'd heard Dorrie was missing, but when he mentioned five years, it was too coincidental."

"He looks a lot different," Brendan said. "It's good to know that. Good work."

Rush blushed again. "Glad I was there, right time and place, sir."

"Are you going to release the video?" he asked Nash.

"I would. I think we need to get his photo out to patrols, and once we do that, it'll leak, so why not? And the public could help. But it's not my decision."

"We want to help," Kellah said. "Angie and I. And knowing he's still around, just like you thought," she gestured to Nash, "it's even more urgent."

"What do you have in mind?" Nash crossed her arms and sat back. No smile now.

"Angie is willing to go out in public, to see if Albert will follow her. Brendan heard her say so. We think he can't resist her."

"Is it true that she's hardly left home since the day she was released from the hospital?"

"Yes, that's true."

"And now she's willing to expose herself this way?" Nash's voice showed she didn't believe it. "Quick, you're part of this?"

"I told Kellah I would only be part of it if you're involved."

"Don't you remember how mad you were when we drove

up to the moving company that Sunday morning and she was standing there? And when she beat us to the warehouse?" Nash's voice didn't rise, but it didn't need to. She was angry. "Don't you remember the penalties for obstructing a police investigation? Kiss your law license goodbye."

"It's not obstruction if you're running it," he said.

"I don't know which one of you is making me crazier," Nash said. "Kellah, you're doing great work at the foundation, but I remember how reckless you were five years ago. You put yourself and other people in harm's way, and I'm not sure you've changed. As for you, Quick, I'm just speechless."

"Don't blame him," Kellah said. "You're right, I haven't changed. But there are things about me you don't understand." She extended her hands, palms up. "But I don't think we have time for all that. Just let me explain what we want to do, then decide."

"And if I say no, you'll just go home and stay there? I doubt it."

"Brendan will make sure I do." She felt him shift his weight, heard him clear his throat, but kept her focus on Nash. "We plan to announce that Angie will begin to play a role with the foundation. She will attend some meetings, become the face of the organization, help with fundraising. We will make her schedule public. Then you can always have people nearby, ready to grab Albert when he comes out. It's even better now that we know what he looks like."

She stopped. She wanted to let Nash absorb it, see the brilliance of the idea, and she was certain Nash would come around. She watched the detective's arms uncross, hands drop to her lap, shoulders loosen. She saw Nash's gaze shift away from the lock Kellah had on it. Kellah turned her head to follow it to Officer Rush.

"I have another idea," Nash said.

18

The next morning, Kellah visited the Auburn family at their hotel. When she left them, she went to the theater where the memorial service would be held. It was the place where Dorrie had become famous overnight, had become, as an obituary said, America's newest star of the most American art form, the musical theater. Now the theater community would say goodbye with song and dance.

Kellah had arranged to have an enclosed canopy set up so the family and the celebrities could go from limo to building without being exposed to cameras and reporters. She wished she could get the teddy bears, flowers, candles, and signs expressing love for Dorrie cleared away from the sidewalk, but she was afraid the optics of that would not be good. Perhaps the Auburns would like these gestures. Some people did, she knew, but not her, when the same had all been for Angie.

Admittance was by invitation only, invitations handled by Dorrie's management agency and the play's producer. A list of the performers who would pay tribute appeared in the morning papers and online, so the crowd of onlookers started to gather early, with both police and private security on hand. Cars arrived and some celebrities sidestepped the canopy to wave at fans, sign autographs, and provide reporters with sorrowful faces and kind words for the talented young woman taken far too soon.

The family's limo came last. Kellah stood by as they moved into the theater. She was aware of the photographers and by-standers who snapped away in hopes of capturing a face in the fraction of a second it might be visible. She was aware that she'd done all she could for them and that she herself was left exposed. Five years earlier, she'd become well known as Angie's friend. When she started the foundation, she had to get used to being its face. She learned to ignore the articles that brought up her parents' deaths and her inherited wealth. But she disliked these free-for-all moments, these times out of her control.

The producer met the family in the lobby and escorted them down the aisle. Kellah slipped into a back-row seat and took advantage of the interval to text Angie. "Where are you?"

"Garden with Guffy. Sun. Quiet. You?"

The night before, when Kellah told them both about Nash's plan, Mike whooped his approval. But Angie, who ought to have been relieved and happy, melted down. She blamed herself for everything, from the beginning and now for see-ing people take risks because she couldn't. Useless, helpless, a waste, that's what she called herself before she took Guffy and went to bed, where she was when Kellah left early in the morn-ing. At least she was up and outside now.

"Memorial about to begin," Kellah texted. "Mike there?"

"Made him go away. Too much hovering."

He wouldn't have gone far, Kellah knew. Maybe to see Bonnie Leland, whose apartment overlooked the garden. Since Bonnie moved in, two years earlier, Mike's world had expanded by one, and so had Angie's. Bonnie visited her when Kellah wasn't home and apparently was good at sitting and not talking. Kellah imagined Mike and Bonnie were together now, watching Angie from the window.

A burst of loud voices in the lobby jerked Kellah back into the moment. The theater seats were almost full and all heads turned toward the noise. She rose and went out to see two police officers force a man to the floor while two more stood over him. They handcuffed him, lifted him, and had him gone so quickly she wasn't sure what had happened. Then someone touched her arm. It was Gen Nash.

"A gate-crasher. According to him, Dorrie is still alive and is being held captive in the basement. He's here to save her."

"God." Kellah looked at the space where the man had lain. "The poor girl had two crazy men after her."

The lights in the lobby blinked.

"I guess they are getting started," Nash said. "Do you have a seat?"

"Just inside, and there's an extra beside me."

They sat together as the orchestra began the overture from Dorrie's show. Nash sat forward and looked around, her gaze sweeping the room.

"You're looking for him, aren't you?" Kellah asked.

"Aren't you?" Nash gave her a quick smile.

"Do you really think he could get in here?"

"He's a shape-shifter."

Kellah rode with the Auburn family back to their hotel. She had arranged with the manager to get them in through a security door from the underground parking garage.

She watched the way they supported each other—the way Dorrie's brothers held their grandmother's arms, the way the father, who used two canes, still sheltered his wife—and she felt alone. A space in the universe opened, but she shut her eyes and didn't look into it.

Ann, Dorrie's mother, took Kellah's hand as they parted. "Thank you," she said. Her voice was hoarse, hushed, and firm. In their few conversations, Kellah had seen that Ann had the strength the rest of them would need. She wanted to tell her, now you know the worst thing. You don't have to be afraid anymore.

"I'll see you tomorrow," she said instead and accepted a kiss on the cheek. When the elevator door closed, she stood a minute longer and told herself that what she absorbed of their grief made her stronger, too. She pushed thoughts of her own mother and father back down into the dark where she kept them.

She had promised Angie she would come home as soon as she could, but she needed time to herself and decided to walk. On the way, she called Brendan to tell him things had gone well. He asked if he could come over and bring dinner. She agreed and he ended the call, "Be careful, Kellah. He can be anywhere."

Albert Darwin, she thought, you're everybody's nightmare, and I swear to be yours.

She stopped at the mailbox in the lobby. Among the bills and catalogs, she found a note about a package for Angie held behind the desk, where anything too large for the pigeonholes went. The package was a narrow rectangle, like a box a piece of jewelry might come in, wrapped in brown paper, heavily taped. The name and address were hand-lettered, printed in squared-off capitals. No return address. Kellah shook her head. Was it starting again, the anonymous and unimaginatively crude messages that had flooded in after Angie was kidnapped? She would open the package in private and dispose of it as she had so many others.

She went straight up to the apartment. It was empty. She looked out the kitchen window and saw Angie on her lounge chair below. She changed out of her black suit into leggings and a tunic, then sat on her bed and cut at the package's tape with nail scissors. The box was so light, she wondered if there was in fact anything inside it. She slid her thumbnail under the tab, opened it, pushed aside crumpled paper and found a plastic bag. The contents puzzled her at first, but at some level her instinct knew what it was. A long thin swatch of pale hair, braided and tied at both ends with skinny white ribbon.

Her cellphone rang from within her handbag. She shook so much she almost dropped it and had trouble tapping the screen to answer. Ann Auburn was on the other end of the call.

"Kellah, we've just received…" Her voice broke in a sob.

"I know. Try not to touch it and I'll call the police." She sat on the bed and stared at the braid. Even though she'd told Ann not to touch her package, she felt compelled to lift the bag and watch the braid slide into a corner, as if to find shelter there.

Suddenly Angie stood in her doorway, Guffy in her arms. "What is that?"

19

When Albert saw that the cops had an announcement to make, something about a dead woman, he knew this would be Dorrie. Finally. It made him sick, how long it took for them to find her. They had found Angel too fast. They said it was because they loved her, but he knew what their love did to her. Maybe nobody cared about Dorrie, nobody but him. He was so fed up that he called Nash and left a message on her supposedly secret number. In the message, he got to say Dorrie's name out loud.

His hand shook when he hung up, not knowing if he'd said enough, or if, honest to God, anybody but him even cared. Either way, it was going to take a while for anything to happen and his nerves were bad while he waited. He decided to trade the van. There wasn't a town in the world where he couldn't swap whatever he'd been driving for something else without bothering about registration, insurance, titles, all that junk. He just had to ask around. Motel clerks, bartenders, some jerk on the street.

He returned the backseat to the van and cleaned it up good. Then, instead of the nice car he thought he'd get next, something Angel would like, he settled for a crummy Forester. It would be OK for a while. To pass time, he drove to the old neighborhood, parked in the alley, and walked around the block a couple of times. The playground at the end of the street looked the way he remembered it with swings and slides and benches inside a chain-link fence. No grass, just gravel and concrete. He saw that the bushes on the far side were gone. There was a basketball court there now. His heart beat faster, like a kid's heart beats when he has run as hard as he can and found a place to hide. Where would that kid go now?

He walked away, dug his fingernails into his left palm, and put his right hand into his pocket so he could touch the knife. He wanted to get away, get off the grid again, but he had to stay to find out for sure that the dead woman was Dorrie. That's when he crossed the cop in the street. The gum, the shoes.

Cops never helped. They came when the neighbor called, and one talked to Dad and one talked to Mom, but nothing ever changed. One time, one of them hassled Albert because the hardware store owner thought he had been shoplifting, but Albert had been too smart. He'd seen the cop car come down the street, slow, like the car itself was on the lookout for him. By the time it stopped and the big ugly man got out, Albert had dropped the pack of utility knives down a storm drain. Soon as he could, he went back to the store and stole more. But ever since, when a cop looked at him, he felt shoved up against the wall by somebody twice his size again. "I'll catch you sooner or later."

He finally got back to the motel and took a shower. He took out all of his knives and arranged them on the bed. He examined them for rust or chips in the blades. Then he took out the bags of hair. Angel's was smooth as ever. Sweet Angel. Dorrie's wouldn't stay in the braid he'd tried to make. He remembered how it looked when she got out of the shower, how it looked when she lay underneath him and said, "Do it and get out."

He went to sleep and when he woke, he turned on the TV. There it was, news that the police would hold a press conference the next day to talk about a woman's dead body. He knew he'd made that happen, made them find her, and he felt like he had power again.

He went to the police headquarters where the announcement was going to be made. A lot of people showed up. Some of them probably didn't even know what was going on. They just saw a crowd and stopped to see what happened. Fine. They made it easier for him to disappear. He wore a new hat, one with a wide brim, and his sunglasses.

It was a thrill, too, to see how stupid the police still were. He'd made a little mistake, running away from that cop who'd seen him step in the gum, but when he heard the voice and realized it was a woman cop, he couldn't stand how she looked at him. Like he was something on the underside of her shoe. If only she'd known how close she'd been to the most notorious, the most wanted. If she'd only known how close he'd come to sticking a knife into her.

He saw the girl with the lemur face, Kellah, standing around at the top of the stairs, above him. Above everybody. Bitch. And there was Nash, the detective he made a fool of five years ago. He wished she knew he was right out there in front of her, so close, but she'd never catch him.

Somebody began to talk into the microphones, talking

about Dorrie. Then he heard his name. It was Kellah. She said his name. That made him smile.

The next day, he went to the theater where the memorial service was. People had left stuff on the sidewalk outside. It was supposed to be for Dorrie. He watched two girls who hadn't even known her cut locks of hair from each other's heads, tie them with ribbons and lay them on top of the heap. And cry about it. A woman with bunches of red flowers in her hands came up to him.

"Want to buy a carnation for Dorrie?" she asked. "Five dollars a stem." He stared at her and she backed away, moving along to rip somebody else off.

He went to the bar in the restaurant across the street so he could watch what was going on. It was the same place he'd waited the first night he ever saw her. He didn't want food but the waiter pressured him so he ordered a burger. The waiter said the restaurant didn't serve lunch until eleven o'clock. Did he want breakfast? He ordered something just to get rid of the guy.

A tent over the sidewalk and up to the theater door blocked his view, but he saw cops coming and going, directing traffic, with black cars lined up and down the street. Kellah showed up and stood there, waiting for something. Jeez, she was evil. Acting like she was in charge, too. Nash showed up but she went down the alley alongside the building. Looking for me, bitch? he whispered to himself.

He wanted to let Nash and Kellah both know he was on to them. He was running circles around them. And he needed to find a way to signal Angel, I'm here for you.

That's when he got the idea. It wasn't easy to think of parting with even a strand of Angel's hair, or Dorrie's, but he decided it was worth it to give up a few strands of each.

In an hour and a half, the doors to the theater opened. A car pulled up and even though he couldn't see who it was, he could tell that several people got in. Kellah walked around the outside of it and got into the front passenger's seat. People started to come across the street then, to come into the restaurant. Time to go to work.

He found an office supply store where he could get what he needed and went back to his room. It took a while to get the packages together. When he had them the way he wanted them, he took photos. Two braids, white ribbons, side by side. He wanted to remember them as perfect this way. Then he had another idea. He took a few minutes to email the photos to a couple of newspapers and websites. That way, the people who got the packages couldn't keep them secret. The world would know.

He put the braids in clean bags and then in boxes, wrapped and addressed them. He went online and found a courier service that would deliver them that afternoon. He felt good, but restless. He checked out of the motel and found one on the north side of the city, where he'd never been before. He asked the clerk where he could get a pizza. But he didn't go for pizza. Instead, he walked a few blocks into the neighborhood behind the place, a crummy section with trash on the sidewalks, where nobody he passed even looked at him. He went into a bar and ordered a burger, no bun, with a side salad and a bottle of water.

"What are you?" the bartender asked, "A health nut?"

Albert stared at him and the man shrugged. Stupid. But when the food came, Albert asked him, "I got a car I may need to trade in. You know anybody who makes it easy?" Sure enough, the bartender scribbled a number on his order pad and gave it to him. As he ate, he looked around the bar. It would have been sweet to see something worth stealing, but the place was a dive. As he left, he pocketed two bucks somebody had left on the table beside the door.

20

Gen found Paul on the couch, his laptop open in front of him, a ballgame on TV. He looked up when she came in and she felt her spirits lift when he smiled at her.

"Is this live or recorded?" She kissed him.

"Live, but I don't care." He muted the TV and closed the computer. "I'm glad to see you." He raised his arm so she could fit under it. She leaned against him and he kissed her temple.

"Your mother called," he said. "She saw all the footage of the memorial. She wants to know if you're getting enough sleep. I watched it, too. Your guy didn't show up?"

"I don't know. My nerve endings vibrated like crazy, but nobody saw him. We had a lot of eyes and cameras all over. I've got people going over the video frame by frame now."

"Did I tell you that I knew Kellah Mace once?"

"No. When?" She sat up and turned to him.

"She was a student of mine. Brilliant. I was sure she'd be a super-star scholar, but she seemed to disappear. Until she became famous, that is."

"She was a little bit famous back when Angie Boone was kidnapped."

"I guess. But it was the foundation that got my attention."

He squeezed her shoulder. "Are you hungry? I can make pasta."

"With your famous vodka sauce? I am a lucky, lucky girl."

Paul started to make a move toward the kitchen, but stopped, saying, "The school year had just ended when Angie disappeared, right? I read some of the fifth anniversary stuff. I remember thinking what awful luck for Kellah, to lose her parents the way she did and then to have this happen to her friend. The media said she was heroic, fearless."

"And they said my partner and I were incompetent. Kellah did some stupid things and they worked out, thank goodness. But I didn't trust her."

"How about now? It seems like she's doing good."

"Yeah, I agree, but she's still hard to read." She stopped herself from saying more, from saying she knew of at least one small falsehood. "I want to change clothes. Pour me a glass of wine and I'll be right there."

"Yes ma'am." He went to the kitchen and she headed for the bedroom, easing out of her suit jacket as she went.

Her phone rang. It gave her a jolt to see Kellah's name on the screen. "What's up?" She sensed it would not be, would never be, a social call.

Kellah explained to her about the packages delivered to her house and to the Auburns' hotel. She was, as always, calm, and Nash knew this was part of what annoyed her about Kellah. She liked to be the calmest person in the room.

"You should go to the Auburns first," Kellah said. "Then come here."

"Yes, of course." She waved off Paul, who'd brought her a glass of wine. "And I'll get somebody over right away to collect evidence." She called the sergeant, gave enough information to let him know what she needed from scene-of-crime personnel, two teams, and then as an afterthought asked, "Is Rush on duty? Good. Have her meet me at the hotel."

She gave Paul a quick hug, whispered an apology, and wondered for the millionth time how cops ever held a relationship together.

It was almost ten o'clock when Nash and Rush got to 100 Parkview. Mike Michaels buzzed them up and met them in the foyer of Kellah's apartment.

"It's good to see you, Mr. Michaels. This is Officer Rush."

"You ladies make a man feel old." He gestured for them to follow him and Nash noticed he had a heavy limp that hadn't existed five years earlier.

"Are you OK?" she asked.

"Doctor says I need a new knee. I don't have time for that."

Nash remembered the impression she'd formed of the room the first time she was in it. It had seemed too grown-up then, too sophisticated for a college girl and her model roommate, and even now it begged for somebody to leave a glass on a table, a half-eaten sandwich, something to show signs of life. She glanced at Rush, who looked around, took it all in with her mouth slightly open, as Mike led them to the pocket door that opened to the library. Kellah and Quick both stood to greet them. Quick looked ill at ease, Nash thought, as if he was still unsure why he was involved.

Angie sat up straight as they came in.

"Hello, Detective," she said. "I'm glad to meet you at last. Please excuse me for not getting up. It upsets Guffy." She gestured to the small dog in her lap. Nash hadn't noticed him until then. His shiny black eyes fixed on her.

"I wouldn't want to do that." She smiled. "This is Officer Cam Rush. She's going to assist us. Did Kellah explain?"

"I'm still thinking it over. I've never been impersonated before." Angie looked Rush up and down.

"Let's all sit down," Kellah said. She sat close to Angie, Quick beside her, Mike on the other side of Angie, their chairs in an arc, so that Nash and Rush faced all of them across a narrow divide.

"I hope the SOC team didn't disrupt you too much," Nash said.

"They were efficient," Kellah said. "They took the box, the wrapping, the contents."

Nash noticed the word. Contents, not hair. "Tell me how it was delivered," she said, nodding to Rush, who took out a notebook and pen.

"A messenger service. I don't remember which one but there was a sticker on the box. Either the courier had been here before and knew where to put it, or maybe a resident told him. Someone wrote a note and slipped it into our mailbox so I knew to retrieve it."

"We want to find the courier. A couple of officers have already talked to your neighbors, to see if anyone remembers him. The package the Auburns got was handled quite a bit at the hotel, including by security, who should have intercepted it. But we'll try for forensics on both. Not that I have any doubt who sent them."

"Of course not. None of us do," Kellah said.

"I want five minutes with this asshole," Mike said. "Five

minutes." He made a sudden motion, a wide sweep of his arm, and Guffy barked. Angie shushed the dog and gave Mike a don't-do-that-again look.

Mike settled back into his chair. "Sorry, Kick. Sorry, Guff."

"I understand, Mr. Michaels," Nash said. "I feel the same way. And Rush does, too."

"You're leaving me out," Angie said. "I have to do something."

Kellah touched her arm. "The first step will be the interview. Only you can do that. Then Detective Nash takes over, OK?" She looked to Nash and smiled. "She has the plan."

21

The motel room looked like a hundred others. All brown and orange and plastic. He put on latex gloves and cleaned the surfaces with wipes. Took a shower, used his own soap and towels, and then stretched his own blanket over the rough bedspread and sat down.

He took an envelope of small bills, ones, fives, tens, out of his backpack, counted them, then added the two dollars he'd snatched. He wrote the new total in pencil on the envelope and slid it back into its zippered interior pocket. He took out the top-spiral notebook he carried in his pocket and added the two to the previous running total. It came to $5,347. He kept only the envelope in the pack. As he accumulated hundreds, he made bundles of $1,000 each and distributed them. Some went into the false bottom of an athletic bag with dirty socks and underwear on top. Some went into a shave kit small enough to hide somewhere in any vehicle. He always kept five hundred dollars in a money belt under his clothes, and two or three hundred dollars in his wallet. What the old man called walking-around money. But the old man had never had money like this, easy to handle, and for sure he never knew how much he had. At least, he'd never known when Albert stole from him.

He wanted to watch the video of the police department's announcement again. He found it on the news channel's website. He muted it until Kellah came to the microphone. Then he played her saying his name over and over. He was ready to move on when a camera angle he hadn't noticed caught his eye. It was the scene behind Kellah while she was at the podium. There was Nash, and right beside her was a tall woman cop, her hat down low over her eyes. All of a sudden, she took the hat off, ran one hand over blond hair, and put it back on. It was quick but enough for him to recognize her. It rattled him. Why did she get to stand behind Nash? What had she told Nash about him? Then he reminded himself, she didn't know who he was, didn't have a clue. And there were a hundred cops around Nash.

He refocused. By now, or soon, those pictures he'd sent ought to be doing their job.

He went from website to website, until he saw what he wanted. The story read, "Multiple news outlets received these photos today. Notes with the plastic bags identified the contents as hair belonging to Angie Boone and Dorrie Auburn. We have not yet verified that identification but have reached out to the police for comment."

The next site he checked was less pukey. It said, "Both of the victims were known for their long blond hair, and both were literally scalped by their sick kidnapper." He laughed because he knew what "literally" meant, and that was a lie. He'd used his knife but if they'd stayed still like he told them, they wouldn't even have gotten a nick. Angel had been so sweet until the minute he had to hit her to get her to sit in the chair. Then she'd gone nuts when he started to cut off the hair. He remembered how a dribble of blood had run down into her eye. After that, she just cried. He wrapped her bloody head in gauze and tape and knelt down beside her.

"I'm sorry, but it was for your own good. Now, I've got to rest, but I'll be back. I'm going to take care of you, always."

But because of Kellah and what happened next, people said he'd kidnapped Angel. But Kellah was the one who'd kept her captive for five years.

Dorrie. He decided he didn't want to think about Dorrie anymore.

He stood up from the bed and went to the closet where his backpack was. He reached in, took out the knife case, and then the bags with the rest of the hair. He arranged the ponytails he'd kept on the floor and put a long knife between them. Then he took pictures. He'd send them out soon, but maybe just to the "literal" people. He liked them best.

22

JULY 2017

"They're ready." Kellah tapped on Angie's door.

Angie came out of her room and stood in the hallway. "Do I look OK?"

They had chosen her clothes together, dark gray pants, a lighter gray silk blouse with a slight V-neck, and a single strand of pearls and pearl earrings that had belonged to Kellah's mother.

"You look great." Kellah hugged her. "You're sure about this, right?"

Angie closed her eyes and drew in. For a moment, Kellah was afraid she would say no, but then she straightened her shoulders and nodded. "I'm sure."

When they stepped into the living room, the TV people stood up or turned around, their attention centered on Angie. Kellah eased away and went to the side of the room that would be unlit, out of sight. Mike was there already with Guffy in his arms. The little dog saw Angie and wiggled to get loose.

"She going to be all right?" Mike asked, nodding in Angie's direction.

"I think so." Kellah rubbed Guffy's ears with her knuckles.

Angie sat on a high stool to get her makeup done. The living room had been turned into a set, two chairs placed so Angie and the interviewer would be knee to knee. The painting that usually hung on the wall behind them had been taken down, and a low table with a large arrangement of flowers provided the backdrop.

The interviewer, Patricia Oregon, came in from the kitchen, her own makeup done, half-glasses on the end of her nose, cellphone in hand. Kellah had chosen her to do this interview because of her ability to put fragile people at ease. She acknowledged Kellah and Mike with a wave. Then she went to Angie and whispered something that made her smile. The two of them moved to their chairs.

"OK, then," the director said, "are we ready for the puppy?"

Mike let Guffy down. He ran to Angie, jumped into her lap, and settled, though with his head up, eyes alert.

Technicians moved the lights and reflectors into place. Would it make Angie uneasy, Kellah wondered, to be hemmed in this way again? Would it remind her of that last big photo shoot and what came later? Under the lights, Angie's face had the old glow, even though its angles were different, softer. The cap of short hair lit up, darker but still gleaming.

"My hands are sweating." Mike opened and closed his fingers.

"Quiet, please," someone called, and it began. Patricia Oregon looked at the camera and went through her introduction, and then turned.

"Why now, Angie?" She had a pink notebook open on her lap. It and the folded glasses she held in her right hand were props her audience had seen her use many times. "You've been out of the public eye for more than five years. You've turned down interviews and there have been no photos or statements from you. Why now?"

The words were challenging but the tone of Patricia's voice and the way she leaned forward were tender with concern. Kellah and Angie had rehearsed for this question, had gone over the answer until it sounded natural. If Angie remembered what to say, if she could pull it off.

"Patricia," Angie said, "I was just a girl going about her life. I had some good luck. I seemed to be able to connect with people through my work, but I didn't want to be just Angel, just a face, a pair of eyes, a head of hair."

Kellah saw that her hands, loose on Guffy's sides, were still. Good.

"Kellah—my friend, Kellah Mace—and I talked about it a lot. I always hoped to use whatever gifts I had to do some good in the world. Then Albert Darwin crossed my path and everything changed."

"After my rescue," Angie said, "I was depressed. I self-medicated. I came to see the world as a trap for innocence, if I may use that word, and for good intentions, so I withdrew. I've been OK, you know, just staying here at home with my two good friends, Kellah and Mike. They accept me for who I am. And I have Guffy." When he heard his name, he looked up at her and cocked his head.

"Our animals are our best therapists, aren't they?" Patricia said.

"This little guy has been mine."

"But?" Patricia extended her right hand with the glasses and made a pulling-in motion.

"But Dorrie died." Now her voice broke and she looked down for a second. "Dorrie Auburn. So young. So talented.

Until Albert Darwin took it all away from her. I realized I may still be able to do something useful with my life. At least, I have that chance, and I should take it. I can show girls and women what not to do."

Her half smile, Kellah saw, was almost like one of the old ones. Or was it a trick of lights and makeup?

"What do you mean, what not to do?"

"Don't follow my example. Be stronger than I've been. You are strong. I thought I was until Albert Darwin came along. Afterward, after what happened, I was afraid of my own strength. Look where it got me, that's what I thought."

"And now you feel that you can be strong again?"

"I do, Patricia, and I'm going to get back into the world. I have one other thing to say. Albert Darwin is evil. If anyone watching this knows where he's been or where he is now, please come forward. Maybe you thought he wouldn't do it again, not after so long. But now you know he will. Experts tell us that people like him don't stop, so please come forward."

Patricia paused before her next question. "When you say you're getting back into the world, Angie, what do you mean?"

"I plan to get involved in the Angel Foundation. I'll do anything I can to help crime victims and their families. I'll be in the office regularly. I'll take part in fundraising events."

She sat back while the director and Patricia stopped to confer, and then tilted her head to the side, looked at Kellah and Mike, and gave them a thumbs-up.

Kellah exhaled and realized how tight her chest muscles had been. Beside her, Mike sniffed and dabbed at his eyes.

"You sure about this, Girly?" he asked.

"Of course." She took his hand and squeezed it.

23

JULY 2017

Albert watched the show on his computer. He watched it, paused, went back, watched it again. Then he muted it, so he could concentrate on her face. He had held that face, touched it. He closed his eyes. His fingers remembered how warm and soft her skin had been. And her hair. It was short. Why was it so short? Maybe it couldn't grow anymore. Maybe he'd made it so it couldn't grow.

I have that power, he thought.

He hated the Oregon woman, how she talked to Angel. He hated the looks of the dog, if that's what it was. Squirrel, maybe. Rat. Then Angel said, "Dorrie." And she said, "Albert Darwin." His heartbeat, like thunder in the room, blocked out all other sounds.

When the storm passed, he started the video again. This time, he stayed calm and he heard, "Dorrie died."

"She wasn't good," he told Angel, "Not like you're good."

He heard "Albert Darwin is evil." That made him mad. Not at her, at the people who lied to her and made her afraid. He could tell the words she said weren't her words. Somebody put them in her mouth.

But he also heard what had been drowned out before. "I am

going back into the world," she said.

At that, he hit pause and studied her face again. She looked different but that was all right. It didn't matter to him. She was still his.

The show continued after the interview. He watched it with the sound still muted. There was a lot of old stuff, video of Angel from before, even before she was famous. High school stuff. Then the ads she'd made and even now, in the Angel Hair one, she looked right at him off to the side where nobody else could see him.

The program showed the newspaper headlines and the FBI spokesperson. And the teddy bears and flowers in front of her house. Kellah and the old guy walking down the street at night, fast, like they didn't want to be seen.

It went on to show Albert's photo, the one Bitch Mom had given them back then. How much did they pay her? he wondered. It was all old stuff. The photo showed him standing between her and some cousin whose face was blurred out. He hardly recognized the fat kid as himself. Did they think anybody would look at him now and see that boy? And the picture of the back of his head. Shaved, with the tattoo. Words appeared at the bottom of the screen, "Photo taken by Angel's friend, Kellah Mace, of man who became kidnapper-murderer."

The show returned to the present. The woman, Patricia Oregon, and some man sat at a desk and talked back and forth. Photos of Dorrie came up, Dorrie in a shiny long dress with her hair up. He didn't like her hair up. Dorrie in costume on a stage, singing to a guy who looked gay but who she was supposed to be in love with. All phony. Then the pictures of her getting out of the car, her whole leg exposed, all of her exposed, and the look she gave the camera, gave him: Help me.

He'd seen this video a lot since then, played it over and over on his laptop. It hit him in the gut every time, every time she asked for help. He'd tried, but they'd made her too crazy by then, and she fought him, made him hurt her, and leave her.

Now it was the memorial service at the theater and famous people crying. Her mother crying. All phony. They hadn't done anything to help her, had they?

A man appeared on the screen, identified by a caption as an FBI imaging expert. He showed Patricia Oregon a three-dimensional model of a head. Albert upped the sound to hear, "…could look like this now, if he let his hair grow out." The model stared out at the viewer, blank-eyed. This is supposed to be me? he thought. He laughed.

The model face was fat, bald on top but with longish hair over his ears. And sideburns. It was shit.

"But," the FBI guy said, "he could have done more to change his appearance. He could have lost weight. He could wear a wig. He could have grown facial hair. Maybe he's taken to wearing glasses."

The model began to morph, to get thin cheeks and a longer chin. It lost the sideburns, grew a ponytail. Added a cap and a pair of sunglasses. Suddenly, it looked like Albert. And that's where it stopped. He was looking at himself.

"We have reason to believe he was in the city as recently as a week ago, when the victims' hair was sent to family and friends." It was the woman detective now, Nash. "He may still be here, or nearby. We consider him to be very dangerous, so we urge anybody with information to call the tip line."

He slammed the lid shut on the laptop. The fuck. He

wanted to throw the thing across the room but got control of himself in time. He just gripped its sides as hard as he could until he saw his knuckles turn white. He let go and flexed his fingers. They didn't know anything. They got lucky with the picture. He would grow a beard. He would dye his hair. It was so easy. They were so stupid. What he was not going to do was leave town. He was going to walk around anywhere he wanted, do anything he wanted.

He opened the laptop again and restarted the video. The show ought to be over but there was one more new person on the screen. A young woman. Blonde. Long hair, but pulled back tight. Pulled so tight it made her cheeks flat and her blue eyes big. Like Angel, he thought. Like Dorrie. He held his breath.

"Officer Cam Rush," Patricia Oregon said, "you encountered Albert Darwin in front of the house where he grew up. Can you tell us about that encounter?"

"Detective Nash wanted someone to patrol the neighborhood, in case Mr. Darwin showed up and …"

He quit listening. This was the cop, the bitch woman cop. And fuck all, there was a jerky video of him almost running away from her, his shoes in his hand. Then he realized, it wasn't jerky, back and forth. The camera she wore went up and down, with her breath.

By dawn, he had figured it out. He had to look different again. He would need another van for a while. He would get the nice car for Angel. If she was going to be back into the world, it meant she wanted to be with him.

But everybody knew what he looked like now. They would be watching for him. And who was to blame for that? Cam Rush. She was a problem.

24

Cam Rush watched the interview and ignored the phone calls that started right away. Her parents. Her sister. Her college friends. They were all going to tell her how good she looked, how well she did. All she cared about was whether or not she could make herself look enough like Angie Boone to lure a psychopath out of his hole. She thought about what had happened in Nash's office with Kellah Mace.

"I can't order you to cut your hair," Nash had said.

Rush responded immediately, "No problem, ma'am."

"Angie's clothes from her modeling days are all in storage," Kellah told her. "I'll find things for you to wear."

"But, ma'am, she was a model. What size did she wear?" She'd felt her hips in her uniform spread at the thought.

"Don't worry," Kellah said. "We can make it work."

Rush felt a little better after seeing the interview. Angie was no longer a size zero, but Rush hoped some of those clothes in storage were loose and stretchy. Whatever, she had her assignment. She also had the appointment to get her hair cut, lightened, and styled like Angie's. Now, she knew more than almost anyone what had happened to Angie Boone.

Nash had handed her the envelope after Kellah left the

office. "This has never been made public. It's my personal copy. The FBI wouldn't let me in when they talked to Angie, but the sheriff was sympathetic. He sent me a transcript. I want you to know what's at stake, so you need to read it. I've got to go to a meeting, so you can stay here. Leave it on my desk when you're done."

Once she was alone, Rush opened the envelope and pulled the stapled pages out enough to read the heading. It was a transcript of the statement Angie gave law enforcement the day after she was rescued.

She flipped through, saw that the questions were brief and the answers long. Twenty-four hours after she was rescued, Angie wanted to talk, she thought. She turned to the last page and the final response caught her eye. It was Angie asking, instead of answering, a question. "What would you have done?"

The transcript began with the date and time and place, a conference room in the hospital where Angie was being treated. The people in the room were listed. Two FBI agents. The sheriff and a deputy. A victim's advocate. A physician's assistant, there to monitor the patient's status. Rush closed her eyes and pictured it, Angie in a wheelchair, an IV in her arm, surrounded by six strangers.

The first questions were about Angie's comfort and welfare. Was the room too warm, too cold? Did she need water? Was she able and willing to tell them what had transpired in the previous two days?

Rush had never heard Angie speak, except in the TV interview she'd just watched, when Angie sounded stiff and rehearsed. The words she now read on the page took on tone and inflection. Slow but determined to get on with it. Close to the edge but hanging on. The collapse into agoraphobia would come later.

"We went to brunch, Kellah Mace and I. We ran into a friend, Vonnie, and her boyfriend. No, I'd never met him before. They said we should meet them later at a party. Kellah didn't want to go. I guess I got a little pushy about it, so we argued. I always want her to get out more. We're like sisters. We only fight because we love each other. I left to go to the gym. The time? I don't really remember. Maybe two? Did you ask Kellah? She'll know."

After this came a series of questions about Kellah and Vonnie and the boyfriend, all with the underlying idea that one or more of them could have been involved in what came later. That irritated Rush. A waste of time and energy. Finally, they let Angie get back on track.

"I took a path that runs along the edge of the park. It takes a little longer than walking on the streets, but it's quiet and shady, so if I have time, I go that way. I don't remember seeing anybody. No, that's not unusual, not there. The path's only a few blocks long so the runners and bikers and serious walkers don't use it. It isn't near playgrounds or the pond, so people with kids don't use it. I don't think it actually connects to any other paths."

Rush wondered if anyone had thought to declare that a crime scene, to get CSI over there. She made a mental note to ask Nash, even though she was sure she knew the answer. No. It wouldn't have mattered anyway, not even just a couple of days later. Still, she thought she might go there herself, to see how it was possible to find such a deserted place in the middle of the city on a Saturday afternoon.

"So, I got near the end, where it comes out on the street, about a block from the gym, and I saw this guy. He was just standing there. He was big. Tall and heavy. A shaved head. I didn't recognize him, and he got mad at me later because of that. He insisted I did know him, that I communicated with him, I don't know, psychically, I guess. I sent him messages in my photographs, he said. All I know is, when I got close enough to pass by him, he held out his hand. I thought he was going to touch me and I pulled back, like this. That's when I saw the knife. He just held it out, on the palm of his hand, like he wanted to show me something special. And he said something like, 'Hi, Angel. It's me.'"

Rush said out loud, "Run, girl."

"Did he threaten you with the knife?" The transcript didn't say who asked.

"Not then, but it was strange. And scary. I had my gym bag over my shoulder, across my body. I tried to get it off, to get it between us or maybe hit him with it if he came closer. But before I could get it clear, he grabbed my elbow. My right elbow, his left hand. He swung me around this way and showed me the knife again. 'We need to hurry,' he said. Something like that. He was calm, but at the same time, he was moving me toward the street."

There were more questions. Did she resist? Was there nobody she could have called out to? Angie's answers here were short. No. No. Rush wondered how she had sounded. Angry at what the questioners implied? Guilty that she'd let it happen? Or maybe all of that came later.

"He had the knife, you know? If I thought at all, it was that once we got out of the park there would be people and I'd scream my head off then. But the van was right there in front of me at the curb. He opened the back and shoved me in before I could do anything. He got in and slammed the door. It was dark inside and the space was small. I was on my stomach and he had a knee in my back. He kept saying, 'Be still. You know I'm here to help you. Be still, be still.' He sounded puzzled, like he didn't understand why I didn't do what he said. I felt like I was in the twilight zone. Nothing made sense. He was getting upset and that didn't seem good, so I decided I'd be still. It wasn't like my thrashing around could accomplish much anyway. Then he bound my hands and feet and forced something into my mouth."

Angie must have shown stress because somebody asked, "Do you need a break, Ms. Boone?"

"I think that's when I left my body. He was hurting me, but all of a sudden, I didn't feel it. I wasn't that girl anymore."

"OK. Let's take ten minutes."

The next question was, "Can you tell us what happened in the van, Ms. Boone?"

"He climbed over me into the front and I heard the engine start. We began to move. I was just glad he wasn't looming over me anymore. I thought, I'll stay calm. I can talk my way out of this. But it was hard to focus, to realize it was really happening. I think it was an out-of-body experience."

Rush wondered how long it was before she crash-landed back into her body again. She knew Angie Boone hadn't been seen in public in more than five years, so re-entry didn't mean return to normal. She's still lost, Rush thought, and that's why I have to do this.

"It was the knife," Angie said, not in response to a question.

Her thoughts unspooled as she talked. "All I could think of was, would he cut me?"

"How long were you in the van, Ms. Boone?"

Damn, Rush thought. Did these people not hear what she'd just said? That had been the guts of it. Would he cut her? A gun wouldn't have been as scary as that knife. She wondered what the transcript couldn't reveal. Was there a pause? Did somebody clear his throat? Did Angie stare down the person who asked, "How long were you in van?"

"I don't know."

"Was it still light when you got out?"

"Oh yes. It blinded me for a minute when he pulled me out. Besides being tied up, one of my legs had gone to sleep and I almost fell over. He had to hold me up. Then he reached down and cut my ankles loose. I looked around and I didn't know where I was, but it was obvious we were in the middle of nowhere."

"You say in the middle of nowhere. You were found in a building."

"OK, not nowhere, but a deserted place. It really made him mad when I didn't recognize it. He told me it was where we met, at that photo shoot. But it looked so different. Even when we got inside, it didn't look the same. By then, though, I knew not to say that."

"How did you get in?"

"There was a gap in the fence. He made me go through it, then go across the yard to a hidden door. We went into a basement. It was dark inside but he had a lamp ready and he took me upstairs to the main floor. He showed me, he'd created a space, a little room, in one corner. He made a big deal of how clean he'd made it. It was like he wanted me to tell him how nice it was, how great he was to do it just for me, so at first, I did."

"What was it like?"

"You already know, don't you? I thought—"

"We want to hear your impressions, Ms. Boone. It'll corroborate what the sheriff and his people reported."

Rush thought Angie must have been getting tired. There was a pause, then a deep inhale, before she went on.

"OK. There was a screen. He said he'd made it. There was a bed, a blow-up mattress, with pillows and sheets on it. A table, folding table, and a wooden chair. A case of bottled waters. A plastic tub that had energy bars in it. And the bucket with a toilet seat attached. He said everything was new and clean, and that this was just for now. Just until I understood."

"Did he say what you were supposed to understand?"

"Oh, yes. In great detail. He said he knew how much I needed him. In all my pictures, I was looking at him and sending him messages. He meant the Angel photos, the shampoo, the eye makeup, all of them. Beginning on the day of the photo shoot, when I spoke to him—something I don't remember at all—he knew it was up to him to save me. He told me everything I'd done wrong. The clothes I wore. The makeup. It was all bad. But he knew I wasn't responsible. People made me do those bad things, but it was all over. I was safe. He must have said that a hundred times. I was safe."

"What were you doing all the time he was talking?"

"Standing there. Looking around. Trying to figure out if I could outrun him, to get back to the basement, outside, and then what? But it was like he read my mind. He said again he knew it wasn't my fault, but I had to be purified. All of a sudden, he said, 'Undress.' You'll think I'm crazy, but until then, I never thought he was going to, you know, hurt me that way. I'd only worried he'd cut my face. For half a second, I was almost relieved, but then I started to shake. I collapsed, I think. I was on the mattress, going to pieces, but my mind was somewhere up in the rafters. I could see myself, but the me that watched didn't feel anything. Then I was naked. He lifted me up and put me in the chair. He wound tape around and around my torso and my arms. I tried to kick and get loose, but I couldn't. I just couldn't."

"We know, Angie."

Was it the victim's advocate who said that? Did anyone hold Angie's hand? Rush knew, from the fact that she was reading the last page of the transcript that it was almost over. She was relieved and could only imagine how Angie felt.

"One more thing, Ms. Boone. Can you tell us about the hair?"

"Why? You know what he did. Do I have to say it?"

"Ma'am, if he touched you with the knife, it moves the potential charges against him into a new category."

"If he touched me with the knife? Well, he did. He said to be clean, I had to be naked and I had to give up my hair. That's when he took the knife and started to shave my head. I was crying and shaking. That made it worse. He cut my scalp. I felt the blood down my neck and down my face. When he was done, he wrapped cloth around my head and taped it. I think he was trying to bandage me, but I don't know. Then he said, 'I'm tired, Angel. I'm going to leave so you can rest and think. I'll come back tomorrow morning, early, and we'll start our new life.'"

"And he left?"

"I heard footsteps. I heard scraping sounds. I didn't hear anything else and I thought, he'll never come back. I'll die here and nobody will ever know."

"We're all relieved that didn't happen, Ms. Boone."

"If you're done, I'll take the patient back to her room now."

Angie spoke again. "I have a question for all of you. What would you have done?"

25

Albert had always hated used clothes because Bitch Mom made him wear them, said he had grown too much and gotten too fat for nice things. But he had to look different, and fast. He could quit shaving, but his beard was slow-growing—blame the old man for that one—and he'd found out when he was off the grid that people saw clothes more than they saw faces. So he went to a thrift store and bought a pair of jeans that were baggy in the butt and too short. He bought a black T-shirt with a Seventies rock-band logo on the chest and an oversized denim jacket. The store had hats for sale but the idea of a hat somebody else had worn was too much. The woman in the shop said it had all been cleaned, but he went straight to a laundromat and washed the stuff in the hottest water. When it was dry, he changed clothes in the men's room. Then he went to a sporting goods store and bought a bright green golf visor. It looked stupid with the clothes and he didn't like that, but the point was people would think who is this douchy-looking guy in the green visor and not see the face from TV the night before, the face all over the Internet today.

Now he could walk around Angel's neighborhood and wait for her to come out.

It was late afternoon. He saw the old guy take the little rat dog down the street to do its business and then go back inside. The man looked a lot older and limped, not as tough as he'd acted five years earlier when he wouldn't let Albert into the building with the roses.

He saw Kellah come home with a man, familiar-looking, but Albert didn't know why. They walked fast, side by side, heads down like they were talking low.

An old woman with gray hair came out and they stopped to talk to her. Kellah hugged her and the man shook her hand. She walked on, pulling a stupid little shopping cart. They went inside.

He saw people who acted as if they lived there go in and out, delivery guys, the mail carrier, a bicycle courier like the one he'd sent with the hair. That gave him a smile.

Traffic grew heavier late in the day. The sidewalk was clogged with people and the streetlights came on. He was tired, about to leave for the day, get something to eat, maybe watch the TV show again—the Angel part—and sleep.

And then Nash showed up, and with her, Rush. But something was different about Rush. Not in uniform for one thing. Her head was bare and he saw her run her hands through her hair. They disappeared inside and he kept thinking about Rush's hair. It had been long and wavy. Now it was short. It had been a reddish-blond. Now it was light.

An hour went by before the street was quiet again. One of the black cars with dark windows pulled up to the curb. Four people came out of the building, Kellah and the familiar-looking man, Nash, and—he felt electricity go through him—a tall blonde. They all wore fancy clothes. She was in a short pale yellow dress. Her legs were long and bare. His ears throbbed at the sight of her. From nowhere, two guys showed up with cameras. Jeez, just like with Dorrie. Bastards. The people got into the black car and it was gone.

Albert stood where he was and absorbed what he'd seen. The women, even Nash, in shiny dresses, naked legs, high heels. But the blonde. He'd gotten that shock feeling, like a glimpse of Angel would give him, but as he thought, he had his doubts. Why did Rush cut her hair? he asked himself. Why did she go in and not come out?

The door of the house opened. The old guy came out again, carrying the little dog this time. The old woman Albert had seen before was with him, her arm linked in his. They went up the street as if they needed to be somewhere. Albert thought how easy it had been to get into Dorrie's building. What if he pulled his knife when the old guy came back, said he'd gut the dog, hurt the woman? The old guy would let him in, but then what? He could see it wasn't the same as with Dorrie.

He wanted to be there when the black car brought them home, but the street was all lit-up shops and restaurants and old apartment houses that were made over to be expensive again. He looked up. Security cameras, all over the place. No alleys, no vacant storefronts to make him invisible. His van was in a lot a couple of blocks away. He went to it, paid the attendant, even though he almost always found a way not to pay, and drove back to Angel's block. He was lucky as the devil again. A delivery truck pulled out of a space right across from the house. He took it, slumped in the driver's seat, and waited.

It was a little after eleven when they came. They all went

inside. He didn't know for sure which apartment Kellah kept Angel in, but only a few windows had lights on in them now. The top floor was completely dark. He was anxious, nervous, and since the street was quiet now, he opened the van door and swung his legs out so that he faced the building straight on. In a minute, lights came on in the fifth-floor windows. He bent over his knees and controlled his breath. When the door opened again, Nash and Rush came out. They wore their normal clothes. He wanted to follow them, but it didn't feel smart or safe.

He went to sleep with his laptop beside him so if he woke, he could check it right away. If Angel had been out in public, somebody would have gotten a picture. He saw it at 3:47 a.m. The man and three women coming out of Kellah's house, getting into the black car, just what he'd seen himself. The story said they were on their way to a private fundraiser for the Angel Foundation, and it said the blonde was her.

He felt flat now, no buzz left. Something was wrong. He focused on the blonde. She was in a shadow and turned away from the camera, but nobody knew Angel's face like he did. The empty feeling became stronger, and he zoomed in. It wasn't her. It was the whore cop, Rush, dressed up, made up to make people think she was Angel. He thought about the TV interview, what she'd said about going out into the world. That was a lie, but they'd made her tell it. She was still a prisoner.

There were more photos later, ones that the Angel Foundation put out, supposed to be from the party, but it was the back of the blonde's head that showed, never her face. Were all those people stupid? Didn't they know it was all fake? Or were they in on it?

His head began to hurt and his eardrums beat jackhammers.

26

As soon as she got out of the car, Kellah looked up. The front windows of the apartment were dark. She hoped Angie was still up. The library, kitchen, and bedrooms were on the other side of the building, so it was possible.

Behind her, a car door slammed and she jumped. Her nerves had been taut all night. Brendan reacted, too. Nash said, "If it's anything, our guys are watching."

"These shoes are killing me," Rush said in a voice that would carry across the street. She stooped to take the heels off, and Kellah sensed that doing so gave her a chance to look around, head down. Kellah caught the small shake of the head she gave Nash when she stood up: nothing.

"Let's go in," Kellah said. "I want to know Angie's OK."

Brendan held the door for the women and Kellah saw him linger a moment, look up and down the street, before he came in.

Mike was in the library, TV on low, a late-night show, his head on his chest. He woke with a gasp when they came in.

"How'd it go?" He sat up and wiped his eyes.

"Fine," Kellah said. "Is she asleep?"

"Don't know. She took Guffy and went to her room when

the news came on."

"I'm awake." Angie appeared in the door, the dog in her arms. Kellah smiled at her and was relieved when she smiled back. "Don't worry. I was just texting Dad. He's been needy lately."

That made Mike and Kellah laugh. "Yeah," Mike said. "Needy of making another million, or what?"

"So, Cam, Gen, how did it go? Did everybody think Cam was me?" Angie called them by their first names rather than Rush and Nash, or officer and detective. It annoyed Kellah a bit that Angie seemed determined to deny the reality of who they were and why they were here.

"Not when they got too near me," Rush said. "Or saw me walk in these." She held the shoes up by their straps.

"We handled it just the way we discussed," Nash said. "We never said Rush was you, but I think a few people thought so, at least when we first went in."

"Was it quiet here?" Kellah asked.

"Yeah," Mike said. "Bonnie and I took His Highness out a couple of times, just to get a look around. Then Bonnie went to her apartment. She made me promise I'd let her know when you got home." He stood up and stretched. "I guess I'll go do that."

"Thanks for being here," Kellah said. "It made me feel better."

He hugged both young women. "See you tomorrow."

Nash took her phone out of the small bag she carried. "I heard from my people all night. The minivan parked out there? It's been there for quite a while. The driver never got out. He opened the door, maybe just to get some air, and closed it just after we pulled up. They ran the plates. The vehicle is registered upstate. We're checking out the owner."

Kellah was aware of Brendan. He'd been quiet all night. At the party, he'd stayed close to her, but she wasn't sure he'd ever looked at her. His eyes were on everything and everybody around her, worried, watchful. She took his hand. "It was good to have you there."

"I felt useless," he said.

"But you looked good," Nash said. He grinned and Kellah felt him relax a little. "And it's time we turned back into pumpkins. Rush, you ready for real life again?"

27

He watched the foundation's website. In ten days, there was going to be another big benefit. This one was to be sponsored by a corporation and its CEO, to be held at world headquarters in the city. The announcement listed the names of big donors. It cost a $1,000 to attend and it was almost sold out. The kicker was, Angie Boone would attend.

He knew they were playing him. But he was too smart. He'd already figured out what to do about the Rush bitch and how to do it. Now he knew when.

It was a quiet time, late afternoon at police headquarters, just after one shift ended and another began. Nobody was coming or going from the underground parking garage. It opened into a narrow one-way alley, dark because the buildings close on both sides cut out the sun. Both ends were lit by daylight or streetlights, but they seemed far away. Albert parked the minivan close to the garage's mouth, not worried about anybody hassling him. There was, maybe, one car every five or six minutes. Latecomers, early-leavers, they all had something else to think about. If anybody thought it was odd to see a vehicle parked in the alley, they ignored it and went about their business.

He rehearsed in his head. He'd followed Rush to work that morning, something he'd done every day for a week. She walked from the subway that day, wearing jeans and a shirt, carrying a duffel bag. She went up the big granite steps and in through the main door. It had tripped him up a few times when he first started to watch her, because at the end of the day, she didn't come out from there.

That's when he'd looked around and found the garage at the back of the building. There wasn't a sign. You had to know it was there. The first time he'd checked it out, his luck was good. He was on foot, in a shadow. He heard her holler at somebody, "No, I'm fine. See you tomorrow," just before she appeared. He guessed going out through the garage saved her walking around the building. That, or wherever she was when she was inside must be closer to the back than the front door. It was not how he'd have done it. Wasn't it supposed to be bad luck, going in one door and out another? Whatever. The alley was perfect for him. And the best thing was, no cameras.

He had followed her. Even without her uniform, she walked as if she owned the street, like when she'd paraded up and down in front of his mom's house. People coming out of a bar stepped back when they saw her. She said something to them, and they laughed. They came his way, two men and two girls, jostling each other, taking up the sidewalk so he had to step aside. They didn't notice him. They were busy with their own bullshit. He tracked her a couple more blocks until he was sure she was going home.

There was no point in tracking her after that. There were CCTV cameras everywhere on the street. And there were oddballs out for no good reason, who might decide to look at him. Besides, it wasn't time. He knew how and where it would happen. As for when, it had to be the day of the big event.

28

It was a few minutes past six when she came up the ramp out of the garage on foot. She wore dark pants, a black T-shirt, a white PD cap, and athletic shoes. She paused to look left for traffic. Stupid, he thought, a stupid reflex with one-way traffic. She swung the duffel bag up, the strap over her head and across her body. If she had a gun, it was in there. Her pause ended and she headed off to the right. He moved. She heard him and turned, but too late. He jammed her against the wall, face first, the bag hard into her gut. He caught her left arm, twisted it behind her, and laid the blade of his knife against her neck on the right side.

"Keep quiet," he said. "Be still."

She had to work to breathe, to get back the air he'd forced out of her. She couldn't do more than whisper, "Who are you?" He could tell, she didn't believe this could be happening to her, and he liked that.

He had to get her to the car and he knew she'd fight him any way she could. She was trained to fight, and he felt how strong her body was, even stronger than he'd expected. But she knew he had the knife now and that would keep her in line. He moved it, cut the bag's strap so when he jerked her away from the wall it fell. He let go of her arm and gripped her shoulder, hard into the big nerve, to force her down. She tried to yell but it was a croak. Then she was on her knees and he let up the pressure just enough for her to pay attention to him and not the pain.

"See the car? That's where we're going."

"Somebody's coming out any minute."

"Then we got to hurry." He held the knife in front of her face, wrapped his arm around her neck and lifted. She was too tall for him to get her off her feet, so her toes dragged when he moved her. They got to the car, the sliding door open and waiting, and that was where she tried to twist away, stomp his foot, swing her elbow, reach for his balls. But she couldn't get out of his grip. Her athletic shoe bounced off his boot. He was too close for the elbow to get any speed. He sidestepped her reach. She was in the car, face down on the floor. He had torn off lengths of tape in advance and stuck them to the overhead liner so that they dangled in reach. It was easy to take off her cap, raise her head with a fistful of hair, yank down tape to wrap her hands behind her back and her ankles. Then he wound tape around her head to cover her mouth. He pulled a pillowcase over her head, twisted it around her neck and tied it. He covered her with the blanket he had ready, then backed himself out. He slid the door closed and leaned against it.

He remembered her bag. Not smart to leave it there because somebody would find it and wonder what was up. He jogged the fifteen feet to retrieve it, returned to the car, into the driver's seat, put the key in the ignition. That was when he heard a car rev up the ramp toward the garage exit. He looked at his watch. It had all happened in three minutes. He was in the driver's seat again and moving.

———

Rush had to breathe. Her chest ached from lack of oxygen, from the slam of ribs against concrete. The tape almost but not quite covered her nose. She resisted panic until at last she felt the smallest release, the slightest movement of her diaphragm. Her lungs drew in what air they could. As they filled, her mind registered pain without order: every muscle, every nerve, every sinew.

Something with heft hit the floor near her head and she flinched. A car door opened, closed. They began to move. She registered the motion as forward. That meant toward the street, away from any possibility of salvation.

OK, girl, she told herself. Get it together. Think.

She was face down on the rough floor mat. Her forehead was probably bleeding but she was sure the abrasions were only skin-deep. Her nose wasn't broken, couldn't be or it would hurt even worse and would be swollen shut. It ran with blood and snot, though. She was glad he hadn't turned her over. On her back, she would drown. One good thing, then.

"You alive back there?" His voice was full of hate.

It gave her the adrenalin she needed to work the blanket around her feet and tug it down until her head was exposed. She rolled onto one side, as much as possible. It wouldn't take long in that position for her arm and shoulder to lose circulation, but it felt better not to grind her nose into the floor with every bump. The van stopped, started again, stopped. City traffic. It took a turn that almost rolled her over again, but she managed to bend her knees and stay on her side.

A cellphone rang near her ear. It was the ringtone she used for Nash, the theme from the old *Law and Order* show. It meant the thing he'd thrown into the back was her bag. It meant her phone was on.

"I guess they'll have to leave a message," he said. "You can tell 'em you were tied up, huh?" He laughed.

She felt a sliver of hope. Maybe it hadn't occurred to him, the phone's GPS left a trail. When she didn't show up at Kellah's apartment in the next half hour, Nash would know she was missing.

29

Brendan got to the apartment at six, his tuxedo in a garment bag, his shaving kit in his briefcase. Kellah met him in the foyer. She greeted him with a light hug.

"We're on edge around here," she said. He understood she meant Angie, who was still unhappy about being left out.

"Is Nash here?"

"She got here about five minutes ago. She's making some calls. Rush texted to say she was just leaving and should be here by six-thirty. Angie has a dress picked out for her."

They started for the library and heard the elevator bell again. Mike and Bonnie Leland stepped out.

"Hi, Bonnie," Kellah said. Bonnie was in her sixties, petite and well-dressed beside Mike.

"I hoped to see you all dressed up for the ball." She kissed Kellah on the cheek.

"Can you wait a few minutes? We're just getting organized."

"We're going for an early dinner at Lacey's," Bonnie said. "I hope we can get Angie to come with us."

"Guffy can come, too," Mike said. "Lacey's saving an outside table for us."

"Angie still hasn't been out of the house," Kellah said. "Not even after what she said in the interview. I don't know that you can talk her into it, but please try. I'm worried about leaving her here alone."

"Where is she?" Bonnie asked. "Let me see what I can do."

They went through the living room to the library. Bonnie and Kellah went down the hallway to Angie's bedroom. Nash was in the library, on her phone. She waved to the men and they sat down to wait.

"I like Bonnie," Brendan whispered. Mike's face lit up and he nodded until Brendan thought he would be dizzy.

Nash ended her call. "Security is in place, here and at the venue. Let's just hope they have work to do."

"You're sure Ape will show up?" Mike asked.

"Sure? No. But there's a chance and we're ready." She looked at Quick. "Maybe this time, huh?"

Kellah and Bonnie reappeared, with Guffy in Bonnie's arms.

"No go," Bonnie said. "She says she has to help Officer Rush get dressed and do her makeup. But we have permission to take His Highness with us, if we promise not to feed him off our plates. And we can bring her cheesecake later."

"Thanks for trying," Kellah said. "And I'll feel better knowing that you'll be with her later."

"We'll cheer her up," Mike said. "And we'll be here when you get back, no matter what time."

He took the little dog in one arm. Bonnie took his other, and they left.

"I'll shave and change clothes," Brendan said. He was eager to get started and needed to do something. Neither of the women answered him. He knew they felt it, too, and that all three of them were lost in their own thoughts and expectations for the night.

Rush was late.

"I don't get it," Nash said. "She isn't answering her phone."

Angie came out of her room and paced. Kellah, also ready for the evening, pretended to read a magazine, but tension radiated from her body. Brendan had on his tux pants and his dress shoes, but still wore an oxford button-down to avoid wrinkling his dress shirt.

"It's 6:45," Nash said. "If she doesn't answer this time, I've got to do something." She headed for the kitchen with her phone.

"I think I'll go to my room," Angie said.

"Can I come with you?" Kellah got up. Angie held up a hand as if to say, don't, but Kellah followed her anyway. Brendan knew, they all knew. Everything was going wrong.

Nash reappeared, her face dark. "Still no answer," she told him. "But her phone's on. It doesn't go straight to voicemail. I called the captain. He's going to get somebody to track the phone."

30

Time and distance were impossible to judge. Rush knew he'd turned right out of the alley. He'd gone straight through a few intersections and the map in her head told her what streets he had crossed, but soon she was lost. He would have a goal in mind, maybe the warehouse across the river, although she doubted it. He must know it had been under surveillance since Dorrie's death. Where else he might take her, she had no idea. All she needed was a small opening, the least opportunity, and she'd make it hard for him, whatever he had in mind.

He stopped once, though he kept the motor running. The door scraped open and she heard his heavy breathing. He was that close and she was helpless. But he didn't touch her or speak. Something scraped across the floor. It had to be her bag. He slammed the door shut and they started moving again.

It wasn't long before the vehicle slowed, stopped, and the engine cut off. Her heart began to pound. The door slid open and he grabbed her by the ankles, pulled her halfway out.

"Sit up." He twisted her legs and she lifted her torso so that she sat on the edge of the van floor, her feet on the ground.

"I'm going to cut through the tape on your ankles so you can walk. You are going to do what I say. Right?"

She felt pressure against the fleshy part of her thigh, near her hip. Then she felt the sting and knew he'd used the knife. The stab wasn't deep, just enough to make her think. She nodded her head. He cut the tape, but the pain was hot now and distracted her. If that had been a moment's opportunity, it was gone.

He gripped her by the elbows, lifted her, and forced her six feet or so across a paved surface. "Step up. Threshold. Stop."

She was inside a building, left shoulder against a wall. It smelled dirty, moldy. She lifted her head as if somehow a sliver of light might find its way through the cloth over her head. None did, and she concluded it was a dark place. He let go of one arm and she could tell he'd stepped away from her. The air pressure changed. He'd opened a door.

"We're going down a dozen steps. You can walk or I can throw you." He nudged her and she felt the floor drop away. She stumbled downward but didn't fall.

"One, two, three," he counted.

She was relieved to get to the bottom on her feet. The air was worse, oppressive, as if squeezed by a low ceiling.

"Sit," he said.

She felt a push against the back of her legs and sat on a hard surface. A wooden chair with a straight back. Her taped hands kept her from being able to sit back.

"Foot here." He held her right ankle to the right front chair leg and she felt him wrap tape around both, and then the other ankle to the other chair leg. "Go ahead," he said. "Try to move."

She shook her head, no. It was the first time she'd been able to oppose him, and she could tell there wasn't any give to the tape. Yet.

"I said, move, bitch." His fist, or something harder, hit the side of her head. She grunted and pitched forward, against the binding around her ankles. She would have toppled face-first to the floor, but he steadied the chair. He wrapped tape around her torso and the back of the chair, layer after layer, her hands pinned between her body and the slats.

When he again said, "Try to move," she did. She tested the space he'd left her. He made a noise in his throat, satisfied with his work, she hoped. She'd found a little wiggle room.

"They will never find you." He hit her on the back of the head.

31

Nash's phone rang. It was the captain. As she answered, she turned to Quick. He was slumped into the big soft chair Mike usually sat in. The sound and her movement brought him around. She nodded as the captain talked, in a hurry now to end the call.

"They found Rush's phone," she said. "Guess where? Remember Big Men Movers?"

"There?"

"There. Her bag, with the phone and her handgun, on the sidewalk outside the fence. Here's what we have so far. A couple of people spoke to Rush as she left headquarters. She told one of them she was going to a party. They made jokes about Cinderella. The sergeant said he told her to wait for a cop to drive her, but she said there wasn't time. She went out through the parking garage. It's a shortcut to a street where she could get a cab. Anyway, she never got here, so something happened. And now they've found her phone."

She watched Quick's face. It went both alert and flat, processing but not giving anything away. She remembered that look and knew he was catching up to her own thoughts.

"It's a message from Ape," he said. "He's figured out that

we've been using her as Angie's double."

"Rush's been on the news." She clinched her fists and tapped herself on the sides of her head. "I should have seen this coming. I should have known he'd try to grab her."

Quick shook his head. "Don't go down that rabbit hole. The thing is to find her. Would he take her across the river?"

"No. He's not stupid. Or even if he did try it again, he'd find out it's off-limits to him now."

He got up, turned his back and went to a bookcase that held framed photos of young Kellah with her parents, and adult Kellah with Angie. "He likes familiar territory, we know that." Quick adjusted the pictures.

"His dad's old restaurant. Darwin's Good Eats," Nash said. She was already calling the captain back. When Quick turned, she gave him a thumbs-up sign. By the time she got off the phone, he had knocked on Angie's bedroom door. She and Kellah came out, Angie serene now, and Kellah troubled.

"Will Cam be here in time?" Angie asked.

"We don't think so," Nash said, then took a deep breath. "In fact, we're afraid she's been kidnapped."

They both went blank, and Angie shook her head. "I told you I should be the one to do this."

"Do you think Ape has her?" Kellah ignored her friend.

"We're going to find her." Nash gathered herself. "I've got to go. I'm sorry, but Rush's welfare is my responsibility. And I want you both to stay home tonight. Quick, you'll stay with them?"

"Of course."

Angie cut him off. "I'm going. To the fundraiser. I made up my mind when Cam didn't come on time."

"It's not safe, Angie," Nash said. "I can't let either of you take the chance."

"But the whole idea is to get him to come after me, I mean, the girl he thought was me. I guess it worked." Angie sank down onto the couch and curled her feet under her. Brendan wondered if she was truly giving up so easily.

"But if he has her, he knows she isn't you," Nash said. "If we ever had him fooled, he knows now. We can't predict how he'll react and we don't know where he is."

"But this event is important, right?" Angie asked. "And everybody expects me to show up, right? Kellah?"

"You haven't left this building in how long?" Kellah's voice was deep with feeling. "We've done everything your way, for how long?"

"Hey, now," Brendan said. "We've got to agree, so Nash can get out of here. We stay put tonight. We take no risks. OK?"

Kellah turned her back on him. Nash felt bad, leaving him with the two women, but by now, the car the captain sent for her would be downstairs.

"I'll hold you to that," she said to Quick. "I'll be back for this stuff." Nash pointed to the rolling suitcase bag she'd brought with her evening dress, shoes, and makeup kit inside.

"And you'll call us?" Angie said. "Let us know when you find Cam?" She gave Nash a brief hug. "Thank you, Gen."

Kellah watched this and felt a twinge. When had Angie last thanked her?

32

He had to sit in the minivan and breathe for a while. It was a hot night and he'd been sweating ever since he'd grabbed Rush in the alley. The basement where he'd left her, it had to be a hundred degrees. He didn't care. She got what she deserved. He had a towel in the back of the van and took time to run it over his head and neck. It would have been good to change clothes but he wore the second-hand ones, his disguise, and didn't have any others.

He wondered what it meant to sweat so much. Was he sick? No, he thought, it was from touching her, the bitch. It had been a long time since he'd had that much physical contact with a human being. He had seen Dorrie naked, wrestled with her, but not for long. Otherwise, he had barely touched her, and surely didn't press against her the way he had done with Rush.

And he had never put a knife into flesh before. Never needed to. He looked down to be sure there wasn't any of her blood on him. He wished he could take a shower and scrub every molecule of her off his skin.

He banged his head once hard against the window and began to drive.

According to the foundation's website, this gala thing was supposed to start at eight o'clock. It was almost that now. He drove toward the glass and steel skyscraper where it was held. The street was blocked off and police moved from car to car. Long black vehicles and fancy foreign cars were permitted to go through but cars like his were turned back. He pulled out into a U-turn so he didn't have to deal with a cop in his face.

Maybe I'll trade for a limo next, he thought. Angel will be safe then. He would drive her everywhere, and nobody would see her through those dark windows. Finally, she'd ask him to stop and she would get out and he would get out. She would take his hands and say, I love you.

He turned into a parking garage, left the minivan, and walked back to the building. If Angel came, he'd see her. Maybe get close enough that she'd see him.

He slowed down when he got near. He wore the disguise clothes from the second-hand store and a doorman who'd stepped out to open a car door gave him a dirty look. Like a guy in a purple coat with brass buttons and striped pants had a right. Albert touched the pocket where his knife was and thought about ripping right through that uniform. He kept walking. Giant planters, five feet tall, five feet deep, were lined up across the front of the building, all the way down the block. Little palm trees and shit grew out of them. It was easy to duck behind the last one. It reminded him of the bushes at the playground, how safe he'd been there. He crept behind the line of planters, toward the front door. The ground was littered with cigarette butts and drink cans. He wished he had something trashy to leave behind. Maybe he'd piss on it all before he left. But now he had to keep watch.

For the next hour, cars pulled up and let people out. Private cars, fancy ones, stopped, and their drivers turned the keys over to parking valets. Albert hadn't thought of that before. A knife in the side of one of those guys and a fancy car could be his. Easy.

He saw unsmiling men and women in plain dark suits. They stood along the sidewalk, five or six feet from each other, both in front of the building and across the street. Their eyes swept the crowd but even though he saw them, they never registered his shape in the shadows. No surprise. He was smarter than the cops again.

But none of the people who swished by him in evening dresses and tuxedos—none of the people who didn't even look down and see him not ten feet away—was Angel. Or Kellah. Or Nash. Or the old guy, or the guy who looked familiar. As the cars quit arriving, as the cops opened the street again and went away, he slid out from between the planters, unhappy, frustrated. Why did people lie to him?

He was only six blocks from where Angel lived. It had been a week since he parked the van across the street and watched for her. Was that a long time, or like no time at all? He didn't know. He remembered he'd thought of getting inside but hadn't seen a way. Now he had to make it happen. He passed by a store window and saw somebody, blank and empty like a ghost, but still somebody. It was his own reflection. Invisible. That was fine.

He knew from the computer, from satellite views and street views, that there was a yard with a wall around it behind Angel's building, but he'd never paid attention to how to get to it.

Now he was in front of the building again. He saw a gap

between it and the building to its left. The dark space was as wide as his body, plus maybe a foot. He eased into it and put his hands out to touch the brick walls on either side. They were damp, like he'd always thought frog bellies would be, but fuzzy, too. Fuzzy bricks? Did something grow on them? He shivered at the strangeness and wiped his hands on his pants legs. He crossed his arms so he wouldn't brush against the walls again, and moved deeper in.

He wanted this passage to bring him into the back yard, but he bumped face first into another wall. It gave him a panicky moment, like he was in a box, a cave, a coffin. But he took a step back and told himself he could turn around and walk out, just like he'd walked in, so he should suck it up and think. This new barrier had to be the wall that went around the courtyard.

He reached out, put his hand flat against it, and extended his arm as high as he could. The wall went higher than he could reach. His heart felt as if he'd just run a mile flat-out, and when he knew he was going to have to climb this thing, it got worse. But he was going to do it. He was going to use his hands and feet on the walls beside him and go up until he could at least see over the one in front of him. And he was not going to throw up while he did it, because Bitch Mom always laughed at him when he threw up.

He had a habit of doing fifty pushups three or four times a day. He was strong. He did it, slowly scaling the wall, and he got to the top. When he looked over, he looked at an empty yard, with rectangles of light from the windows above scattered across it. He knew now the wall was about twelve feet high. If he went on up, got on top, he could hang down and have a drop of only a few feet. Then what? Hell if he knew, but he felt good again.

33

After Nash disappeared behind the elevator doors, Kellah remembered something she hadn't thought of in years. When she was a child, she believed those doors were magic. They took people away, they brought them back. Except when they didn't. As if he knew, Brendan put a hand on her shoulder.

"Do you wish you were going with Nash?" she asked him.

"No," he said, and then, "Maybe. I don't know. But I'm glad to be here with you."

Angie walked past them, silent, toward the library.

"Want something to eat?" Kellah asked him. "I made you eggs once, remember?"

"I remember everything."

He sat while she took eggs and bread out of the refrigerator. "I should remodel this kitchen one day. Mims liked it like this, but sometimes they had parties, and the caterers complained. Of course, I never have parties here."

Then she stopped. "I'm not sure why, but I'm remembering a lot tonight. Little things." And she felt tears burn behind her eyes. She leaned against the counter and all of sudden, she cried. Brendan had his arms around her, his head pressed against hers.

"We can start over," he said. "If you want to."

She didn't want to talk about that. "Do you think Nash will find her?"

"Every cop in the city will be looking for her, I know that. And Nash has a good idea about where to look. Just like she figured out where Angie was. You got there first, but still, she knew."

She stepped away from him, just far enough to reach for a dish towel and wipe her eyes, not far enough to break the connection. "Where is she going?"

"Do you remember when we talked to Biggers, Ape's boss? He told us about a building Ape's mother owned, thought she'd sell for a million one day?"

"I remember."

"Nash and I got search warrants for that place and his mother's house. We went to the building first. It was empty, but it would be a good place to hide somebody, so that's where's she's gone."

"But what if she's wrong?"

Before he answered, the door swung open and Angie stood there. She wore a long midnight-blue dress, one that fell free from shoulder to floor. It was unadorned, except for translucent beading along the deep V-neck. Kellah remembered it from the Angel days, when it had floated away from the model's thin body. Now it rested on the curve of her hips.

"This is what Cam was going to wear."

"You look beautiful," Kellah said. "I could take a picture, send it to your dad."

"Or you could get dressed so we can go to this damned party." She pointed to Kellah, then to Brendan. "You've got your tux, right?"

"Angie," Kellah said, "you heard Nash. She wants us to stay here, safe."

"And you always do what somebody tells you? Did you before?"

"It was different." She turned to Brendan. "Tell her." But he was quiet for a long moment.

"If you mean it, Angie, I'll take you," he said.

Kellah felt it as a blow to her solar plexus. "No. No. She never leaves the house. She …"

No other words came to her. He embraced her. She couldn't raise her arms either to push him away or pull him in.

"It'll be OK," he said. "I promise."

"You want us to start over? If you take Angie away from me, it will be the end. Of everything." She whispered it into his chest and didn't know if he heard it or not.

"No," he said. "It won't."

When he let her go and left the room, she was cold. She looked at the eggs broken into a bowl and poured them into the sink. If they were really going to go, to leave her and go, she didn't want to witness it. She went through the pantry to the old back stairs and took them down to the ground floor. There was no light under Mike's door, so she guessed he wasn't back from dinner. Unless he'd stopped in at Bonnie's apartment.

Or disappeared, like everybody else.

She couldn't remember the last time she'd gone alone into the garden. It was always with Angie, to toss a ball for Guffy, or sit in the shade. The outer limit of Angie's world. Until tonight. Maybe the garden would be her sanctuary now. The door opened on both sides with a code on the keypad, a change made for Angie's sake. In the early days of her self-imposed confinement, she would go out there in a daze and forget her key. The electronic beeps seemed loud to Kellah, the green light that flashed when the lock opened too bright. The city was never quiet, never dark, and in summer, never cool. But the space here was soft and the air fresh. She stepped out into it and let the door close behind her.

34

Once he landed, he saw the door, ran to it, and tried it first thing. He wouldn't have been surprised if it opened for him, but no luck this time. The keypad wasn't lit, but he felt it. Maybe fingers had worn some of the numbers more than others, maybe that would reveal the code. But he couldn't take the time to figure that out. The lobby door was glass. The lights were on inside. If anybody came to the street-side door, they'd look right across the lobby, straight at him. The same if anyone was getting off the elevator. He heard a sound and saw a door he hadn't noticed—small and off to one side—and somebody came into the lobby.

He jumped off the landing and for the second time that night hid behind bushes like he had when he was a kid. Safe again.

He expected whoever was in the lobby would go out to the street, but next thing, the door to the yard swung open and somebody stepped out. It would be perfect if Angel came out to meet him, but this person was on the small side. A woman, he thought. He patted his pocket. The knife was there. He'd wait until she went back inside. Maybe he'd use the knife to make her let him in, too. He'd bet that the odd door she'd used led to a stairwell, and he could climb until he found Angel.

The woman made a noise that startled him. A groan, a moan. Something like pain. Then she walked across the yard, through a patch of light that fell from a window. Then back to dark, back to light. He saw how the patches were in a line and the nearest one came from the first floor. The next one from the second floor. The one farthest away, that would be from the top floor where he was now sure Angel was kept.

The woman stood in that one now, turned back to look up, and he knew who she was. Kellah Mace. Bitch. He didn't know why she felt pain but he was glad. She raised her hand all of a sudden, like a wave to somebody up there, and then dropped it. His eyes adapted to the light. Black hair over a white face, pinched like a little animal's. What had he thought of before? Oh yeah. A lemur. Stupid thing from TV. Bitch Mom said so cute, she wanted one.

Kellah went to a lawn chair, one of the long ones you could lie down on under a tree in the middle of the yard. She sat on it and pulled her feet up so that her knees were up in the air. She wrapped her arms around them and made that noise again. More pain. Her phone rang. She took it out of a pocket, looked at it, and threw it out onto the grass. He laughed and she heard. She turned her head left and right, not knowing where the voice came from. He came out from where he hid and walked straight toward her.

"Who's there?" she asked.

He didn't answer. He got close to her and stood over her. She'd put her feet on the ground but he felt huge. And good.

"I know who you are," he said. "You know who I am?"

She stared up. "I can't see you. You're in the shadows. Step back."

She was lying. She knew. She just wanted him to back away. But he didn't. He leaned down so his face was closer. "Where's Angel?"

She moved like she wanted to get up but didn't dare. Then she slid backwards on the lounge chair as if she'd go off on the other side, but she stopped that, too. She wasn't totally stupid. She saw he could reach her, grab her, whichever way she tried to go.

"Where's Angel?" he asked again.

"She isn't here. She's gone out."

He snorted. "Liar. You always lie. And you make her lie. She said she'd be out in the world, but then it was that cop. You think you can fool everybody."

He heard Kellah breathe in and out fast, like she was trying to control it. That meant she was scared and was trying to make him think she wasn't.

"How did you get in here?" she asked.

He shook his head. "She's upstairs, right? You're going to open the door for me and I'm going to go up and save her."

"She went out. She went to a party."

"No. I was there. She didn't come."

"Things got confused. She just left a few minutes ago."

"No. The cop was supposed to go, wasn't she? The cop who looks like her, but I took care of that. Where do you guess she is now?" He used his voice to make it sound like it was a big mystery.

"You mean Cam Rush? Detective Nash knows where she is. She's going to find her in the deserted building your mother owned."

That made him step back, just a little. How the shit did she know that? Kellah moved fast, swung her legs over the chair. He reached to grab her and she ran for the door. He was faster. Tackled her. She hit the ground on her stomach and he knew he'd knocked the breath out of her. The problem was, he'd landed hard, too, and took her heels under his diaphragm. He got onto his knees and reached into his pocket. The knife wasn't there. He had dropped it. He looked around, had to find it.

She moved, tried to crawl away. He grabbed her feet and yanked them until she rolled onto her back. She sucked air and he got his hands around her throat. But his brain yelled at him, stop. He needed her to get inside the house.

He let up. "Tell me the code for the door."

She coughed and choked, and shook her head, no. He hit her. He grabbed her hair and shook her head back and forth. When he let go, she lay still.

"I didn't hurt you. Not that bad. Get up." He held his own side, where a rib ached, but he stood, grabbed her arm, and hauled her up. "You open the door."

Her cheek was bleeding now. And her mouth. She looked him in the eyes and he saw a look he'd seen before but couldn't think where. Then she screamed, hoarse and broken, but loud.

"What's going on?" The woman's voice came from above them, from a window in the building. "Who's out there?"

"Call 911," Kellah called. Then she dropped her voice and said, "You are nothing." That's when he remembered the look. It's how Bitch Mom looked right before she laughed at him.

"I'm going to kill you." He wanted the knife, wanted to feel it go in deep, come out ragged, go in deep again. The way he'd stabbed Rush, just so many times more. But all he had were his hands. They'd do.

Then he lay on the ground with lights inside his head like fireworks, like strobes, like his brain was on fire. He wasn't sure his eyes worked but he opened them and saw the old guy.

"You move, I'll kick your ugly head in again." It was the old guy. With the bad leg. Albert tried to remember which leg that was. He lay still. He needed to let the fog clear. When he turned his head, it was like a miracle, like the devil's luck. He saw the knife on the ground, not far, not far.

"I give," he said. "Just give me space to breathe."

And like an idiot, the old guy shifted his weight. That was all Albert needed to roll toward him, come up fast, punch him hard in the leg, right on the bad knee. His fist met bone and hurt like hell but he was tough, he could take it, and the old guy went down in a heap. Howled. Albert wanted to laugh but he had to get the knife. He had it. The blade came out like it was all the beauty the world ever held, and he dug it deep into flesh.

Weight hit his back and knocked him sideways. Fists pounded the sides of his head and a voice raged in his ear. Fingers dug into his eyes. He dropped the knife again so he could grab his attacker's hands. They released suddenly and the weight fell away. His eyes hurt more than anything he'd ever felt and he was on his knees trying to shake the pain away when a wrecking ball slammed into his side and he collapsed.

Screams, sirens, lights, blood. Someone lifted Kellah, gently this time, wrapped her in a blanket and walked her away. She looked back and saw Mike on the ground. Nothing made sense. She spoke to the person who held her. "Where's Mims?"

"Who? Oh, honey."

She recognized Bonnie's face. "I mean, where's Angie?"

"I don't know."

"Can I call her? Where's my phone?"

"I have mine." Bonnie held it out. "Do you know the number?"

"I can't remember. Oh, God, what's happening?" She watched while paramedics lifted Mike onto a gurney and moved it toward the building. "I have to go with him."

"Honey, you're bleeding yourself. You need to stay still."

Then it was Genevieve Nash who held her. "I'm so sorry, Kellah. Sorry I wasn't here."

Kellah tried to remember where Nash had gone, and why.

"We found Cam Rush," Nash said. "She's alive, she'll be OK. They've got Mike on his way to the hospital. And Ape, too. These guys need to look at you, see about your injuries. Then we'll talk."

Two EMTs lifted Kellah onto a gurney and made her lie back. They strapped her on and began to roll it toward the building.

The lobby was full of people, residents of the building and others she didn't recognize. She held out a hand and Nash took it. She heard a whine and looked up to see Bonnie holding Guffy. Bonnie's face crumpled and she cried into the little dog's fur.

They went to an ambulance parked out front and lowered the gurney to load it on.

"Come with me?" Kellah asked Nash. She saw Nash's eyes cloud and blur.

"I'll see you there. I'll be right behind you."

The doors closed and one of the EMTs began to talk to her, ask questions, while he cut off her clothes and swabbed at the blood.

35

She woke up cold and reached for the comforter that should be there on her bed.

"She's awake," somebody said. She opened her eyes. The walls were the wrong color and the window wasn't where it should be. When she tried to sit up, a hand on her shoulder stopped her.

"Girly." It was Angie's voice, hand, face.

"Where am I?" Her voice was thick and the words were mush.

"In the hospital." Somehow Angie knew what she asked. "You need to be still. Brendan's here."

His face was gray. He had deep creases in his forehead. His eyes were red and wet. It was hard to look at him, to see him like that, so Kellah turned back to Angie. It was the blue dress with the beading that made her remember.

"It really happened," she said. "Mike?" Did the sounds she made convey what she meant? She wasn't sure until Angie answered.

"Kellah, Girly, Mike died. They got Ape, but he killed Mike."

"And you almost killed Ape," Brendan said.

Kellah was home. Her bruises were vivid yellows, blues, and deep purples. She had a black eye and four tiny black sutures between her nose and upper lip. But most of the blood that soaked her clothing that night wasn't hers. It was Albert Darwin's, from when she stabbed him. And some of it was Mike's, from when she held his head in her lap. But it hadn't helped. He died. The words curled back on themselves endlessly in her brain. The worst thing. Again.

Angie and Brendan were there all the time, with cups of hot liquids, with ice cream, with faces that only sapped more and more light out of her days. It was worse when they told her they loved her. Bonnie came, sat with her and held her hand.

When Kellah asked, Bonnie told her story.

"When we got back from Lacey's, we went right up to your apartment, but nobody was there. We didn't understand, where was Angie? Mike was upset. He kept saying, 'Where're my girls?' I said, 'Let's go to my place and make some calls. We'll figure it out.'

"I left him in my living room and went to the bathroom. You know how it's at the back of the building. While I was in there, I heard an odd sound that seemed to come through the exterior wall. It was a scrabbling sound, like something trapped and trying to get out. I opened the window a little and I heard a groan as if somebody strained to lift something heavy, and then a thud. I went out to the living room and told Mike. He opened the drapes, and we saw the shape of a man run across the lawn right below us. 'I'm going down there,' Mike said and I was afraid for him to do that. I said, 'No, call 911,' but before either happened, we saw you come out of the building and go to the lounge chair. We knew you were in distress, honey, but we didn't know why, and you were supposed to be gone by then. So where was Angie? Where were Brendan and Nash? Then we saw him walk toward you. Your head was down. You didn't see him coming. Mike handed me Guffy and told me to make the call. He moved faster than I thought he could on that knee of his, but it was you down there, his Girly. I opened the window and called, so Albert would know somebody was watching. Then I was on the phone, describing what I saw. I saw it all."

After that, they were quiet when they were together, or sometimes they talked about Mike.

Nash and Rush came to see Kellah. Brendan and Angie were with her. Rush wore a scarf to cover the stitches in her head.

"They say I was concussed," Rush said. "But I fell off a horse once when I was a kid. That was a concussion."

"But you're alive."

Rush nodded. "I am. And so are you."

"I'm sorry we couldn't come over sooner," Nash said. "I was cautioned not to talk to you while the department investigated how we wound up with you and Rush in the hospital, a guy from the Most Wanted List almost dead, and, poor Mike."

"Are you in trouble?" Kellah asked.

"I should have had Rush under surveillance every second and I know it. She should never have been alone, once we exposed her. Then my bosses figured out how the lack of CCTV cameras in the alley behind our own building came into play and they're less interested in placing blame. But it's the second time Albert Darwin has left me looking pretty stupid. I don't care. He can't do any more damage, thanks to you."

"Brendan," Kellah turned to him, "can I amend the statement I gave? I want to say whatever I can to help Nash."

It must have been the right thing to do because Nash smiled at her. "Thanks, Kellah. But that's not why I came. I need to make peace with you. It doesn't have to be today, but when you're ready, I can tell you the story."

"I'm ready."

"Nothing's going to change," Brendan said. "There's no hurry."

"Stop protecting me," she said and Angie laughed.

"Ignore them," Kellah said. "I want to hear it."

"That's what I thought you'd say," Nash said. She took a deep breath. "When you stabbed Ape, you missed major organs, but not by much. They had to operate to clean the wound and see how much damage was done. When he was out of ICU, we Mirandized him and charged him, and he began to talk."

Kellah looked from face to face while Nash told her what Ape had said about the years after he kidnapped Angie and the weeks after he kidnapped Dorrie. She listened but judged the impact of the words by how Angie absorbed them, by how Brendan's face got darker.

"I don't know how he climbed that wall," Nash said. "I've looked at the space and I couldn't do it."

"Crazy gives you super powers," Rush said.

"We still don't understand how he knew certain things," Nash said. "He likes to talk, to let us know how smart he is, but if we press him, he shuts up."

Rush made a circle with her finger, like a replay of what she'd just said. "But he's charged with serious felonies, state and federal, starting with kidnapping, ending with felony murder."

"Will Angie have to testify?" Kellah asked.

"I'm more than ready," Angie said.

"He could plead," Nash said, "but I'm not sure the DA will offer him much."

"It'll be years before this gets to trial," Brendan said. "And we'll all be there with you, Kellah. You won't be alone."

She closed her eyes and pressed her lips together to keep from telling him he was wrong. So wrong. She was alone.

And she didn't want to tell him that she'd really tried to love him. She knew if she couldn't love him, she couldn't love anyone, but she wasn't sure it was going to work. She didn't think she could take the risk of losing anyone else.

PART 7

After and Then

36

Genevieve Nash took two weeks off and spent them on the Outer Banks of North Carolina with Paul. She called her mother every day.

For Kellah, the days went by and the bruises faded. Brendan went back to work but came to her house every evening, bringing food from Lacey's and bottles of wine. Kellah had her personal assistant bring her laptop over so she could do some work, but she couldn't concentrate and slept a lot.

One morning, she found fresh flowers in the living room, stargazer lilies.

"My mother's favorites," Kellah said. She touched the petals and rich golden pollen came off on her fingers. "Did Brendan bring them?"

"No," Angie said, "I got them when I went to the market this morning. You've told me a million times how you loved the fragrance when you were little."

"I did?" She didn't remember ever saying that. And then she realized what Angie had just said. "You went to the market?"

"Yep. Put on my big-girl panties and everything." She sat down on the loveseat. "Have you ever thought about redecorating in here? I mean, does it feel like you?"

"I hadn't thought. Do you think I should?"

"You either have to go back to the foundation or get another hobby. Interviewing designers could be your new hobby."

"Kick, you make the foundation sound like it's my hobby."

Angie looked at her, head cocked. "You said it, Girly, not me."

"Everybody says I should take all the time I need. I mean, Mike died. He was my last connection to Mims and Pops, and he died, Angie. To save me."

"I know. I know better than anybody what it means to have someone who'd do anything for you. Now it's my turn. Go to work. Tomorrow. No, today. It's not noon yet. Get dressed and we'll both go."

Angie put Guffy inside a tote bag and zipped it up. He yipped. "Get used to it," she told him. "You're a working dog now."

"You want to take him to the office?"

"He can't stay home alone." They were silent, both thinking of Mike again.

They took a cab to the foundation's offices, where Kellah had to endure mobbing and hugs from her staff. Her assistant followed her into her office.

"Detective Nash called yesterday to see if we can help a woman whose husband was killed by a drunk driver last week. The drunk is—get this—a judge, so the woman, whose husband wasn't documented by the way, is afraid she can't get fair treatment. Three kids under the age of five. And since everything that happened, donations have picked up. Lots of them in Mr. Michaels's name."

Kellah and Angie were recognized on the street. People took

pictures with their phones. If Angie saw, and if she felt feisty, she yelled, "I'll double what *The Daily* will pay. Call me first."

They worked together through the summer and fall. Brendan and Kellah argued. She said he should quit coming over, he said she should accept him in her life. Angie said, "If you don't want him, I'll take him," until Kellah made her stop.

In November, Angie said, "Maybe I should go see Dad for Christmas. I'm expecting to hear he's single again, and he'll need me."

"We haven't spent Christmas apart since we were fifteen."

"I know." She was combing Guffy's coarse waves. "It's not the healthiest thing, is it?"

Angie's father sent her a first-class ticket. Guffy went with her. Kellah spent her first night alone in the apartment and decided to sell it. Then she thought of Bonnie and changed her mind. She would sell the art and furniture and redecorate instead. Maybe Bonnie would like to move in with her.

She went to Lacey's every night for dinner, taking Bonnie with her when she could, and worked every day, including Christmas. She was not surprised when Angie called to say she thought she'd stay a little longer in L.A.

The realization came slowly to Kellah, how wrong Cousin Irene had been about the worst thing. It was still out there, somewhere. She would have to live the way she had before Albert Darwin came along. Unafraid.

ACKNOWLEDGMENTS

I find that gratitude is a deep well that, if used right, never runs dry. I hope I come close because my life is full of all the best people. I am grateful.

I am grateful to my Gaskin and Esthimer families for epitomizing what it means to be family. My mother and father taught me to love stories, books, words. There is no way to thank them enough.

I am grateful to the Parkerettes: Alyce, Anne, Ellen, Jan, Jean, Mary Erwin, Nancy, and Norbie, a wonderful group of women who have been with me since 1969. We have grown up together and aren't done yet.

Shirley Drechsel has been a special supporter as the best business partner and friend a person could have. She encouraged me to take the leap.

I am grateful to Girls Writing: Joyce Allen, Paula Blackwell, Kim Church, Rebecca Duncan, Ruth Moose, and Pat Walker. Or as I call them, the best six-headed editor in the world. We see each other through, from roughest first draft to the best the story can be. We do it with laughter and lunch, too.

Georgann Eubanks and Donna Campbell, thank you for creating the community that is Table Rock Writers. Special thanks to teachers I met there, Darnell Arnoult and Dawn Shamp.

Lisa Whittemore and Steven Esthimer are excellent proofreaders. It's an uncommon brain function and I'm glad they possess it. Any errors that remain are mine.

The writers who have trusted me to edit their work, and in many cases, to publish it, deserve special thanks. You have been my best teachers and I am proud of what we have done together.

Barbara Lorie was my first writing teacher and remains a wonderful friend. I still use the lessons the late Max Steel taught me.

Independent bookstores bring readers and writers together. Thank you, booksellers.

Thanks to Karen N.V. Owen and Kelly Prelipp Lojk for deft editing that made this book better and design work that made it beautiful. Thanks to Barbara Tyroler for her talent and for making me look good.

You, the reader, should know, I am grateful to you for completing the cycle.

NORA GASKIN is the author of two previous books, *Time of Death: The True Tale of a Quest for Justice in 1960s Chapel Hill* and *Until Proven: A Mystery in 2 Parts,* based on a true crime.

As the founder, editor, and publisher of Lystra Books (an eclectic and growing publisher, based in Chapel Hill, North Carolina), Gaskin has stewarded more than twenty books into publication.

Add to that resume her editing byline for *Carolina Crimes: 21 Tales of Need, Greed, and Dirty Deeds,* a terrific anthology of stories set in North Carolina and South Carolina, with an introduction by Jeffery Deaver, published in 2017 by Down & Out Books.

She is a lifelong resident of Chapel Hill, Durham, and Chatham County, North Carolina. She loves the Piedmont landscape with its hills, woods, and curves that keep viewers from seeing what's ahead. It's the perfect place for a mystery/suspense writer to live.

www.ingramcontent.com/pod-product-compliance
Lightning Source LLC
Chambersburg PA
CBHW061020120726
47910CB00006B/2028